DEATH AT DAYTON'S FOLLY

Virginia Rath

DEATH AT DAYTON'S FOLLY

VIRGINIA RATH

COACHWHIP PUBLICATIONS
Greenville, Ohio

Death at Dayton's Folly, by Virginia Rath
© 2019 Coachwhip Publications
Introduction © 2019 Curtis Evans

Published 1935
No claims made on public domain material.
Cover image: Snowflakes © Vadim Cherenko

CoachwhipBooks.com

ISBN 1-61646-470-4
ISBN-13 978-1-61646-470-7

THERE'S GOLD IN THEM THAR BOOKS!
The Detective Fiction of Virginia Rath

Curtis Evans

"[Virginia Rath] creates well-flavored human beings and she recreates atmosphere. She is ingenious and she has humor and she plays fair with the reader."
—"The Browser," Marshall Maslin

"[Virginia Rath is a mystery] author who actually seems to know something about character delineation—in plain English, the people in the story sound and act like real folks."
—"A Book a Day," Bruce Catton

In her day as a detective writer Virginia Rath (1905-1950), who published thirteen mystery novels in the dozen years from 1935 to 1947, was a popular and respected name in mid-century American mystery. A native Californian, Rath set both of her detective series in the Golden State. The five Rocky Allan novels detailed the criminal investigations of a handsome, homespun deputy sheriff in a rural northern California county not far distant from Reno, Nevada. The eight novels about Michael and Valerie Dundas, a suave male couturier and his charming wife who continually encounter murder, are contrastingly set, with a few exceptions (like *Murder with a Theme Song*, a sleuth mash-up which partly takes place on the home turf of Rocky Allan, who also appears in the novel), in the sophisticated precincts of San Francisco.

Although Virginia Rath died too young at the age of forty-five and her novels, which were never reprinted in paperback, fell out-of-print after her death, once they had been widely praised by noted reviewers like *San Francisco Chronicle* crime fiction critic Anthony Boucher and popular syndicated columnists Bruce Catton (later a Pulitzer Prize winner for American history) and Edwin Marshall Maslin. More recently, eminent crime writer Bill Pronzini observed in 2008 to Steve Lewis of the website *Mystery*File:* "I think you will like the Virginia Rath novels. Good, solid, Golden Age plotting, background and characterization." Now, after a lapse of over seven decades, Virginia Rath's formerly neglected detective novels finally are back in print. There is, it seems, life in the old seam yet.

Virginia Rath's detective novels are steeped in California color because Rath, a child of the Golden State, knew her section of California through and through. Born at her parents' Manhattan Ranch in Colusa County on September 1, 1905, Virginia Anne McVay was the only child of William Nelson McVay and his wife Grace Rawlins. William was a son of California "Argonaut" Joseph McVay, a Tennessee native who, after an initial lone foray to California during the '49 Gold Rush, at the age of twenty-two with two of his brothers boldly crossed the Great Plains in 1850 to prospect for gold. After remuneratively mining for several years with a partner named Henry Nelson, Joseph with Nelson brought a large head of cattle to Colusa County, about one hundred and twenty miles northeast of San Francisco. In 1872 Joseph wed Nelson's nineteen year-old niece and ward, Mary Ella Nelson, a native of Virginia who was a full quarter-century younger than her forty-four year-old husband. Together Joseph and Ella reared three children before retiring to San Francisco, where they respectively passed away in 1905 and 1909.[1]

William Nelson McVay, who was born to Joseph and Ella in 1875, was educated at Oakland's

Sackett's School and Depeu and Aydelotte's Business College. William ranched in Colusa County until October 1906, about six months after the San Francisco earthquake. At that point he opportunistically moved with his young bride, Grace Rawlins, and baby daughter, Virginia (who presumably was named after his mother's home state), to the Bay City's upper-middle-class Haight-Asbury District, which had survived both the quake and the conflagration which followed it intact; and for the next six years he lucratively engaged in general contracting. In 1912 the family returned to Colusa County, settling at a 450-acre, family-owned ranch located on the bank of the Sacramento River, about five miles southeast of the little town of Princeton.

Virginia McVay graduated from Princeton high school in 1921 at the age of sixteen (her class had but fourteen students) and thereupon entered the University of California at Berkeley, where she majored in American history, with an emphasis on the Civil War. After her graduation from college in 1926, Virginia moved to Plumas County, where she taught history at Portola high school in the Sierra Nevada Mountains, about one hundred and forty miles east of Princeton and fifty miles northwest of Reno. Although the town of Portola owed its inception two decades earlier to the lumber industry, the town's modest growth began in 1909 when it became a stop on the Western Pacific Railroad's Feather River Route. Running water and electrification came to Portola only gradually, while the town's wooden sidewalks and dirt streets were not replaced with concrete and asphalt until 1928, two years after Virginia's arrival. Yet however much Portola may have been lacking in some forms of modern progress, old sins abounded: a red light district at the southeast end of town had been in existence since 1910, and by 1930 there were thirteen saloons, where patrons could try their luck at slot machines, poker, dice, blackjack and keno.[2]

"I went there [to Portola] with two ideas firmly entrenched in my mind," Virginia later recalled of her less assured younger self in an interview with San Francisco journalist Nancy Barr Mavity, who was herself a former mystery writer. "First, I was convinced that I would never marry. Second, I was determined that I could not stick it out for more than one year." In the event, Virginia had endured employment at Portola High School for three years when in 1929 she married Carl Henry Rath (1903-1968), a strapping young telegrapher employed by the Western Pacific Railroad. The grandson of German immigrants, Rath had been born in Chicago and was the great nephew of prominent

Ludington, Michigan lumber merchant William
Rath. In her crime fiction Virginia sometimes
seems to draw on her husband's personal background, as in *Death Breaks the Ring* (1941), the
title of which references square dancing, when Valerie Dundas divulges that her husband Michael
first learned square dances "in Wisconsin in a
lumber-mill town years ago."

For the next two years, before they relocated
to San Francisco, Virginia and Carl Rath resided
five miles to the east of Portola in the little town
of Beckwourth, named for James Beckwourth, a
mixed race California pioneer who many decades
earlier had discovered the Beckwourth Pass, the
lowest mountain pass in the Sierra Nevada. Carl
continued to telegraph at the railway station while
Virginia taught school and banged away at home
at her typewriter, trying to score a hit in the fiction market. In this endeavor she found her and
her family's experiences in rural northern California of inestimable value, for they finally gave her
a publishing hook. By the mid-Thirties regional
or "local color" mysteries had achieved consid-
erable success in the United States, but typically
they were set either in the American South or in
New England. Rural northern California offered
jaded mystery readers a new wrinkle in murder.

"I would not exchange my five years in that environment for anything I can think of," Virginia avowed to Nancy Barr Mavity in 1936, when she was in the midst of successfully publishing her Rocky Allan mysteries, which she set in a sparsely populated patch of northern California that happened to bear a great resemblance to Plumas County.

In her Rocky Allan detective fiction, Virginia made use not only of the experiences of her pioneering Grandfather McVay and his family. The intense "restorationist" religiosity of her mother's family (her father's family was merely mildly Methodist) found its way as well into her second mystery, *Murder on the Day of Judgment* (1936). Virginia's mother Grace was the daughter of Thomas Franklin Rawlins of Elk Creek, California, a Christian (aka Disciples of Christ) minister, merchant, postmaster, farmer and journalist originally from Texas, where the Rawlins clan had been instrumental since the 1840s in spreading the Christian word throughout the north central region of the Lone Star State.[3]

Thomas' father William "Elder Billy" Rawlins was similarly a Christian minster and correspondent of the *Gospel Advocate* (though Elder Billy's obituary in the *GA* noted regretfully that during his lifetime he had entertained "many peculiar views which . . . crippled his influence as a teacher of Christianity"); and his grandfather Roderick Rawlins, born in Massachusetts in the year the American colonies declared independence from Great Britain, had been baptized by the great Christian evangelist Barton Warren Stone.

Unlike the zealous Reverend Stone and her earnest Rawlins forbears, Virginia Rath seems to have been rather more attracted to the material mysteries of detective fiction than to the metaphysical problems of religious faith. Virginia recalled that while there had been "few books" at the McVay ranch in Colusa County, where she had resided from the ages of six to sixteen, there providentially were to be found on the shelves there some mysteries by American author Anna Katherine Green, which Virginia, like the once similarly captivated detective writers Agatha Christie and Carolyn Wells before her, had devoutly "absorbed." From an early age she also, judging from comments made by characters in her novel *The Anger of the Bells*, read fiction by Edgar Allan Poe, father of the detective story, even though grisly Poe horror tales like "Berenice" and "The Black Cat" gave her nightmares. ("You hadn't ought to been readin' stuff like that when you was so young," a character chastises a young woman writer who admits having perused Poe as a child, to which she responds: "I suppose not, but no one censored my reading. Probably if they had I'd have read the books on the sly.") "I always wanted to write detective stories from the time when I was a little girl on a ranch in Colusa County," Virginia reminisced to Nancy Barr Mavity. "I like the people in them. . . . Characters and setting come first with me, then the action begins to crystallize."[4]

Less happily, there were certain morbid and tragic experiences in the lives of Virginia and her husband which the author left unmentioned in interviews, though these too may well have inclined her to writing about something so macabre as murder. In 1924, when Virginia was but eighteen years old and attending the University of California, her forty-eight year-old father died after taking an overdose of his heart medicine. Similarly, Virginia's husband lost his father at a young age. Carl was not yet two years old when Chicago businessman Miles Emil Rath passed away from acute appendicitis at the age of twenty-nine. Around this time one of Miles' brothers died from typhoid fever and another was fatally struck by lightning while conversing on the telephone in his house during a thunderstorm. The Rath boys seem to have been singularly ill-starred by fortune, though Carl, at least, survived to the age of sixty-five.[5]

Having precociously written fiction from an early age at the lonely ranch at Colusa, Virginia at the age of sixteen had completed a novel during her freshman year at the University of California, which she naively submitted to the reprint publishers Grossett and Dunlap, simply because, she explained, "she had seen so many books with that name on them." During her college years Virginia worked on the school newspaper and published fiction with the UC Berkeley *Literary Review*, but at the time she planned, as a history major, to write biography. She was fascinated with the Civil War period, her mother's family having come from Texas and her paternal grandmother, Ella Nelson McVay, having belonged to the United Daughters of the Confederacy and claimed relationship with *the* Virginia Nelsons, one of the so-called First Families of Virginia. In Virginia's youth the most prominent representative of this branch of the family was author Thomas Nelson Page, a noted contributor to the southern Lost Cause ideology (i.e., the egregious romanticization of "old plantation days" as a time of caring masters and contented slaves.) However, Virginia cannily came to realize that, as she put it, "a biographer has to be a first-rate detective—especially as the prime function of biographers, memoirists and diarists seems to be to conceal and distort all clues as to what actually happened." She concluded that "my interest in . . . extricating facts from a tangle of misleading inferences was ready-made to apply to a detective story." Perhaps indicating Virginia's skepticism about family legends, her sleuth Rocky Allan, who comes, like Virginia's maternal forbears, from Texas, divulges in the novel *An Excellent Night for a Murder*: "My mother . . . came from Virginia. Her folks were dirt poor but they all had a very high and mighty way about them."

The first fruit of Virginia's fascination with detective fiction found its way into print in 1931, when *Complete Detective Novel Magazine* published a garishly illustrated 60,000 word mystery (credited to Virginia Anne Rath) titled *The Murders at Hillside*, about a series of grisly crimes which in classical fashion strike what the magazine termed "a gay house party." Having published her manuscript with a pulp fiction magazine, it never occurred to the ingenuous author that she might additionally have sent the novel (as in fact did many pulp fiction writers, including no less than Dashiell Hammett) to an actual book publisher. However, after Virginia and Carl moved to San Francisco, where he had taken another position as a railroad telegrapher, she continued writing, producing short stories and novelettes, though with little success. In 1934 she completed another detective novel, which this time she planned to submit to a publisher, under the title *Murder in the Stacks*, on account of the titular murder taking place in the library at the University of California. However, she was cast down one day when her husband brought home a newspaper clipping announcing the publication of a novel by Marion Boyd under that very same title, wherein a murder takes place in the library of the University of Miami (Ohio).

After this distressful and demoralizing experience, Virginia determinedly made it her mission "to read practically every detective story published, for fear her own ideas may have occurred to someone else first." Happily that same year she hit upon the idea of setting a detective novel series in rural and rustic northern California. Nobody had yet taken *that* idea, it seemed, although a couple of years earlier the late Earl Derr Biggers, creator of Charlie Chan, had set the final Chan opus, titled *Keeper of the Keys*, at scenic Lake Tahoe. The next year Virginia submitted her new novel, under the title *Death at Dayton's Folly*, to a major American mystery publisher, Doubleday, Doran, who promptly accepted the novel and published it shortly before the author's thirtieth birthday. Virginia's dream of being a true published detective novelist before the age of thirty had been attained just in the nick of time.

During these years in Frisco, Carl worked at the railroad station between three in the afternoon and eleven at night, allowing Virginia evenings to work unhindered on her detective novels. She aimed at typing a thousand words every night until her current book was completed. In this fashion she produced thirteen detective novels, with eleven of them (all published by Doubleday, Doran) appearing in the seven years between 1935 and 1942. Aside from her aforementioned initial pair of novels, *Death at Dayton's Folly* and *Murder on the Day of Judgment*, these Doubleday, Doran titles were *Ferryman, Take Him Across!* (1936), *The Anger of the Bells* (1937), *An Excellent Night for a Murder* (1937), all of them with Rocky Allan as sleuth, and the Michael and Valerie Dundas mysteries *The Dark Cavalier* (1938), *Murder with a Theme Song* (1939) (where Rocky Allan plays a substantial role), *Death of a Lucky Lady* (1940), *Death Breaks the Ring* (1941) (where Rocky has a cameo telephone conversation with Michael), *Epitaph for Lydia* (1942) and *Posted for Murder* (1942). There then came four fallow publishing years, followed in 1947 by a final pair of Dundas mysteries, *A Shroud for Rowena* and *A Dirge for*

Her. These two titles appeared in Ziff-Davis' Fingerprint Mystery line, a short-lived, though good quality, detective fiction imprint, which unfortunately folded the following year. Although Virginia Rath lived three more years, the once prolific author published no more new detective novels in the span of time which remained to her.

However, in 1950 Virginia made an impressive final stab at the mystery genre that she had proudly made her literary home, when she notably contributed to the "Theo Durrant" crime novel *The Marble Forest* (1951), collaboratively composed by no less than a dozen members of the northern California chapter of the Mystery Writers of America, including Anthony Boucher, Lenore Glen Offord, Darwin Teilhet, Dana Lyon, William Worley, Richard Shattuck and Eunice Mays Boyd. Each contributor to the novel was assigned a different character about whom to write in individual episodes, on the assumption that his or her character was the villain. From these chapters "ringmaster" Anthony Boucher selected the true culprit and wrote the denouement accordingly, revealing to all and sundry the fiend's identity. This interesting experimental crime novel, which concerns the horrific kidnapping of a four-year-old girl who is buried alive in a casket and has but a few hours to live, was well-reviewed and seven years later made into a film, *Macabre* (1958), which was produced and directed by renowned ballyhooing B film impresario William Castle, maker of such fondly remembered schlock horror classics as *The House on Haunted Hill* (1959) and *The Tingler* (1959), both starring Vincent Price; brazen *Psycho* knock-off *Homicidal* (1961); the Robert Bloch scripted *The Night Walker* (1964) and *Straight-Jacket* (1964), respectively starring faded Hollywood stars Barbara Stanwyck and Joan Crawford; and *I Saw What You Did* (1965), based on the Ursula Curtiss suspense novel *Child's Play*.

Tragically Virginia, who at the beginning of 1950 had been honored with election as president of the MWA's northern California chapter, died, after a sudden fatal illness of five days' duration, on October 26 of the same year, shortly after completing her section of *The Marble Forest*. The forty-five-year-old was survived by her husband Carl and her mother Grace Crowder, though she left no children and her books were largely forgotten after her death, despite the important contribution to regional American mystery which they constituted. In her mysteries Virginia Rath may largely have dispensed with, as Nancy Barr Mavity noted, the customary, clichéd trappings of Golden Age crime fiction, but in them she had importantly pointed the way to the future of detective fiction, making murder happen to credibly presented people in authentically detailed surroundings, all the while making sure not to sacrifice the fun of teasing readers with a carefully clued murder puzzle to solve. For the classic crime fiction fan such books truly are as precious as California gold.

THE BALLAD OF ROCKY ALLAN

Virginia Rath's first series sleuth Rocky Allan, the Roderick Alleyn of Plumas County, California, made his investigative debut in 1935 in *Death at Dayton's Folly*. Rocky's impressive initial outing is Rath's most traditional tale, concerning as it does murder at a family house party at a snowbound country mansion. Rocky, we learn, works on a railroad as a fireman, or stoker, in addition to serving as a deputy sheriff in a mountainous rural northern California county with two main towns (and rivals), Merton and Brookdale, the county seat. My guess is that Rath's barely fictional county is based on Plumas County and the railroad town of Portola, where Virginia Rath taught school for several years in the late 1920s and early 1930s, and Quincy, the seat of Plumas County. (This becomes clearer in the later books.)

Rocky is the son of a Texas farmer, like Virginia Rath's maternal grandfather, whose restlessness prompted him to leave the family homestead at the age of seventeen, eventually ending up in California, though he admits that he "never did get entirely rid of that [Texas] way of talkin'." The strapping deputy sheriff and railroader, who in some ways seems to have been modeled on Rath's husband Carl, is "six feet of hard flesh and muscle," blond-haired, leonine and tanned, broad-shouldered and narrow hipped; and his name "Rocky" is a nickname derived from the occasion when a man hit him on the jaw, succeeding only in busting his own hand. "It made me kind of dizzy for a minute," Ricky reflects nonchalantly of his opponent's long-ago punch, "but I knocked him cold." He also is better read than people who do not know him think. His adversaries soon learn not to dismiss him as some country bumpkin or hick from the sticks sheriff.

What a paragon of manliness, then, is Rocky, who rather resembles a roughhewn, homespun version of Ngaio Marsh's highly romanticized posh policeman sleuth, Roderick Alleyn. Rocky—whose real name is Nathan Bedford, the name being derived from the notorious Civil War cavalry general ("Granddaddy fought under him in the Civil

War")—even has providentially received a size-
able inheritance from a relative, in the manner of
those Golden Age British gentlemen sleuths, who
invariably are kissed by the gods of fortune. After
the death of his Uncle Bill, who worked for the
Santa Fe Railroad, the year before the events detailed in *Death at Dayton's Folly* take place, Rocky
inherited from him "near to ten thousand dollars."
He admits "it's come in right handy." (It should
have indeed, being worth about $180,000 today.)

When Death strikes the swanky gathering at
Dayton's Folly, a rambling, isolated former hotel
turned country house (one is reminded of Stephen
King's *The Shining*), Rocky is providentially on
hand, having agreed to ride with a trucker friend
delivering supplies to the mansion during a sudden heavy snowfall. Helping Rocky to solve the
case is a genteel San Francisco private detective
of sorts, Theophilus Pope, Virginia Rath's nod
to the gentleman amateur detective tradition in
Golden Age detective fiction, as exemplified by
such figures as Lord Peter Wimsey, Albert Campi-
on, Ellery Queen and Philo Vance. "I knew a guy
named Oh-Be-Joyful, once," Rocky observes politely on learning Pope's pretentious name. Despite
their different social backgrounds, the two men
work like gangbusters together and even manage
to solve, with the power and phone lines failing in

the perilous blizzard, the dreadful murder at Dayton's Folly (and the second one which follows it), before the county sheriff, Jake Thompson, even appears. Rocky also finds love with one of the persons of interest in the case, beautiful red-haired nurse Eleanor Gannon—this despite the fact that Eleanor is implicated in the lurid affair up to her lovely eyeballs.

In the second Rocky Allan detective novel, *Murder on the Day of Judgment* (1936), Rocky and Eleanor are married and have only recently returned from an extended sojourn to the Texas farm of Rocky's father when they receive an invitation from Theophilus Pope to come help him out on a case at a rural campground called "Coon Hollow," located just outside the Butte County line near the city of Chico. (Actually Pope chauvinistically invites only Rocky, but Eleanor, like any wife worth her salt as the feminine half of a Golden Age mystery couple, insists on coming along too.) It seems that the notorious Sapphira Barlow, a charismatic septuagenarian fortune-teller from flaky Los Angeles (and a Victorian-era prostitute to boot), has descended on Coon Hollow with her dubious entourage, insisting that the end of the world is at hand. (Cynics say things got too hot for her in LA.) Death does indeed come as the end for several of the people at Coon Hollow,

putting Rocky and Pope together again on another strange case, which they similarly solve before
Sheriff Jake Thompson makes it to the crime scene
(though Sheriff Jake appears in the last chapter).
The ingenious detective novel—in which Virginia
Rath in creating her criminal milieu effectively
draws upon the religious zeal of her own maternal
ancestors, who were prominent in the establish-
ment of the Christian Church in nineteenth-cen-
tury America—marks Theophilus Pope's exit from
the series. Rocky could handle things by himself
from hereon.

Rocky stays at home with Eleanor in the town
of Merton to solve a vicious double murder in the
third Rocky Allan detective novel, *Ferryman, Take
Him Across!* (1936). Both of the novel's murders
take place in the early morning aftermath of a
Hallowe'en costume party at Merton High School.
Bizarrely, one of the murder victims has had an
antique coin placed in his mouth, recalling the
legend of Charon, mythological ferryman of the
dead. Many Mertonites point fingers of suspicion
at musician "Jazz" Mitchell, whose band played
dance tunes at the spooky masquerade, because
the hotheaded Jazz seemingly was involved in a
scorching love triangle with the victims. However,
Rocky thinks he knows better, in this clever mystery where the author advantageously draws on

her own teaching experiences in Portola. Strik-
ingly portraying the petty rivalries and backbit-
ing that can assume such outsized importance in
small-town life, Rath gives *Ferryman* the persua-
sive atmosphere of a village *Gaudy Night*. (Far less
appealing is a needless subplot about a murderous
escaped black convict on the loose in the vicinity.)

Rocky goes back on the rural road again in
his fourth mystery, *The Anger of the Bells* (1937),
which takes place primarily in the "ghost" mining
town of Slacktown, aka Gold Gulch. Sheriff Jake
Thompson has retired to live with a son in San
Diego, leaving Rocky and Eleanor in possession
of his house in Brookdale and Rocky as his likely
successor after the next sheriff's election. Eleanor
Allan is on a trip to San Francisco with a girlfriend
from *Ferryman, Take Him Across!*, but taking her
place as Rocky's investigative sidekick is Rocky's
widowed father, Robert Edward Lee Allan. (The
Allan family, like many white southerners of their
day, does indeed venerate dead Confederate gener-
als.) The elder Allan is on a visit to California from
Texas, where, we learn, oil has been discovered on
his farmland. (Dollars seems to rain down from
the heavens on this fortunate family.) Providing
dubious comic relief are the malapropisms of one
Mary Anne, the Chinese-American cook of Slacktown's hotel owner, Kitty Featherstone-Quinn,

who comes to Brookdale to entreat Rocky to investigate the ghostly ringing in the night of bells in the tower of Slacktown's old schoolhouse. A big black cat named Sultan plays a key role in the affair as well. Happily Eleanor shows up later in the novel, along with Jazz Mitchell, newly deputized by Rocky, who has despaired of the abilities of his other deputies, like the aptly named "Dud" Williams, introduced in *Ferryman, Take Him Across!* One is reminded of the droll country mysteries of Bill Crider.

Sheriff Rocky's fifth and final leading appearance as a sleuth takes place in *An Excellent Night for a Murder* (1937), wherein he solves the slaying of a strange man visiting Brookdale from San Francisco. Recalling *Death at Dayton's Folly*, the stranger's murder implicates a wealthy, snooty local family, the Graydons, heirs of the late Joshua Graydon, founder of the Graydon Lumber Company, who loftily hold themselves apart from the little folk of Brookdale. Virginia Rath mentions that Brookdale, despite being "only the county seat of a small mountain county," has "a very impressive courthouse," the building of which was spearheaded by Joshua Graydon. This likely is a reference to the actual Plumas County Courthouse in Quincy, a grand classical revival edifice completed in 1921, the size and cost of which, notes the website of the

California Supreme Court Historical Society, "was considered so exorbitant for the county that there was talk of recalling the board of supervisors." Eleanor appears in the novel, where we learn that she is expecting the couple's first child. Meanwhile Rocky enjoys for once having an able deputy working with him on a case. This ardent young man is Andy Duncan, an enthusiast for medical jurisprudence and a devotee of R. Austin Freeman's Dr. Thorndyke detective novels. A decided complication takes place, however, when it turns out that Andy is in love with one of the Graydon women. Rocky knows what that is like from his own amorous experiences with Eleanor in *Death at Dayton's Folly*.

The Rocky Allan series formally ended after only five novels, yet Rocky and Eleanor both resurfaced in *Murder with a Theme Song* (1939), a murder mash-up in which Michael and Valerie Dundas, a suave San Francisco couturier and his wife who debuted as sleuths the previous year in *The Dark Cavalier* (1938), meet Brookdale's first couple. This novel should really be considered the sixth Rocky Allan mystery. In it Rocky plays every bit as active a role as Michael in the investigation of a murder in San Francisco and a murder on Rocky's own home turf, both of which seem to have their roots in the year-old abduction from his home of wealthy nine-year-old hellion Frederick Armstrong, Jr., who seemingly has never been seen again since. This event recalls both the real-life Lindbergh kidnapping case (1932) and *Murder on the Orient Express* (1934), the famed Agatha Christie novel which drew upon the Lindbergh case. (Is it a coincidence that Christie's kidnapped child was named Daisy *Armstrong*?) It also partly anticipates Virginia Rath's final work, the collaborative novel *The Marble Forest*.

The title of the *Murder with a Theme Song* is derived from the cheerily macabre strains of the popular French-Canadian song *Alouette*, which makes a menacing leitmotif in this exciting case. There is even a cameo appearance by the Allans' rambunctious young son Robert Edward Lee, Jr.—dubbed "Shay," Eleanor explains, "on account of a shay is a very small engine with a very loud whistle"—and the debut and sole appearance of Sing Toy, the Allans' imperious Chinese housekeeper.

This could have been the beginning of a beautiful sleuthing friendship between the Allans and the Dundases, but Rocky only makes one additional, cameo appearance in the Dundas mystery series. This is in the novel *Death Breaks the Ring* (1941), where late in the tale he takes some questions on the telephone from Michael—all the while trying to fend off his toddler son Shay, who is crawling on his back and grabbing him by the hair—about an important facet of Michael's amateur investigation into a murder at the Summit House resort hotel, likely located in Sierra County, south of Plumas. The Dundases are in fact returning from a visit with the Allans (Michael refers to them as "friends in Brookdale, which is over on the Feather River Highway"), by way of the small towns of Sierra City and Downieville, spending time, Michael grumpily complains, "wandering back and forth between two supremely unimportant hamlets known as Calpine and Sierraville," because "Mrs. Dundas wanted to view a little more of the infinite monotony of mountain scenery." At Summit House they become enmeshed in murder yet again, though happily Rocky, we learn, puts in a good word about Michael with the local sheriff, Fred Payne, and Michael's phone conversation with Rocky finally puts the amateur sleuth on the right track. Rocky remains a rare railroader to the last.

Notes:

[1] Although I did not locate Joseph McVay in the 1870 census, his partner Henry Nelson

that year was worth about $635,000 in modern dollars.

[2] See Rebecca Rhode, "The History of Portola," at https://www.ci.portola.ca.us/portola-history.html, City of Portola-California.

[3] Restorationist Christianity calls for returning the faith to it early, apostolic roots in the first Christian centuries.

[4] Another exchange which takes place in *The Anger of the Bells*—this one between sleuth Rocky Allan and his father, whose regional ancestry seems to mimic Virginia Rath's—suggests more of Virginia's possible childhood reading:

Rocky grinned at his father. "What was that book you caught me readin', Dad, the time you set me to copyin' one of the worst 'begat' chapters in the Old Testament to take my mind off it?"

"It may have been the copy of Boccaccio's stories [in the *Decameron*] one of my mother's Virginia uncles—the one 'at read Greek—brought back from Europe before the [Civil War]. Well, that was kind of foolish. I reckon you already knew ever'thing you could learn from that book, bein' brought up on a ranch and all, even if it wasn't expurgated. It may've been *Madame Bovary*, though. Your mother always kept that Boccaccio hid pretty well."

[5] One of the pallbearers at William McVay's funeral, Clifford Lee Crowder, a bank book-keeper at the First National Bank of Chico, would in 1930 marry William's widow Grace, after his own wife died the next year, 1925, at the age of forty-five.

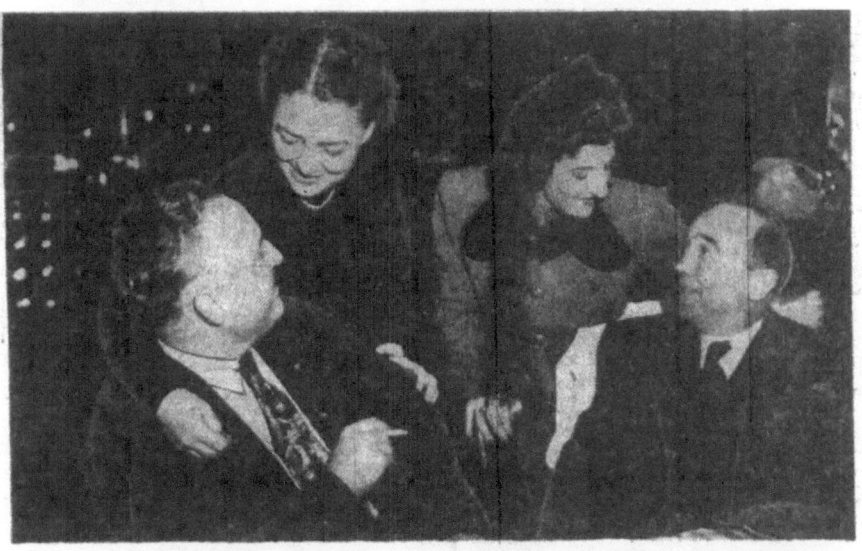

Lower photo (left to right): Husbands Carl Rath and William Faulkner, seated, are "best friends and severest critics" of mystery writer wives Virginia Rath and Florence Faulkner. Mrs. Rath is secretary and Mrs. Faulkner treasurer of Northern California "Mystery Writers of America, Inc."—Tribune photos.

VIRGINIA RATH

DEATH AT DAYTON'S FOLLY

To
Carl
who does not like
detective stories

PART I
DEATH ON A SNOWY HILL

Dick Barnes, who drove truck for one of the town's oil companies, met Rocky Allan in front of the Greek's restaurant. It was not snowing then, but the sky was an ominous dark gray, and the east wind lashed coldly at unprotected flesh.

Dick said: "I got to go out in this, down to Rio Linda with a special order. How's to go with me, Rocky? I don't know if I'll get there or not, the way the roads are."

"You wouldn't expect me to be able to lift that truck of yours out of a snowdrift, would you?"

"If she once gets in, I'll have to leave her and walk back," Dick said gloomily. "Then the company will pester me for a report about how it happened. Still, sometimes an extra fellow can help out if the going's tough. Not that I blame you for staying home."

Rocky considered briefly. "Oh, I reckon I'll go. I get kind of fed up with settin' on my tail in that boardin' house. Where 'bouts is your buggy?"

The truck was just around the corner from the Greek's. Dick had already put on the side curtains.

"They had the snowplows out between here and Greenleaf," Rocky said, climbing into the cab. "That road ought to be all right till it snows again. I don't know what they've done on the other side of Greenleaf. They don't care if the road's passable there or not."

The heavy car moved slowly down the deep-rutted main street of the little mountain town. Dick said:

"It's between Greenleaf and Rio Linda I'm worryin' about, even if it's only three miles. Well, four or five by the time you get into Dayton's Folly."

"Hunh? Is that where we're going?"

"Yeah. I wouldn't be making this trip for anybody but a guy with pull. Fellow by the name of Leale."

"I think I've heard of him. He used to be a lumber man himself if he's the one I mean. I think he had an interest in the mill up here." Merton owed existence to the fact that it was a railroad division point and possessed one fairly large lumber mill. "Has this fellow bought Dayton's Folly?"

"They'd ought to call it Leale's Folly if he has. What anyone would want with a barn like that—"

"I heard old man Dayton meant to make a hotel out of it, but it isn't in a good place for a summer resort." Rocky lighted cigarettes for both of them. "What're you taking them?"

"Furnace fuel. He's got money, I understand. Think he just leased the place last fall, but he had a furnace put in. I guess it was colder'n they figured on, so we got this hurry-up order. Damned nuisance!"

Rocky said absently: "Sure is." Then: "Rich guys are funny I wouldn't mind goin' down South to get out of this weather for a spell. But Leale, he leaves a nice comfortable house in San Francisco an' comes up here to rough it." He grinned. "With a furnace in the house, of course, and I reckon a whole pack of servants."

"Not many. I was talking to Wharton at Greenleaf yesterday. They hired Sarah Powers to cook for them, and they brought a butler or something like that with them. And a nurse—" Dick stopped suddenly, looked at Rocky, and said: "Hell! I forgot—"

"Forgot what?"

"Well, didn't you know that red-headed nurse that was in the hospital here for a month?"

"I knew her. She was a swell girl," Rocky said evenly. "Eleanor Gannon, you mean? She relieved one of the regular nurses about two months before I landed in the hospital."

"Oh yeah. How," Dick said very tactfully, "is your shoulder?" He was referring to a broken shoulder Rocky had received in an automobile accident three months before.

"Not bad. I'll be back to work in another month."

Rocky moved one shoulder slightly and wondered if he would go back to work so soon. The damn thing ached when it was cold, like it was now. Probably the company doctor was right to keep him out of service another month. It was a bad time on the road right now: slides and washouts. They didn't want any firemen with bum shoulders, and things were so tight in winter that he'd probably get very little work anyway.

Dick chuckled suddenly. "How's law and order going to be kept in Merton tonight with you gone, Rocky? Say, how'd old Thompson ever come to appoint you deputy, anyway?"

"Oh, I've done some hellin' around at various times, but he could have worse deputies than me," Rocky said good-naturedly. "He knew I'd be in town, for one thing. Williams is a good enough constable, but you can't tell when he'll get soused to the eyes. I haven't had to do anything, 'cept to tell Pete Miller he'd better marry that Parker girl before her old man got out his shotgun. Winter's a bad time for that kind of thing: there ain't anything else to do aroun' town. Who's Eleanor Gannon nurse for in this bunch?"

"The old man's sister is an invalid, I understand."

"Damned funny place to bring an invalid."

"That's what I thought. She can't be very bad off. I guess the furnace was for her."

"Maybe. Eleanor had a lot of high-class friends in the city, probably. Her dad must have had money once. Maybe she already knew the Leales. How's the driving?"

"Not bad if you watch it every minute. It's going to snow again, though. Good thing Leale got his order in when he did."

The road was white glass between jagged mounds piled up by the snowplows. The truck skidded ponderously as they went around a curve. Dick fought to hold it on the road and swore exhaustively.

But Rocky was thinking about Eleanor Gannon—"Carrot-top," he'd called her once, thinking she'd resent it. She hadn't: she probably knew her hair was pretty even if it was the kind of red that had a gleam of orange to it. A tall girl, not too thin, with long gray eyes. Too smart to marry a roughneck tallow-pot. Not that he'd ever asked her to marry him—or anything else.

Dick switched on the lights though it was only a little past four o'clock. He repeated:

"It's going to snow. How many feet would you say we'd had, Rocky?"

"There's not more than two, now it's settled. Couple of cars managed to get into Reno yesterday. But they said another good storm'd close the roads for quite a while."

"Good thing if it did," Dick grunted. "If cars can't run the small dealers don't have to have gas. I tell you, those roads out in the valley are hell. You can't tell when you'll go through one of those bridges out there. Well, here's Greenleaf."

Greenleaf was a large red mill, a snow-covered mountain of sawdust, a company store, clubhouse and cafeteria, a row of three-room houses that had nearly forgotten they had once been painted green. There were homes of company officials on a slight hill to the left of the road, and a small hospital. Light showed only in the hospital windows. Dick said:

"Doc Ames is staying here, Wharton says. All the company officials are gone, but there's a few of the mill families here. Ames thought he'd better stay. He's the nearest doctor for any of the folks down at Humber, and there's quite a few families there."

"I never met Ames. I've heard he's a good guy."

They crossed an old wooden bridge over a swollen stream. The road here had not been scraped recently, but still the truck managed to crawl along. There were forty miles between Greenleaf and Brookdale, the county seat, but Greenleaf people did not try to go to Brookdale in the winter months, so the county authorities paid little attention to the road in that section. Rocky said:

"You'll just about make it and that's all. I don't know that road into Dayton's Folly. How did this bunch get in there?"

"They came on the train, and it made a special stop at the Rio Linda station. You know: that little shack near the track. They'd wired Wharton, and he had his car to take 'em up to the house. The old lady and the luggage, that is. He'd already taken up a bunch of groceries that they sent on ahead."

"How many of them are there?"

"Oh—well, the old lady and Miss Gannon and old man Leale and a son and daughter, I think. No, two daughters and two other men, seems to me Wharton said. Boy, if it really starts to snow before I get unloaded and back to Greenleaf, me and you will be spending the night there."

"It hasn't really started yet," Rocky said, looking out at a few white flakes floating lazily past the truck. "It's still 'most too cold to snow. That looks to me like Rio Linda station ahead of us."

All down the river between Greenleaf and Brookdale were scattered summer camps and cabins, a few pretentious, most of them not. When

George Dayton, a retired lumberman, had built his eleven-room log mansion, he had thought to compete with the two hotels some fifteen miles farther down the river. He had died before he acquired any paying guests, and his son had been trying to sell Dayton's Folly ever since.

It was too far from Brookdale, too far from the hotels, and too large for the average family. And lonely, some people would think. They were crossing the railroad tracks now, and before them was a gated bridge with a large "No Trespassing" sign. Rocky got out and opened the gate, noting as he stood aside that the trees on the hill they must climb were so thick that he could not see the house.

He looked doubtfully at what he could see of the road and, climbing back into the truck, said: "You'd better put her in low, fella."

"I am. It's not such a steep hill, though. I guess we'll make it."

The road curved up gradually; small diamonds of hard snow spun away from the truck's grinding wheels. They came at last in sight of the house sitting, tree-encircled, on the hill. Lights winked from its windows, but it had the lonely air of a misfit; too large, too dark, too elaborately fashioned for its setting of tall pines.

But there were gay voices and laughter outside. Dick looked and said simply:

"Jeez, some folks are gluttons for punishment. I see the old man put in lights too."

The long sloping hill on one side of the house was a perfect place for coasting, and a high-powered light had been installed on a tree at the hill's top. There were three sleds and six people there; a great many gay colors in knitted scarves and jackets. A sled whizzed down the hill, swerved, and up-ended in a snowbank.

It was Eleanor Gannon who scrambled up, laughing, and gasping. Her blue cap had fallen off, and her hair was brilliant against dazzling white. Some young fellow had been with her, steering the sled. It was hard to see what he looked like in the dusk, that far away from him.

Dick stopped the truck in front of the house and got out. Rocky followed, because his feet were numb with cold and he wanted to see this Leale bunch close up.

There was a girl, a tiny little thing with yellow hair under a red beret. Pretty as a picture, even in one of those funny one-piece suits that looked more like a baby's sleepers than anything else.

Her voice was clear and high, like a child's, as she said: "Your turn now, Daddy. I'll go with you."

She didn't look toward them, but she had seen them. She was—posing, that was it. Rocky grinned a little and looked curiously at Alfred Leale.

A short man, somewhere in the fifties but sturdy and vigorous in his movements. Gray mustache, shaggy gray eyebrows, a strong, square face reddened by cold. He turned and called to Dick:

"Be with you in a minute. This is my last trip down."

He fumbled with gloved hands in his inside breast pocket. "I think we've all had enough for one day, Norma. I'll take you down once more when I've had a bracer."

Eleanor was climbing slowly up the hill now, well to one side of the smooth track beaten down by the runners of the sleds. She held her cap in one hand, and snowflakes melted when they hit against her hair. She saw Rocky, and her eyebrows lifted. She waved to him.

The young fellow who had steered their sled followed behind her. Over under the light two men were kneeling down, repairing another sled. Rocky looked toward them. He could not see their faces, but one was very tall, he thought—

Then for an instant it was as if everyone and everything were frozen by the cold. This was an icy dream: that Alfred Leale put the flask to his lips and drank, took what was only the beginning of a forward step, and fell face down in the snow. But the figures in the frozen tableau moved.

Norma Leale gasped, "It's his heart!" and knelt down, tugging impotently at a thick mackinawed shoulder.

Feet crunched on the snow. Eleanor was stumbling as she tried to run uphill. The man who turned Alfred Leale over on his back was tall and very thin; the one just behind him had a neat black mustache, small hands and feet.

Rocky thought: "Jeez, what funny things you notice—" Somehow he was standing by Leale now, with Dick just behind him.

Norma Leale said: "He'll be all right, won't he? He shouldn't have stayed out so long."

The man who faced her over her father's body shook his head. He said flatly:

"He's dead, Miss Leale. And I think he was poisoned."

II

An instant of silence, then Norma Leale screamed and kept on screaming, shrilly, hysterically. Eleanor, reaching the top of the hill at last, stooped down for a handful of soft snow and threw it in the other girl's face.

"Stop that!" She lifted Norma to her feet. "Come over here."

She forced her down on the sled under the light globe, standing between her and any sight of Leale's body.

The flask, small and flat in a covering of pigskin, had fallen from Leale's hands into the snow. There was a brown stain by it, but when Rocky picked it up there was still some liquor in it. He said:

"I reckon we'll want to keep this. How about what went out on the snow?"

The tall man looked up at him curiously, still kneeling beside Alfred Leale. "Only a small amount of liquor will be needed for analysis. You say 'we,' Mr.—"

"Allan. Yeah, it's kind of funny," Rocky drawled, "that I happen to be a dep'ty sheriff. Want to see my badge?"

The incredibly long brown face had small wrinkles around its mouth. They stirred as if the man might be amused. He said:

"Oh no, I don't think we need to see your badge. It's really very—convenient, your happening along. I suppose it won't be easy to get in touch with the authorities. But that can wait. Keep the flask, Mr. Allan. Miss Gannon, will you take Miss Leale into the house? If necessary, tell the other women what has happened."

Eleanor nodded. "Come on, Norma. No, you won't have to tell your aunt or Beatrice. You can lie down."

"I suppose that even in these circumstances the social amenities must be observed." The tall man got to his feet, brushing snow from his heavy corduroy trousers. "This"—he indicated the younger of the two men behind him—"is Mr. Leale's son Joseph. And his cousin Mr. Dunn. My name is Pope."

Joseph Leale looked like Norma; not at all like their father. His face was delicately handsome, fair skinned, his mouth indecisive. His voice was like Norma's too, rather high pitched. He said:

"But, Pope—his heart was bad! You don't know—just because he took a drink that he—he—"

Dunn's teeth were chattering, and he beat his gloved hands together, but he looked at Joseph scornfully.

"You know as well as I do just how bad Alfred's heart was," he said. "And that was—not bad at all. Mr. Pope probably knows more than you do, Joe. Alfred hired him as a secretary, but he didn't need a secretary. So—" He shrugged.

Pope said: "That's true. He didn't need a secretary. But he was—cautious when it came to confiding fully in anyone."

Rocky felt Dick moving restlessly behind him. The snow was falling fast now on Alfred Leale's still face. They didn't have any time to waste: it was going to snow the night through. Rocky turned to Dick.

"Dump that oil out and then go back to Greenleaf and send Dr. Ames up here. I reckon we'd better have him come. After that you'll have to get home best you can alone. If you don't hustle you'll never make it. You," he said to Joseph Leale, "give him a hand with the oil. Now, Mr. Pope—"

"Yes?"

"Think we'd better take him into the house?"

"I don't see what else there is to do. If I might suggest—"

"Sure; anything you like."

"Dunn had better go ahead, then. And clear the way, I mean. Keep the elder Miss Leales out of the hall."

Dunn said: "I'll do what I can, but you know Beatrice and Cousin Georgina. They—well, I'll try."

He started toward the house. Dick turned to ask:

"Sure that's all I can do for you, Rocky? Jeez, I'd like to help, but if I get stranded with this truck—"

"I know. You got to get back. We'll phone the sheriff. I don't know," Rocky said, looking up at the whirling white sky. "I'm afraid we're in for it. The sheriff can't get a train till tomorrow morning, and if it snows all night— We'll make out, Dick. Get going."

The stiff roar of the truck's motor was in their ears as they took up their inert burden. Joseph Leale stumbled ahead to open the front door. He said nervously:

"Who's going to tell Beatrice? Someone's got to—and Aunt Georgie. I don't want the job."

The hall was long and dark and smelled of damp cold. Rocky made out two mounted stags' heads that served as hatracks, and a steep stairway not far from the front door. The first door to their left was closed, but as they passed it a woman's harsh voice cried:

"I tell you I will go out there! I've got to see— You're not going to keep me from him now, though you always tried to when he was alive!"

An older, softer voice said: "Miss Gannon, throw some cold water in her face if she doesn't stop that yelling. This is no time to be dramatic, Beatrice."

Pope murmured: "I think you won't have to break the news to Miss Beatrice, Mr. Leale."

Joseph looked startled at the title; he had seldom been called Mr. Leale. He said:

"I suppose they heard Norma scream and Eleanor or Hal had to tell them. It's this front room, Mr. Allan."

He did not go into his father's bedroom. Rocky watched Pope draw a sheet gently over the dead face. He said:

"I more or less took charge back there a while ago, Mr. Pope, because it kind of seemed to me I'd better, being's I was right here. But I don't know anything about what you do when people are murdered, less'n it's in an open fight. What do you think we'd better do first?"

"I suppose," Pope said, "that we will want to look around in here, eventually. I don't think that's the first thing we should do, but we had better lock the doors."

"There's a connectin' door over there."

"Yes, that leads into Joseph Leale's room." Pope locked it and handed Rocky the key. "Better keep that—and this one to the outside door." He nodded down the hall. "I can't see that it will be of any importance, but I'll explain to you—Miss Norma has the room opposite her father's; Miss Beatrice is next to her. There is a connecting door between those rooms too. Next are the bathrooms, one to each side of the hall, and they can be entered only from the hall. Then Dunn and Austin have the next rooms, opposite each other. Austin is the— well, call him the butler if you like."

Rocky grinned briefly. "I always hankered to see a real live butler."

"Austin isn't that. He's a— Never mind." Joseph swayed a little. "I think I'd like a drink," he said thickly.

"I wouldn't," Pope said, "drink any liquor that doesn't still have a substantial and unbroken seal on it."

Joseph went a shade whiter. "My—God! I'd forgotten. Pope, if he was poisoned, how did it get in his flask? He never left that lying around, and he filled it just before we went out this afternoon."

"I'm glad to know I remembered correctly. I thought he did."

"Now we're gettin' somewheres," Rocky said. "I guess this is your first most important thing: What was in that flask? I thought it smelled like it might be brandy."

"It was. That's what he always drank. Not an expensive brand," Joseph said irrelevantly. "Just— Oh God!"

Rocky looked at him with patient contempt. He thought: Well, I reckon folks do talk like that sometimes, after all. He said: "Well, what now?"

"He was the only one who drank brandy," Joseph whispered. "We all took whisky; everybody here. Everyone knows that. He'd be the only one who would fill a flask from that decanter."

"I noticed that too," Pope said sadly. "And I think—but you had better get your information first hand. It doesn't matter what I think."

Rocky had already a shrewd suspicion that what Mr. Pope thought might matter a great deal. He said to Joseph:

"Well, do you remember if the bottle was already open when your father filled his flask from it? Was there any left over?"

"The stuff was in two decanters on the dining-room sideboard," Joseph said. "One of whisky and one of brandy. Austin saw to keeping them filled, and of course there must have been some left over in the brandy decanter. Father's flask wouldn't hold more than a pint. We all went in there—I mean, Mr. Pope, Hal, and father and I did—and filled our flasks. We put them right in our pockets and went outside."

"So that the brandy in the decanter must have been poisoned, because no one had a chance to poison what was in his flask? And the brandy was there all the time," Rocky said, "for anyone to get at?"

It was Pope who nodded. Joseph wet his dry lips and stared at the wall.

"Whyn't you lie down for a while?" Rocky said. "If you don't want to talk to any of the women folks—"

"No—no, I don't. Not yet. I—I think I will—lie down. Pretty soon—I'll come down—"

"He's kind of a weak sister, I'd say," Rocky remarked as the door to Joseph's room closed. "Hysterical or something, though I suppose this is a big shock. Maybe we'd better see if we can find that brandy decanter?"

"I wonder if we will," Pope said. "Though how anyone could take that chance— Walk softly."

His whisper was too late. A peremptory voice said:

"Mr. Pope? Well, come in here and bring that sheriff person with you."

Pope shrugged helplessly. "One minute, if you don't mind, Miss Leale. We must get that decanter of brandy, for safety's sake."

"You needn't bother. The minute Eleanor told me what had happened I sent her in for it. Come on in here. You're rather slow," Miss Georgina Leale said, "with your precautions for people's safety. Is this your sheriff?"

She did not look like an invalid, though she was small and very thin and must have been more than ten years older than her brother. Her gray hair was beautifully waved, but her brows, thick as Alfred Leale's, had been left untouched by beauty operators to meet across her beaky nose. From under them, eyes of a peculiar dead black regarded Rocky until he felt his ears growing warm.

"Well," she pronounced, "he doesn't look to me like he'd be any force as a detective, but he's a handsome young brute. Don't glare at me, sonny. Eleanor tells me you and she have met. This is my niece Beatrice; half sister to Joe and Norma."

Beatrice Leale muttered unintelligibly in a voice thick with weeping. All her colorings were indefinite: sallow skin, brownish hair, brownish eyes. Yet she escaped neutrality because she was so definitely not good-looking, with her narrow mouth and high cheek bones and body that was thin above the waist and too wide in the hips.

She sat huddled up on a small couch near the airtight stove whose warmth, superimposed on the furnace heat, made the room insufferably hot. Besides the couch there were a bureau, two tables, and at least three chairs, in the largest of which Miss Georgina sat, dressed in a quilted robe, wrapped in a gay blanket, her shoulders protected by a pink afghan. She motioned toward the table nearest her.

"There's your decanters," she said grimly. "Both of 'em. Eleanor brought both because one is empty and clean as a whistle. The other's got a little whisky in it, as you can see. I didn't do any tasting, but it's the one that held brandy that's been washed out. What do you think of that?"

Rocky said, because evidently Pope was not going to speak: "I suppose the kitchen would be where you'd go to wash something? Have you talked to Sarah Powers yet?"

"No. Have her in here, and we'll ask her about it."

"Oh, I reckon I'll go in there and see her myself pretty soon."

"Nonsense, young man! Have her come in here where I can— Do you mean to tell me—"

Rocky's drawl became a little more mellow than usual. "I reckon maybe I'd better talk to Sarah alone, Miss Leale. Wasn't you and her and Miss Beatrice alone in the house this afternoon?"

Miss Georgina's black eyes came alive. "Are you, insinuating that we—that I—"

Eleanor said smoothly: "You know you mustn't excite yourself, Miss Leale." But she grinned at Rocky and Pope as she stood behind Miss Georgina's chair with her back to Beatrice.

"Excite—fiddlesticks!" But Miss Georgina thought better of it and managed to droop against her pillows again. "Austin was somewhere around," she said. "Chopping wood, probably. It hurts his dignity to have to do it, and he's no good at it, but we have to keep warm. The house is a tomb."

Beatrice winced at the last word. "About those decanters—Aunt Georgina sent me to the dining room for some port a little after four," she said. "And they both had liquor in them then."

"And I'll testify she didn't have time to do anything but get the port and come right back here. Mr. Pope!"

Pope started; looked away from the two cut-glass decanters. "Yes, Miss Leale?"

"Why did my brother hire you? He didn't need a secretary."

"So several people have observed. I was not hired as a secretary but as a—shall we say safe-guard?"

"A private detective, I suppose you mean?"

"I'm not a detective," Pope said. "I was recommended to your brother as a man of discretion who has had some experience with murder."

"Indeed! And why did Alfred need a man of that kind around him?"

"Well, wouldn't one be naturally inclined to think that he considered himself—in danger?"

"You mean he didn't tell you anything. Nonsense!" Miss Georgina said, lowering her shaggy brows. "Still, I admit that Alfred was very cautious and inclined to be close mouthed."

"I found him so. There may be something in his papers that will help us. He brought that steel box with him."

"Oh yes, so he did," Miss Georgina said very carelessly. "I'd forgotten that. Well, you'd better just bring that down to me and I'll look over whatever's in it."

"Just as Mr. Allan wishes." Pope added: "Mr. Leale's bedroom is locked now," and Rocky took his cue from that.

"Sorry," he said. "You can see things when we've looked 'em over. There might be something you'd hide out on us."

Because he found the old lady's angry glare rather unnerving, he looked over her head toward Eleanor and Beatrice. Though he was encouraged by Eleanor's quick little nod of approval, it was Beatrice's expression that held him longest. She was glad he was going to look at her father's personal papers—but Miss Georgina was saying:

"This is absolutely ridiculous! A small-town deputy sheriff prying into my brother's personal affairs—"

"Folks most generally," Rocky said, "have to put up with whatever authorities happen to be handy when they—when there's a murder committed, ma'am."

"Then I insist on seeing the sheriff before you do anything!"

"I got no control over nature." Rocky stepped to the window and pulled aside the curtains. "You can see that, can't you? I got a kind of a hunch that's going to keep up all night. No one's going to be drivin' here from Brookdale, and it's even money the train never gets up the canyon."

"But they told us—"

"The public'ty department tells you a hell of—a lot of things that ain't so. We got no snow sheds on this road. An easy grade, but a bad storm starts slides. The train'll be plenty late if nothin' else. I'll phone the sheriff, and he'll try to get here. Might order out a couple tractors."

"I see," Miss Georgina said with sudden calm. "We're isolated, is that it? And except for you happening along— Well, perhaps Alfred thought this was as good a way as any." She shivered and drew the blanket more snugly over her knees. "Eleanor, put some more wood in that stove."

Rocky, who had been sweating plentifully ever since entering the room, backed hastily toward the door. He said to Eleanor:

"They mentioned something about Leale's heart, and Dunn said it wasn't really bad. Is that so?"

"Yes. The very slight trouble he had couldn't possibly have killed him. Mr. Pope, if it was poison, what was it?"

"I'm not a toxicologist," Pope said. "Your guess is as good as mine, child, and probably the same as mine. I don't know how much the doctor will be able to help us when he comes."

Miss Georgina said: "Young whippersnapper!" and Rocky was uncertain whether she referred to him or Pope. But Eleanor smiled again.

"Dr. Ames was here this morning," she said. "He seems very capable, but his bedside manner isn't all that can be desired."

"I thought he was very disagreeable with Auntie," Beatrice said.

Rocky turned back to take possession of the decanters. "I reckon there aren't any fingerprints on these?"

"Mine, at the very tops of the necks," Eleanor said. "But we looked at them carefully. Even the stopper was shining and sparkling clean, and they are so heavily cut that they wouldn't show prints, anyway."

"Well, we'll have to keep 'em. I guess we'll go to see Sarah Powers and this fellow Austin. He been with you very long, ma'am?"

"Five years. He's another man of discretion," Miss Georgina said nastily with a look at Pope. "A very useful sort of fellow, though—in the city. Don't you keep that cook talking too long. We're supposed to have dinner at seven."

"Would you like me to make you some beef broth, Miss Leale?" Eleanor asked.

"Maybe you'd better. I feel faintish, and I guess I can trust *you* not to drop anything in it."

Beatrice gave a strangled sort of gasp. "I'm going to—to—lie down—" She brushed past Rocky, and they heard her running up the stairs.

"She thinks I'm heartless. Maybe I sound that way. She was the only one who ever did care for Alfred," Miss Georgina said. "The rest of them are just scared."

III

Rocky stopped in the cold hall and wiped his forehead. He thought Pope looked a little as if he were smiling. It was hard to tell: a smile was a curved line, and all the lines of this man's face were long and straight. But he said:

"That was a good bit of work, Mr. Allan: refusing to let Miss Leale conduct her own inquiry."

"Oh, well, cracks about small-town sheriffs kind of stick in my craw. I don't know anything about this business, but she could 've doped the brandy, couldn't she? I reckon she can walk?"

"Yes, though she never does unless she has to."

"Was the door I saw in there to another bedroom?"

"Yes, a quite small one. Miss Gannon has that, to be near her—patient. I think the rooms must have been intended for a library and den. There's a lavatory in Miss Leale's room, too. Here is the telephone if you want to use it now. Give me the decanters and I'll wait for you in the dining room. It's at the end of this hall."

A small card was thumbtacked above the old-fashioned telephone: "Two rings, Greenleaf; one ring, Humber." Rocky smiled wryly. You got Merton through Greenleaf, but the Greenleaf telephone service ceased when the mill closed. Humber, a somewhat more permanent lumbering town, had a line to Brookdale but no direct line to Merton. Leale's order for oil must have taken a lot of relaying to reach Merton.

Humber took her time about answering. Rocky remembered that the telephone board was in some private house, along with a branch of the county library. He rang three times before Humber said unenthusiastically:

"Operator!"

"Get me the sheriff's office at Brookdale, will you? Or his house if he isn't in his office."

Humber was suddenly interested. "The sheriff? Is it serious? Because I haven't been able to get Brookdale for an hour. The line's down somewhere, I guess."

"Son of a—"

"Are you addressing me?" Humber said acidly.

"No! No, ma'am! But it's serious. What time do you close up?"

"Eight o'clock is when we're supposed to close. But I guess I can make a special effort, Mr.—"

"Allan. Rocky Allan."

Humber cooed: "Oh, Mr. Allan! I know you. We danced together two three times one night in Brookdale. I'm Maudie—"

"Say, that's swell. I didn't know you worked the board in Humber." Who the hell, Rocky wondered, was Maudie? "Well, listen—there's been a death here; maybe a murder. Yeah, that's what I said. Well, if the sheriff and the cor'ner don't get word in time to catch Number Six when it goes through Br00kdale in the mornin', it'll be another day until they get here. Roads bad down your way?"

"Terrible! And the way it's snowing now I don't think they could even get through behind a tractor and plows. I'll do my best to get hold of Brookdale. Trouble is, unless they call me, they won't know the line's out. But I'll keep trying—Rocky."

"You do that and call me back." Rocky hung up the receiver, said simply, "Whew!" and went out to where Pope was waiting in the dining room.

"I suppose it isn't unusual for the telephone wires to go down in a storm?" he said when Rocky had reported his conversation with Humber. "I wouldn't worry about it. I don't believe a sheriff and coroner will be of any great aid. There's your sideboard. I haven't touched anything."

Looking out the windows Rocky saw that there were enclosed porches on both sides of the room. Old man Dayton had probably thought it would be nice for people to eat out there on warm days, for the dining room itself was rather small. The living room that he knew to be opposite Miss Georgina's room must take up a good deal of space.

There was a clock on the sideboard; hands bisecting its face. "Six o'clock. Seems later," Rocky said. "It wasn't quite five when we got here. Ord'narily it'd take the doc about fifteen minutes to get here, but right now I'll look for him when I see him."

He tugged at the doors of the lower section of the sideboard. There was nothing on top but the clock and a clean and empty cocktail shaker and glasses. On the underneath shelves were two full quart bottles of whisky, labels unbroken, a half-empty bottle of vermouth and one of gin, a squat bottle of crème de menthe from which one small drink had been taken, half-a-dozen quart bottles of sherry and port, two of which had been opened.

"They didn't stint themselves any," Rocky said.

"No. They brought two boxes of liquor; the un-opened one is the larger. Leale did not buy expensive brands, however. Miss Norma is the one who drinks the crème de menthe."

"There isn't any brandy here, not even part of a bottle. I suppose you didn't notice how much brandy there was here when the stuff was first put out?"

Pope frowned. "No, I don't think I did, though I have an idea that I saw three pint bottles."

"What time did you all get here?"

"Yesterday morning."

"How soon was all this stuff laid out like this?"

"We had drinks as soon as we could after we got here. The house was infernally cold. By the time we had lunch, Austin had everything in order: that was his job. Whether he filled the decanters from bottles he had previously put here or whether he brought brandy from the box the liquor was packed in, I don't know. But I do know that Alfred Leale took a nightcap of brandy from the decanter last night and suffered no ill effects from it."

"What time was that?"

"About ten o'clock. He drank cocktails with the rest of us, but so far as I know that was all until he drank from his flask out there on the hill."

"So that any time after ten o'clock last night someone could 've put poison in that decanter? Or in a bottle Austin filled it from unless the seal wasn't broken till he did it. I guess we'd better talk to this Austin—"

A pleasant voice said, "You wanted to see me, sir?" and the door between dining room and kitchen swung back into place. "I'm Austin, sir. Mrs. Powers has been telling me what has happened."

Rocky had expected this man to look like the butlers and valets you saw in moving pictures, but he didn't, in spite of his deferential air. He wasn't bad-looking; he had thick brown hair that could not quite be kept from curling, and his features were good. His body was compact and muscular too, though he was saying with a rueful look at his hands:

"I was in the woodshed, sir. There is only a wood stove in the kitchen, and they want fires in the living room and Miss Georgina's room. The logs all have to be split, and I'm afraid I'm not very good at it."

"It's a knack," Rocky said. "I'll show you how when we get time. We want to find out about this booze, Austin. Mr. Pope says you had two boxes of it."

"Yes sir. I packed them myself. When we got to the house yesterday, it was so cold that everyone took a drink, but that was out of their pocket flasks; Mr. Joseph's and Mr. Dunn's. Mr. Leale had his packed in his bag, empty. Then someone suggested hot toddies, and I opened one of the boxes and heated water as soon as we got the fires started, and Mr. Joseph mixed the toddies."

Rocky looked helplessly at Pope. Did they want information of this kind or was he wasting time by listening to it? Pope said:

"I remember that. Then, when we were thoroughly warm, we helped you start the furnace and went upstairs to unpack. What did you do then?"

"Well, sir, Mrs. Powers had come by that time. There was a misunderstanding, and she was late, but she got here about ten and took charge in the kitchen. So I unpacked the box of liquor that was already open and placed it as you see it now. I filled one decanter with whisky and one with brandy. The decanters hold a little more than a quart. I used one quart bottle of whisky and two pint bottles of brandy."

"How many bottles of brandy was in the lot?" Rocky said.

"Three pints, sir—not very much, but only Mr. Leale drank brandy, and there is more in the other box." He looked at Rocky uneasily. "I'm still rather in the dark, sir. Mr. Dunn was quite short with Mrs. Powers. She thought, though, that there was at least a suspicion that the brandy in Mr. Leale's pocket flask was poisoned."

"She's right. So now you see what we're trying to get at?"

"Yes. Yes sir. There were cocktails and wine for dinner and luncheon both yesterday and today. Everyone drank those," Austin said. "Last night Miss Norma took a small glass of crème de menthe. Mr. Leale had a glass of brandy before he went to bed last night. And he—or some of the others—must have had one or two drinks during the day yesterday. Because I was able to put the third pint into the decanter last, night after dinner."

Rocky said: "You mean—before he had his nightcap?"

"Yes sir. But evidently only that drink was taken out of the decanter after I last refilled it, because it was nearly full after lunch today. I knew they were planning to go out to coast, and Mr. Dunn said they had better carry something to keep out the cold and patted his pocket. The whisky decanter was nearly empty though I'd refilled it more than once. I"—Austin smiled faintly—"drank what was left and filled that decanter. But there was no more brandy in the sideboard, and I knew there was enough in the decanter for Mr. Leale to fill his flask if he carried it. He never did except when he was—well, roughing it. Tramping, you know, or out in the cold like this."

"And then," Rocky prompted, "they came in and filled their flasks?"

"I didn't see them, sir. I did hear people talking in here when I was in the kitchen, but that wasn't immediately after lunch."

"No," Pope said, "we sat in the living room for some time. It was nearly three when we came in here."

"And of course, sir, that brandy was in the decanter all night and all day, and as I said before, I'm almost certain no one had taken anything out of it after Mr. Leale did, about ten o'clock last night."

Rocky sighed. "Yeah, I get that. Did you wash that decanter?"

"No sir. I noticed it over there just now and wondered—"

"Someone washed it. Any idea who could 've done it?"

"No one did it until after three-thirty, sir. I was in here then; the clock being where it is, naturally I looked at it. The whisky decanter was as it is now, and the brandy decanter as it would be after Mr. Leale had filled his flask from it. Everyone was outside then, I thought, except Miss Georgina and Miss Gannon—"

Rocky said: "I thought it was Beatrice Leale who stayed with the old lady."

"She was with us at first," Pope said. "But she said that it was too cold for her and left us after about an hour and sent Miss Gannon out." He added flatly: "Joseph Leale was rather anxious that Miss Gannon should not have to spend the entire afternoon in the house. When Miss Beatrice finally came in, Miss Norma said: 'Oh well, she likes to be self-sacrificing.'"

Austin's lashes flickered a little. "I straightened things in here and then went out to split wood," he said. "I came in twice: that is, through this room to go to the living room with loads of wood. But I didn't notice the decanters either time because my arms were piled so high with wood that I couldn't see very well."

"That's all right: Beatrice Leale says the decanters still weren't washed a little after four. You'd have to have water to wash the thing out clean, and the kitchen would be the best place to get it," Rocky said. "We'll have to talk to Sarah Powers."

"Yes sir. She has a bedroom off the kitchen. I suppose she was in one of those two rooms all afternoon. She was in the kitchen the second time I came through it but not the first."

"Oh! And if she was in the kitchen the same time as Beatrice Leale was in here, Beatrice couldn't

have washed the decanter in there even if the old
lady didn't say she came right in and right back to
her." Rocky looked at Pope. "You all were out of
the house about two hours, but some of you must
've had to come in again during that time."

Pope smiled faintly. "Oh yes. I didn't, or Mr.
Leale, and Miss Gannon didn't leave us after she
came outside. Joseph Leale went in with Miss Beatrice and Dunn about twenty minutes later, and
Miss Norma a very short time before you arrived."

"Then all of them were in the house for a while
some time. But some of them came in before the
decanter was washed, if Beatrice Leale is telling
the truth. Joseph, at least, unless he was in the
house long enough to come in here after Beatrice
took the port back to the old lady. I suppose,"
Rocky said, "that whoever washed that decanter
wouldn't have to have poisoned the brandy in it,
but it'd look damned suspicious. Do you know
what time it was when you came through here
with the wood, Austin?"

"I'm afraid not, sir. But I suppose the first time
was somewhere near four and the second half an
hour or so later."

"I see."

But Rocky did not see anything except that
anyone could have poisoned the brandy in the decanter and that apparently the decanter must have

been washed between four and about five-fifteen. Little as he wanted to, he would have to talk to the old lady again. He had an idea her hearing was pretty good. She'd hear, if she didn't see, people come into the house to go upstairs or along the hall. He'd have to talk to the whole bunch of them and ask them a lot of questions, and likely they would all be very careful how they answered. Eleanor might be some help—Eleanor and Pope.

"We might's well go in the kitchen and talk to Sarah Powers," he said. "Did you have something you wanted to do in here, Austin? Set the table? Well, go ahead."

Sarah Powers was fussing capably over a number of steaming pots on the large wood range. It was a relief to see someone like her, Rocky thought; the kind of person he understood. She was an engineer's widow; one of the cooks at the Greenleaf cafeteria when the mill was running.

A fat little woman with a bush of yellow-white hair and very round blue eyes. She was a little indignant now because Dunn had been "so snappy. Just told me Mr. Leale was dead and might 've been poisoned. Murdered, I s'pose he meant? Then he told me to find Austin, which he could 've done himself. Well—" she rattled the stove lids expressively—"I never, did like this outfit."

"That's interestin'." Rocky sat down by the stove. "Why not?"

"I don't like city folks much," Sarah stated. "But if they wanted to pay me sixty-five dollars whether they stayed a month or not, that was just sixty-five dollars I never counted on getting. I warned Si Wharton to tell 'em I was just a good plain cook—"

"None better anywhere," Rocky said.

"Not in my way. But last night that little blond girl comes in and wants can-apes and hor deeooovers—"

Pope's mouth twitched, and Rocky judged Sarah's French pronunciation must be at least original. "She said somethin' about me wrappin' bacon around olives and then broiling them and a lot of other fancy ideas. I went right to Mr. Leale and he laughs and says not to pay no attention to her but to humor the old lady if she wanted special things, because he was payin' me extra for that, but to give the rest of 'em good filling meals and let it go at that. He seemed a real sensible gentleman, though he was kind of stand-offish."

"Where were you all this afternoon? After lunch, I mean."

"Well, it took me quite a while to get through, because the kitchen needed a lot more cleanin' done." Sarah looked approvingly at her immaculate woodwork but complained: "Can't keep the kitchen floor clean with people trackin' in snow all the time. I took a lie-down when I'd finished. That was just a bit after three-thirty. I slept some and got up about four to look at the kitchen fire."

"Then you didn't hear anyone come into the kitchen in that time?"

"No, except Mr. Austin come through with wood while I was layin' down and then again after I was up. That door's to my bedroom. Them two on the other side is to the cellar and back stairway."

Rocky was not listening now. He turned to Pope and said apologetically:

"I kind of thought, seeing's people had all night and morning to dope that brandy in, it would 've been easier to find out who washed the decanter."

"Yes, I thought that would be the easier task," Pope said. "You haven't questioned the others who were in the house after four. They may be able to tell you something, but frankly, I'm not hopeful that they can—or will."

"I feel like that too. I mean that they're pretty apt to keep their mouths shut. Hell! they almost got to. Someone here has to be guilty. They can't claim any outsider sneaked in. Isn't there something called exclusive opportunity?"

"It's a term quite often used in murder cases. Why?"

"Well, even if we found out all the times after ten last night that folks was in the dining room—besides at meal times—what's that mean? Someone could 've sneaked down at night. If we found out somebody had been seen doing that it'd look suspicious but it wouldn't prove that person did the poisoning. And as for just bein' in that room sometime this mornin'—" Rocky lifted his broad shoulders disgustedly.

"Perhaps you will do better, working from the standpoint of motive. But even there— Don't be impatient," Pope said, looking out at the white swirl of snow. "It seems—rather useless."

"Say, I keep forgetting to ask where you sleep. You accounted for all the others."

"There is a small guest cabin back there." Pope nodded toward the kitchen door. "I'll show you."

The boardwalk was thick with powdery snow, though someone had evidently shoveled it off earlier in the day. The walk split a few yards from the house, its shorter branch running "to the woodshed," Pope said. "This is the cabin; very comfortable when there is a fire in the stove. Four beds, as you see. I suppose you will have to sleep here unless you intend keeping guard in the house."

"I like this place better'n the house," Rocky said. "Only I don't exactly see why you were stuck out here. Were you?"

Pope said: "I haven't begun to tell you of my acquaintance with Alfred Leale. It's too long a story. But the man was annoying. He wouldn't give me his full confidence, and I think he regretted having brought me along. When he was assigning rooms I suggested that I sleep out here. Like you, I don't care for that house. Besides, that was the time for Leale to say he wanted me inside. I tried to force his hand and failed. He was rather amused at my tactics or really was glad to have me away from the house."

"Well, how did he happen to—" Rocky stopped, listening. "I guess that'll have to wait. I think that car coming must be the doctor."

IV

They could hear the sound of a car's straining engine and the whir of wheels slipping in snow when they stepped outside again. The noise ceased abruptly, and Rocky said:

"I reckon he's stuck. We'd better go lend a hand."

He plunged through the unbroken snowdrifts at the side of the house, reached the road, and presently saw the faint glimmer of a flashlight through the white dusk. Dr. John Ames was behind the light and furiously angry as he toiled up the hill.

"Stuck? Of course it's stuck!" he snapped. "I got off the road; couldn't see through this snow and the car's in up to its hub caps. God knows how I ever got this far. Are you Allan? I've seen you in Merton. Your friend gave me your message. I was getting ready to start when Tony Pinelli came in to say I was wanted to deliver his wife's eighth child. I had to go, and Tony lives down below the mill where you can't take a car in winter, so we had to walk."

"Well, you made pretty good time, spite of that."

"I said it was her eighth, didn't I? The baby was wrapped in a red flannel undershirt, and Mrs. Pinelli was drinking soup when I got there." Ames grinned briefly and wiped snow from his face. "Anyway, I'm here, and it looks to me as if I'd remain here for the night. I can walk to Greenleaf in daylight, but I can't risk it in the dark. Barnes said it was Leale who is dead. I suppose I'd better see him at once?"

"I reckon you had. We locked his room. I think we'd better get that steel box the old lady spoke about, don't you?"

Pope nodded. "Since she wanted to look at it herself, perhaps you had better take charge of it. There might be other keys to that bedroom; to any of them. I suppose the key to the box is still in Leale's pocket."

They were in the front hall now, and Ames grimaced toward Miss Georgina's bedroom door.

"I suppose," he murmured, "that that old Tartar made things unpleasant for everyone?"

"Kind of. Is she really sick?" Rocky asked.

Ames snorted. "She's old enough to tire easily but damned if I can see anything else wrong with her. I told her so and she nearly took my head off. You lose the proper bedside manner for cases like hers after you've been ten months in a lumbering town."

He stood back to let Rocky unlock the door of Leale's bedroom. "I guess her brother heard echoes of the fracas because he stopped me afterward to suggest that I'd better humor the old girl. Well, let's see—"

He put down the bag he carried and pulled the sheet from Alfred Leale's face. While Pope remained beside the bed, Rocky opened bureau drawers and looked over their contents. Nothing in them but neatly arranged stacks of shirts, underwear, and handkerchiefs. An unloaded .22 automatic and an unopened box of cartridges beside the handkerchiefs. Ames straightened up, said:

"Well, you've given me an easier job than I'd hoped for. Cyanide. Did you suspect that, Mr. Pope?"

"Why do you think I should have, any more than anyone else?" Pope countered.

"Oh, I don't know. Miss Gannon probably had some suspicions too. But you seem," Ames charged, "to be more or less—at ease in this situation."

Pope said: "I'm no expert, but I have seen a death by cyanide and I know the characteristics. Besides, it was available—as I shall explain later. May we take his keys?"

"Oh, of course. Everything in his pockets, if you like. I have no authority, anyway. I suppose you've notified the county authorities, Allan?"

"Tried to. The line's gone out between Humber and Brookdale. The operator said she'd keep trying to get them. Say, do you know her—the operator?"

"A husky female with buck teeth. Why?"

"I—just wondered. I remember her now. She steers like a battleship, dancing."

Rocky turned over the miscellaneous heap of articles Pope was placing on the bureau: a key ring, four creased and dirty envelopes, two handkerchiefs, fountain pen, cigarette case and lighter, pocket knife, loose change. He singled out the smallest key on the ring, opened the square steel box on the bureau, and looked at the orderly piles of papers inside.

"I guess this can wait," he said, putting the letters from Leale's pockets and the pigskin-covered flask in the box before he locked it. "I've got the flask he drank from, Doc. Could you analyze the brandy that's left?"

"If I ever get back to Greenleaf, I suppose I can. I have a lab, of sorts. But the stuff was obviously poisoned. According to Barnes, he drank and fell over. Save it for the coroner. He'll have to have it analyzed and a post mortem done if," Ames said grimly, "he ever gets here." He walked over to the register, stooped and turned it off. "You don't want any heat in here."

"I never thought about that," Rocky said. "I don't see anything else of his in here that looks worth takin'. I'll keep this strongbox in my own hands till we get time to look it over. What time is it?"

"Seven-five. Where," Ames asked, "are all the family?"

Rocky grinned. "I guess they must all be lyin' down, though I don't know about Dunn. Miss Gannon brought Norma Leale in right away, and Joseph got kind of sickish—"

"He would. And the very—plain Miss Leale who looked at me so reproachfully when I couldn't consider her aunt a very sick woman?"

"The old lady was finally a little too much for her and she decided she'd lie down too," Rocky said. "Dinner's supposed to be at seven, the old lady told us."

The brassy notes of some sort of gong, vigorously beaten, rang through the house. Pope said:

"I imagine Mrs. Powers rang that, in a bad temper. Austin's touch is very artistic. We'd better go down. Yes, I'd lock the door again."

Eleanor was in the hall, outdoor clothes discarded for the crisp white of her uniform.

"Mrs. Powers is cross because no one wants dinner—downstairs," she said with a rueful smile. "I've taken Miss Georgina her tray and brought something to Norma and Beatrice. Harold Dunn has gone down, and Joseph. You'd better go too, and not wait for me. But I do think you'd better see Norma and Beatrice after dinner, Dr. Ames. You won't try to go back to Greenleaf tonight, will you?"

"No, I'm not fool enough to try to walk. I'll see your patients—now, if you like."

Eleanor shook her head. "There's no reason to delay your dinner. And while Norma is rather hysterical, that's nothing serious. Beatrice—well, she refuses to eat and she doesn't want to see you. I'll talk her out of that."

"She will too," Ames said as they went downstairs. "I'm glad she's here to keep some balance in this crazy household. I knew her slightly when I was in the city," he added. "Met her at the theater one night with a friend of mine who was interning at Lane-Stanford."

In the dining room they found Joseph Leale unhappily regarding the bottles on the sideboard shelves. Harold Dunn, already seated at the table, was watching Joseph with a derisive grin.

"Take a chance," he said. "Very likely no one meddled with anything but the brandy. It's a quick death if you want to risk it but I'm sticking to what's left in my flask. I know that's all right."

Joseph shuddered and sat down as Austin entered the room with a tray loaded with soup plates.

"The bottles that have unbroken seals ought to be safe, hadn't they?" Joseph said, addressing Pope. "And I mixed cocktails from that half-empty bottle of gin and vermouth."

"That was at one o'clock," Pope said discouragingly. "Personally, I think nothing but the brandy was poisoned. But I don't know."

"But how could it be when the seals aren't broken?"

"Oh—" Pope got up, went to the sideboard and came back with a bottle of whisky—"what you call seals are, in this case, only a strip of paper glued down across the cap or cork of the bottle. The glue on this one seems to be a little damp."

His long slender fingers were working dexterously at the government tax label as he spoke, and finally he held it up, untorn. There were smears of glue on the sides of the bottle near its neck and in another instant he had pasted the label in place again.

"You see? Of course, according to Austin, the brandy must have been poisoned in the decanter."

"Why?" Joseph said.

"Because your father had a drink from the decanter after Austin last refilled it. If we are to believe that Austin is telling the truth—" Austin smiled slightly and went back to the kitchen—"and I don't see why he should not be—none of the three bottles of brandy that were used could have been poisoned in the bottle."

"Then why all this hocus-pocus about the labels?" Dunn said.

"Mr. Leale was wondering if it would be safe to drink this liquor. Well, I'd like at least to examine it first. I don't like poisoners," Pope said sadly. "They make me very nervous. There is no use in being foolishly reckless. Someone may have wanted to make absolutely certain that Leale would die."

"Or even some of the rest of you," Rocky suggested rather maliciously. "You'd better lay off that unopened box of booze too. Or maybe I'd better smash the works."

Dunn said: "God, what an awful waste!"

"Yeah, ain't it?" Rocky thought: I'll bet he would think that. He didn't get those pouches under his eyes drinking water. Be interesting to see what happens when that flask of his is empty.

Joseph looked suddenly hopeful. "Well, if Austin should be lying—I don't say he is, but if he should be and that brandy was poisoned in the bottle—someone besides one of us could have done it."

Pope looked at him with an air of polite regret. Dunn pulled peevishly at his small mustache.

"Don't be a sap, Joe. Even if Austin had any reason for lying about how he filled the decanter, still your idea is all wet. That liquor, as everyone knows, came from De Rosa's and was packed and sent off that same day. You aren't—"

He stopped as Eleanor came in and sat down. She looked unfavorably at her cold soup, pushed her plate aside, and said:

"Go on with what you were saying. I heard the last part of it. Have you decided those government tax labels aren't any protection to a bottle that has only a cap screwed on the top?"

"Mr. Pope has just demonstrated that," Ames said. "Did you think of that? Bright girl."

"If Alfred hadn't been so tight he'd have bought the better brands, that have lead foil or cellulose around the necks. Anyway, Joe is now trying to prove the brandy was poisoned in the bottles, so he can assign responsibility to De Rosa or some of Alfred's old business enemies," Dunn said unpleasantly.

"I didn't suggest De Rosa: that's foolish," Joseph said.

But there was something so uncertain about his defiance that Rocky decided: He's pretty well under Dunn's thumb, but he's got more nerve when Eleanor's around.

Austin was removing soup plates now and bringing in roast lamb, rather overdone.

"You sent the boxes away," Joseph persisted. "Where were they until the expressman came for them?"

Austin did not pretend not to have overheard their previous conversation. He said:

"The liquor was delivered to the back door, sir, in two boxes, but they were not nailed down on top because we wished to be certain the order had been correctly filled. I checked against my list; nailed up the larger box. Then I was called to the other part of the house, and the smaller box—the one we opened when we arrived here—was in the kitchen for an hour or so before I had time to fix it."

"I suppose Joe would like to prove Lupita—the cook—doped up the brandy," Dunn jeered.

"She was doing her marketing, sir," Austin said seriously.

"Well, I looked at the stuff myself, Joe. So did Beatrice. I heard Cousin Georgina tell her to see if they had sent enough port. And Norma asked me about her precious crème de menthe, and I told her I hadn't noticed if there was any," Dunn said. "So I suppose she went to take a look. But this is all a waste of time, except that I agree with Pope that poisoners may be no respecters of persons and I don't care to risk drinking any of that stuff."

"In case of emergency, sir, I have nearly a quart of whisky in my room," Austin said. "I bought it myself and have had one drink from it." He left the room again.

"Well, that's something," Dunn said. "Our admirable Crichton—" He looked toward Rocky; began kindly: "A character in a play, Mr. Allan—"

"Yeah, by Barrie. I can read," Rocky said blandly, "with some help on the big words." Eleanor giggled, and Dunn gave her an unfriendly glance.

"I read that play in the hospital," Rocky went on. "It was mighty interestin' how this butler was able to—to act so much better in an emergency than all the ladies and gentlemen. Where were you, Mr. Dunn, after you told Mrs. Powers what had happened? Why didn't you go find Austin yourself?"

"Why should I? Oh, I don't know—I was rattled, I suppose. I didn't want to answer a lot of questions, and I didn't know where Austin might be. I went up the back stairway to my room. Frankly, I was hiding from Cousin Georgina. I'd have been a convenient scapegoat; she always has to blame someone for anything unpleasant that happens. I did look in to see Norma, poor kid. Patted her shoulder a bit. How is she?"

"All right." Eleanor quite obviously had little sympathy to give Norma. "It would be nice, Joseph, if you'd at least say good-night to your aunt."

"Oh, sure I will," Joseph said quickly. "I suppose it was an awful shock to her."

"She stood it remarkably well."

Dunn said: "Miss Gannon is being diplomatic."

The sneer was for both Eleanor and Miss Georgina. More than likely, Rocky thought, Dunn had made a pass at Eleanor and been told where to head in. Dunn looked like he'd go for any pretty woman. Joseph was different, and maybe he was just the type a decisive person like Eleanor would want to marry. He was good-looking and he must be well off, now.

Rocky scowled at his coffee cup and turned to a covert scrutiny of Pope. Now that he had taken off his heavy leather jacket you could see how very thin he was. But there would be plenty of muscle about those angular shoulders. His face was long and brown and melancholy; very nearly a caricature of a face. Yet there was something attractive about it; you wanted to laugh and for some reason you didn't.

Rocky decided suddenly that since it was doubtful if the sheriff would be here by morning he'd let Pope direct things. He hadn't said much, but Rocky felt that the man would know what was best to be done. Probably—nothing.

They might get some place by considering motive, Pope had said, and that sounded reasonable enough, but he couldn't know what motive any of these people had for killing Alfred Leale until he knew more about them. Pope could tell him a great deal, and very likely Eleanor could—if she would. But it was just as likely that she would feel she owed her employers some loyalty. No, not that so much. They didn't treat her like just a hired nurse, so perhaps she considered them her friends, and she was the kind who stuck to a friend.

Joseph, having forked his apple pie into bits without eating any of it, said abruptly:

"Well, I guess I'll go see Aunt Georgina," and eagerly: "You're coming, Eleanor?"

"Not now. Tell her I'll come in an hour or so. I want," Eleanor said deliberately, "to talk to Mr. Pope and Mr. Allan."

"She would," Dunn said. "Nurses see and hear—things. And tell them, I suppose."

"In the circumstance of a particularly cowardly murder, yes. Have you some incident in mind," Eleanor said pleasantly, "that you particularly don't want me to tell?"

"Certainly not. But outsiders don't always—understand a family as its individual members understand each other."

"Seems to me," Rocky said amiably, "that families that go around poisonin' each other are right likely to be misunderstood by the gen'ral public."

Dunn reddened angrily, and his small white hands tightened on his fork. Rocky waited for the explosion, but Dunn said nothing. Rocky let Austin refill his coffee cup, thinking: Dunn's afraid of any guy bigger than he is. Not Joseph, because he's soft. And not me, at first, because he thought I was too dumb ever to know what he was talking about. He drank coffee and was quite pleased with the result of his skirmishes with Dunn. Pope said:

"By the way, Austin, what did you do with the empty bottles?"

"They're in the snow, sir. To the right of the kitchen. Garbage and trash disposal seems to be rather a problem," Austin said apologetically. "Mr. Leale said we should build an incinerator, but we haven't had time to do that. So I threw the empty bottles and other odds and ends into the snow."

Pope nodded. "Is there a fire in the living room?"

"Yes sir. It's been burning for more than an hour, and it's quite pleasant in there. I must say that the furnace alone doesn't seem to heat the house satisfactorily."

"Wait till it quits snowing," Rocky said. "That's when it's really cold. Fifteen or twenty below, most likely."

Austin shivered and glanced involuntarily at his reddened hands. Joseph, who had seemed unable to get himself gracefully from the room, mumbled:

"Well—I'll see Aunt Georgie and then go in the living room."

"I suppose," Dunn said, scowling at Pope, "that is where you want me to go? All right."

Pope looked reflectively at the door Dunn slammed behind him and took his fourth cup of coffee. Ames said:

"What a remarkably nasty disposition that fellow has."

"Not always," Pope said mildly. "He is usually quite good company."

"So are all pampered pussy cats so long as they have their cushions and cream," Eleanor said. "They spit and claw when they're disturbed."

Ames laughed. "Very likely you're right. Shall I see your Miss Leales now—the younger ones?"

"Miss Georgina doesn't need you. I'll take you to Norma and Beatrice. She—Beatrice—really must sleep. Then I'll come back here to talk to you two."

Pope said: "I like that girl. Her story should come before mine because she knew the Leales before I did. My idea is this—that we have no clues and are not likely to discover any. Tracing the source of the poison in this sort of case is usually one's best chance, but even if we were in the city where we could work on that angle, it would do us no good, because Joseph Leale dabbles in chemistry and has a very well equipped laboratory in the Leale home."

"The hell you say!"

"Yes. Anyone here or anyone who ever came to the house could have entered that room. He was not careful about locking it. So it seems to me that we have only one sort of material with which to work—that is, the people concerned."

"I managed to figure that out for myself, only I couldn't put it in those words."

Rocky was thinking he liked to hear Pope talk. He had a deep, pleasant voice and an odd sort of accent. It wasn't just exactly like that of an Englishman Rocky had known, but there were resemblances. He was unprepared for the man's sudden question:

"If you don't mind telling me—why are you called Rocky? I always have a great curiosity regarding the origin of nicknames."

"Oh—" Rocky grinned—"it was a guy that hit me on the jaw that started people callin' me that. He busted his hand. It made me kind of dizzy for a minute, but I knocked him cold."

"I see." Pope looked appraisingly at Rocky's six feet of hard flesh and muscle; his broad shoulders and narrow hips. "I see," he repeated.

"My real name is Nathan Bedford," Rocky confessed. "After the cavalry general, Forrest. Granddaddy fought under him in the Civil War."

"Texas or Arkansas?"

Rocky laughed. "Texas. I haven't been there for ten years, but I never did get entirely rid of that way of talkin'. My dad's a farmer, but I had an uncle was a railroader. Got killed on the Santa Fe last year. Somehow, I couldn't settle down. I lit out from home when I was seventeen and finally ended up on this road. Since times got hard there ain't so much work in winter times. Uncle Bill left me near to ten thousand dollars, and it's come in right handy."

He stopped, rather abashed at having talked so much about himself but suspecting that Pope was one of these people you did talk to, because he gave you his entire attention. Pope murmured:

"Nathan Bedford. My given name is Theophilus."

"I knew a guy named Oh-Be-Joyful, once," Rocky said courteously.

To his surprise, all the long lines of Pope's face moved upward in an unmistakable grin. He took off the large tinted glasses that had hidden his eyes, showing them to be very blue, very alert.

"How comforting," he said, polishing the glasses on a napkin. "I will remember that—and here's Miss Gannon."

Eleanor said: "Dr. Ames very diplomatically went into the living room. He prescribed for Norma and Beatrice, and I think they will sleep all right tonight. I settled Miss Georgina for the night, too."

"Why are you worried about this Beatrice?" Rocky said.

"Oh, Norma cries and screams and lets off steam. Beatrice is a repressed type, and she lies rigid and stares at nothing. Besides, she was almost too devoted to her father. Why have you been so damned formal with me, Rocky Allan?" Eleanor said severely. "As if we'd never met before."

"I didn't know—I thought maybe—"

"You thought wrong! You're a friend of mine, aren't you? Don't you suppose I've told everyone you are—if you thought I wouldn't care for them to know it? You're perfectly ridiculous! And I didn't know you'd been in the hospital."

"Didn't you?"

"No, or I'd have written to you. What happened?"

"Oh, Bob Wright and I drove to Reno. You knew Bob a little? He always did drive like a fool. Tire blew out when we were goin' aroun' a curve at about fifty. Car rolled over three times."

"Were you both hurt?"

"Kind of. Bob died. I busted my shoulder. Well," Rocky said abruptly, "where do we begin?"

"With whatever Miss Gannon has to tell us," Pope said.

PART II
"SOMEONE WISHES ME DEAD"

Eleanor absent-mindedly pulled out the four hair-pins that were needed to hold the curling ends of her hair in a loose knot.

"I can think better this way," she said. "I don't want to waste time telling things that aren't important."

Rocky found it hard to take his eyes from that shimmering mop of hair. He wanted to run his fingers through it, as Eleanor herself was doing. But she was saying:

"I met Norma Leale in 1928. My father was fairly well-to-do then, and he sent me to a girls' school in Berkeley. I was seventeen and Norma was fourteen and had one of these intense school-girl crushes on me.

"It's odd that kids in school don't talk very much about their homes or parents. Norma and I never met each other's parents. But I remember that at that time her father had not retired from business and was not at home a great deal. She spoke of Beatrice, who is ten years older than Norma, and of her aunt, not very affectionately. Of course, from a flirtatious and spoiled fourteen-year-old, that wouldn't mean much.

"Joseph and I are the same age, and I met him when Norma brought him to a school dance. He was in his last year of high school, and he took me out several times that year. He was going to Stanford the next year, and I suppose our friendship would have continued if poor Daddy hadn't been so enthusiastic about Trans-America. I did start to Mills College, but by Christmas time I could see I was going to need to earn my living as soon as possible.

"So I entered a hospital as a student nurse, and it was lucky for me that I wasted no time about it, for my father died in six months and I had nothing. That's how I lost touch with my old friends. I was," Eleanor said tolerantly, "determined to be very independent. I saw too many other girls whose families lost money hanging onto the edges of the old crowd and accepting favors gratefully.

"Well—I've been on my own for more than three years now and am not quite so touchy. So I was very glad to meet Norma in San Francisco about a month ago and go to lunch with her."

Norma led the way to the Palace, ordered without any study of the right-hand side of the menu, and then wasted her food when it came. She looked to Eleanor, after six years, simply like a grown-up fourteen. She was suddenly rather glad for the hard experience of those six years that had made her wise enough not to envy Norma.

She was even less inclined to do so as Norma talked on and on, for the old admiration that had made her give Eleanor her confidence at fourteen seemed automatically to reassert itself, in spite of a slight tendency toward condescension now and then.

The condescension was for Eleanor's brief answer to Norma's, "Darling, wherever have you been? No one seemed to know." And then: "But, my dear, how simply dreadful for you!"

But Eleanor restored the old relationship with her crisp, "Not at all. There are worse things than knowing you can earn your own living."

"It's wonderful that you can. I wish I could. But I'm so helpless." Norma looked at her bonelessly soft hands. "And it's really Father's fault, even if I am naturally lazy. He has such old-fashioned ideas about women, and I get so tired of being absolutely dependent on him and having to keep within my allowance when he has so much money."

Eleanor looked at Norma's mink coat and said dryly that she imagined the allowance was rather a generous one.

"But it isn't! Thirty-five dollars. Of course, I can charge all my clothes and things, but Father goes over the bills, and he has just one car and none of us can use it. Joe is on an allowance too."

"Oh yes. What is Joseph doing?"

"He often speaks of you, Eleanor," Norma said sentimentally. "He tried to find where you were— he was going to Stanford, you know. But he got in with a fast crowd and didn't make his grades his second year. He was in an automobile wreck after the Big Game, too. Of course, everyone was drinking and it got in the papers and Father was very angry."

"Is your father at home all the time, now?"

"Oh yes. He sold his interest in the lumber mill in Lassen County. I don't know if it's better or worse since he's home. Of course I've only been out of school three years. There wasn't any use my trying college. I thought I'd have a good time but I don't," Norma said pettishly. "We have lots of money and no social position at all. It makes me sick. Father's first wife never tried to break into things, and my mother just had two babies and died."

"Oh, you must have some friends," Eleanor said mildly.

"But not—exciting ones. Joe knew lots of people, but Father won't let him bring them to the house. Joe has to sneak out to meet them. I went with him once or twice."

"I should think," Eleanor said generously, "that there would be scads of unattached males buzzing around you."

"Oh, enough," Norma said complacently. "But there are only two that Father approves of, and they are earnest young business men, so unexciting. Eleanor, I'm so unhappy!"

"You must be, not to eat these stuffed chicken breasts, considering what they're costing you." Eleanor helped herself from the dish between them. "Who is the man?"

"I can't tell you—yet. Because, while I know you wouldn't tell, I just can't risk Aunt Georgina or Beatrice—or anyone—knowing. Beatrice hates me."

"Does she? That's nice."

"I mean it! She hates me because I'm pretty and she's homely and can't get married. Father's cousin Harold, who lives with us, is three years older than she is, and once we thought they might get married. Six—oh, about six years ago. But Harold likes me now. I wouldn't have him as a gift, but I don't mind teasing Beatrice."

"I'll wager you don't. Sisterly affection."

"You needn't look that way. She's only my half sister, and she's always trying to set Father against me. And Joe too, though he can get around her if he takes the trouble. Father's fondest of her, but she's always afraid he might not be. And she doesn't have to stick to an allowance, but she doesn't want to spend money. I hate her too," Norma said calmly. "Shall we have strawberries?"

"In January? They'll have no taste. I prefer French pastry. But I take it," Eleanor said when the waiter had come and gone, "that your father doesn't approve of the man? Or does he know about him?"

"Yes, Father knows, because—George insisted on telling him we were going to get married sometime. He's wonderful—George. I think he could improve me a lot," Norma said unexpectedly. "He knows all my faults and tells me about them, and I don't mind. But he hasn't a decent income yet, and Father said we must wait. He doesn't really like George, though he has only seen him once and can't give any good reason for not liking him."

"Your father can't keep you from marrying, you know."

Norma widened her eyes. "Oh, but Father wouldn't give me one cent if I married without his consent, and I'd be of no use to George if we didn't have enough money. Father said he didn't want his name mentioned again and I was not to see him. Of course I did, sometimes. But not lately, because he got a job in the South and doesn't even write very often. Doesn't dare to, I mean."

Eleanor shrugged. "Well, my dear, you know best. But I can't break down and weep over your sad plight. I suppose you haven't told Joseph? You two used to be good friends."

"We still are. But I wouldn't dare tell him because he might blurt it out to someone. Harold, maybe, and it would be awful to have Harold know. He has too much influence over Joe. I don't see why Father doesn't realize that. I could tell him a thing or two about Harold, but Father won't let us carry tales. Poor Joe hasn't anything to do except when he fusses around with chemicals. Chemistry is the only thing he was ever good at, and Father let him fit up a lab. Maybe he'll invent something some day," Norma said hopefully. "Are you through?"

"Yes, and I have some shopping to do. You wouldn't be interested in it: just uniforms and white stockings. It's been nice to see you."

"But—Eleanor! Why didn't I think about it before? Let's sit in the lobby and I'll tell you."

Eleanor looked at her watch, thought, "Oh well, I may not see her for another six years," and let Norma drag her to a high-backed chair in the lobby.

"It's this," Norma began eagerly. "Aunt Georgina plays at being sick. No, she isn't really. She just wants attention. Well, sometimes she has a nurse, but right now she hasn't and she wants one. It's really an easy job. She just wants someone starched and white around for a few hours. She goes to bed early and has breakfast late."

"Yes, but from your own account, my dear, your surroundings aren't exactly—harmonious."

"No, but it might be worse, and I was thinking how nice it would be for me and Joseph to have you there. Well, you can laugh, but I don't see why it would be as hard as taking care of a really sick person."

"I suppose it wouldn't be, if your aunt— Why did her former nurses leave?"

"Oh, she didn't quarrel with all of them. Usually she just decides she is feeling better because she thinks that Beatrice is getting too independent about running the house. She really does it all, anyway, but Aunt Georgina wants to give the orders. Really, it would be an awfully easy job.

You don't have to do any cooking or anything like that, and we could have some good times."

Eleanor hesitated, thinking of her last case, that of a gentle old lady who had very slowly died of cancer. She did not particularly like to nurse a person who was not really ill, or to mix business with pleasure in the way Norma suggested, but she was rather tired.

"Besides, we may all go up to the mountains for a while," Norma went on. "You'd like that, wouldn't you?"

"Nothing better, but does your aunt go on excursions of that kind?"

"She wouldn't let us leave her behind. We always have to go everywhere in a family party. It gets so tiresome! And I don't suppose we'll get to go where we want to. That's partly my fault."

"Why is it?"

"Well, last summer Father let me go with some people to a hotel in the mountains near a place called Brookdale. One day we were riding and passed this old house they called Dayton's Folly. It was for sale or rent, but no one would buy it because it was so big. Father has been talking about getting a place in the mountains, and I mentioned this one to him. I didn't suppose he'd be interested, but he went and leased it with the privilege of buying. He didn't consult any of us. I'm afraid if we go anywhere it will be there, and it will be lonely in winter time. It's just like him not to take us some place like Tahoe. But if you were along, that would help."

"Thank you. I've been up in that country, and it's lovely. I'll interview your father if you like," Eleanor decided suddenly. "Or will it be your aunt I must see?"

"Both. Because if I just spoke about you to Aunt Georgina, she wouldn't consider you, just to be contrary. If I speak to Father first it will be all right. Tomorrow, about two?" . . .

The Leales lived on Broadway in a somber brownstone mansion. Eleanor's first thought on seeing Dayton's Folly was that the two houses were in some subtle way deeply akin. In neither of them did you ever feel completely warm and at ease. Neither house had ever truly belonged to anyone or been loved. Flowers did not like to grow in the back garden of the Broadway house for all the impassioned labor of the little Japanese gardener. When you went there you were careful not to walk across the lawns or to pick the flowers without asking permission.

The place was imposing, however, spacious and well kept, though the furnishings were a trifle old-fashioned. Another proof, Eleanor thought, waiting to see him, that Alfred Leale's taste in all matters was rigidly imposed on his family. She decided that she would dislike him heartily, though she knew Norma well enough to discount a great many of her remarks.

But, reluctantly, she was forced to admit that she liked the man. And pitied him at the same time, because while he was so obviously concerned for the well-being and happiness of his household you soon understood that he was quite certain that he always knew what was best for them. He could not see why they did not recognize this omnipotence and was angry when they did not. The old-fashioned household with a kind and sometimes indulgent father as its unquestioned master was his ideal.

He looked at Eleanor approvingly, however, when Norma introduced them.

"Of course, you will have to see my sister, Miss Gannon, but I'll take you up to her, and I'm sure there will be no trouble. I suppose Norma has told you that she is not seriously ill." His eyes twinkled a little; he was evidently not quite without humor. "Norma has been telling me about you, and Joseph has spoken of you. I'm not surprised that his memory has been longer than usual. It will be very nice for Norma to have you here. I certainly cannot become very enthusiastic about most of her friends."

At a remark of this sort from her father, Norma might turn sullen or she might only laugh, as she did today, having a point to gain and choosing to "humor Father." She said:

"I knew you would like Eleanor. Then it's all settled?"

"If Miss Gannon cares to stay and your aunt agrees. We'll go up to see her now."

Norma murmured some excuse and did not go with them. As they went up the stairs Leale said:

"I admire your pluck, Miss Gannon."

"There are thousands of girls like me."

"Not all with your early upbringing. I was wondering what Norma would have done under similar circumstances. I suppose I have made things too easy for her and Joseph, but it would be taking work from those who really need it, to throw them out into the world. Georgina, here is Miss Gannon. You know, I spoke to you about her last night."

Miss Georgina said: "Is that your own hair, girl? But I suppose it is. You couldn't get that shade by dyeing. You'll give some color to this room, and you look capable. Did you bring your things with you?"

By the end of her first week there Eleanor had shaken herself into the routine of the household—a routine evolved by Leale and Miss Georgina and imposed on the others. Breakfast at eight, luncheon at one, dinner at seven, and one must be at the table at the designated hours or go without. Anyone who meant to lunch or dine elsewhere was expected to notify Leale at the breakfast table and, in the case of Norma and Joseph, to tell him where they were going.

Miss Georgina had her own schedule—breakfast at ten, what she termed a "snack" at noon, another snack at three, and dinner at six, leaving Eleanor to have her meals with the family. Her work, she admitted, was almost negligible but sometimes exasperating.

Miss Georgina expected that at some time during the morning she should be visited by every member of the family and to have those who were at home come in to see her after dinner She had a stock list of symptoms which she recited in answer to their dutiful questions regarding her health.

These rather amused Eleanor, but she was too forthright to enjoy being forced to corroborate Miss Georgina's statements. The old lady ate enormously, slept remarkably well, and kept full charge of all the housekeeping activities.

Beatrice received orders for the day when she visited her aunt in the morning; orders whose execution was no small task, for Miss Georgina was an old-fashioned housekeeper, and besides Austin and the cook there was only one other servant.

"You didn't dust behind the pictures in the living room, as I told you," Miss Georgina would say. "See that you do it today. I don't know where you get your slipshod ways."

Beatrice flushed and said nothing, but afterward she muttered to Eleanor in what was a rare outburst:

"I don't know how she guesses I didn't dust the backs of those pictures, and it's perfectly ridiculous that I should have to! Norma never does one thing, and Aunt Georgina expects there should never be one speck of dust in all this big house."

But while Eleanor, pitying the older woman, had made friendly overtures, she soon understood that being Norma's friend was enough to spoil her chances of becoming Beatrice's. She saw more of her while on duty than of anyone else in the house, for Beatrice was always faithful and even found time to read aloud to her aunt in a flat, expressionless voice.

"I don't enjoy her reading but it's good for her," Miss Georgina said when Eleanor tried to take over this task. "She likes to mortify the flesh and be a martyr. She likes keeping house too, whatever she may say. What else has she got to do? Of course she'd rather not take any orders. Fine mess things would be in if she didn't. She's got no executive ability. It makes her mad when I guess she hasn't done something I told her to do."

She looked shrewdly at Eleanor as she said this. Eleanor was quite certain by now that Miss Georgina was not gifted with second sight but that she was given to midnight ramblings about the house. Partly, she supposed, by way of exercise, but mainly to discover whether her orders were carried out. Eleanor could not help saying:

"If I were Beatrice I'd wonder why you always— guess right."

Miss Georgina chuckled. "You're a smart girl. Go on being smart—and discreet."

II

Those nocturnal prowlings of Miss Georgina's rather annoyed Eleanor, however. In spite of its solidity there were a great many noises in the house at night, and sometimes she found herself strangely nervous. Her room opened into Miss Georgina's, but she was forbidden to enter the old lady's room after she had settled her in bed at nine o'clock.

Miss Georgina might read for hours after that, but it was understood that Eleanor was off duty then. The halls were dark at night because Leale saw no reason to light them after he had gone to bed. And there was something rather eerie in the idea of Miss Georgina's wandering about the house, inspecting the backs of pictures and several catch-all closets that she expected Beatrice to keep in perfect order.

But it might not always be Miss Georgina who came softly along the hall. Several times, she knew, it was Harold Dunn. He had a latchkey and more or less came and went as he pleased, but he came softly when the hour was past midnight. So far as Eleanor had been able to discover, his only income was a small allowance that Leale gave him.

"Because Harold's father loaned Father some money once when he needed it," Norma said vaguely. "He did have a job until four or five years ago. I mean, he did sometimes. Then he had pneumonia, and he coughs a lot whenever he thinks he might have to go back to work."

Dunn did sometimes sit for several hours in front of an old typewriter and afterward would announce that he had started a new story. Now and then he managed to finish one, Norma said, "but they always come back from the magazines he sends them to."

It was Eleanor's opinion that Dunn intended to try very hard to marry Norma. Just now he assumed a very charming older brother attitude toward her. But of course he did not know about the absent George, and Norma could not resist any sort of masculine admiration. When she responded prettily to Dunn's flattering table conversation it was painful to watch Beatrice.

Apparently no one else did, and Eleanor tried not to. Yet it was not so much an old affection for Dunn as hate for Norma that she thought she saw.

Beatrice centered all her repressed and thwarted power to love upon her father. She, at least, was the sort of dutiful and housewifely daughter of whom Leale approved. And he was her one strength; however scornful the others might be of her, she was the only one whom he never criticized, the only one whom he treated as an adult.

"And she gets nothing from it," Norma said bitterly. "She's worn the same fur coat for five years. She does it so she can remind Father of it when I want a new one. I suppose if I'd be nice to her I could get her to use her influence with Father for things I want to do, like having a car. But I— will—not!" Norma said, grinding her white teeth together. "Not if I ride on street cars for the rest of my life!"

Joseph was not so scrupulous. A careless compliment or half an hour of ordinarily pleasant conversation from him was enough to enlist Beatrice's help whenever he wanted it. His point gained, he would ignore her again, though he never jeered at her as Norma and Dunn did. Beatrice never seemed to learn by experience but caught eagerly at what came her way.

Eleanor had to agree with Norma that Dunn did possess a great and probably unfortunate influence over Joseph. She also wondered why Leale did not see it, but Dunn's attitude toward Leale was perfection. He never argued with him and appeared to have the utmost respect for Leale's wishes and opinions. Dunn and Joseph seemed never to have the same evening engagements, but Eleanor knew that they often met after they had left the house.

"Poker game," Joseph explained on one occasion. "I wish I had Hal's luck." He frowned darkly. "Not just at poker. There's a gambling joint where he takes me sometimes. Of course, the old man doesn't know anything about that."

"So I supposed. How do you get in at night?" Eleanor said. "You have no key."

"Hell of a thing, isn't it? Twenty-four and can't have a latchkey! Well, Dad goes to bed at ten and Austin at eleven. Austin is a good guy, so he keeps his mouth shut when I'm not in by the time he locks up. Lets Father think I was. And I had a duplicate of Hal's key made. What else is a guy to do?"

"Go to work."

"Doing what? Dad could get me a job in some mill, but what's the point in it? I don't need to work; not that kind of work. If he wasn't so stubborn— After I'd flunked out at Stanford, he swore he wouldn't send me anywhere else, though I promised I'd do better. That wasn't very reasonable," Joseph said. "Was it, now?"

"No-o, it doesn't seem so to me."

"Because I really would have got down to work and stuck to it. And I think he's sorry he swore I couldn't have another chance, but he won't go back on his word."

It was at this point that Eleanor hesitated and finally decided that she need not tell Pope and Rocky Allan the rest of that conversation.

They had been sitting on a stone bench in the garden, and Joseph took her hand suddenly.

"I could get out and dig ditches, Eleanor, if I had you to work for. And I wouldn't have to, because the old man likes you. Couldn't you marry me? Honestly, I never did forget you."

"Boys usually remember the girls they thought they were in love with at seventeen. But that's a long time ago, Joseph."

"I know you mean I never tried very hard to get in touch with you," Joseph muttered. "But I was only a kid, and the minute I saw you again— Of course, there was a girl I got mixed up with. Dad never knew about that. If he had— It was fairly serious but we made a clean break."

"I understand perfectly. I'm not expecting to marry a young saint, Joseph," Eleanor said impatiently. "Just a man with some backbone."

She did not add that she doubted that he would ever dig ditches for her sake. She was quite certain that Alfred Leale would not oppose their marriage. But she got up abruptly and started back to the house.

"It's time I got back to Miss Georgina. And don't look so doleful. I'm really very fond of you, if you would only grow up a little."

"I would, if we were married," Joseph insisted, and while he had let her go that afternoon his first proposal had not been his last.

But she needn't tell Rocky or Pope. She supposed they both knew that Joseph was in love with her. His attitude toward her made that almost embarrassingly evident. Rocky was looking at her now with a queer little smile. He had odd eyes for so blond a man; yellowish brown instead of the blue you looked for. Yes, he guessed what she hadn't told him about Joseph and herself, and it was better that he should. She wouldn't tell him, either, that Harold Dunn had assumed that a nurse never slept in her own bed when a man's was at her disposal and that he hadn't managed to forget what she had said to him. Rocky probably suspected that, too. His air of amiable simplicity was very deceiving; it made people underrate his intelligence. She went hastily on with her story.

Leale probably did regret his harshness when he saw Joseph bored and idle or working only at uncertain intervals in his laboratory. But he would never give anyone a second chance, Eleanor felt, once having made sure the first chance was a fair one. Miss Georgina said:

"Al's stubborn and close mouthed. He's not a happy man. Maybe he never has been, but when he was working to get on in the world he was too busy to know whether he was or not. His first wife was a queer stick and his second a silly doll-baby. Norma and Joseph are like their mother, but they've got enough of Al in them to make them ornery. Of course Joe can get around me. I'm old enough to like to have a good-looking nephew be nice to me sometimes."

"And a good-looking cousin?"

"Harold?" Miss Georgina snorted. "Utterly worthless. Oh, he has charming manners when he wants to use them. His mother was my mother's cousin, you know. She was bone lazy, and Harold takes after her. I guess you gave him a lesson? Good! I had to discharge one little slut of a nurse because of him."

Eleanor said: "Does Mr. Leale know that?"

"I don't know how much Al knows about Harold, but I don't tell him anything. Men will be—men," Miss Georgina said. "Yes, I've got old-fashioned views. Don't believe in a double standard, and neither does Al."

"Why didn't you marry, Miss Georgina?"

The old lady looked pleased. "So you think I might have? Well, that's true, but the man died, and I followed tradition and remained faithful to his memory. I can't," she said wistfully, "even remember clearly what he looked like. Oh well. Has any more been said about this trip to the mountains?"

"A great deal has been said but nothing has been decided. Norma and Joseph want to go to Tahoe." Eleanor had found by now that she could be frank with Miss Georgina regarding anything but her alleged invalidism.

"So we'll probably go to this place—Dayton's Folly, is it?—if we go anywhere. I'd rather stay home, but Al's been hankering to see snow again. Anyhow," Miss Georgina said, "we're going to clean house this week."

"Why?"

"Why? What are houses for but to be cleaned? My mother never went away for any length of time that she didn't clean house first."

The house was accordingly cleaned, from top to bottom, attics, cellars, closets, and shelves. There was only one room that Miss Georgina did not dare to meddle with—the kitchen, where a fat Spanish cook possessed absolute authority. No one interfered with Lupita, who had a fearsome temper. Eleanor thought it spoke well for Austin that he and Lupita never clashed.

"Austin," Beatrice said on one of the few occasions when she was willing to talk to Eleanor, "is the only competent servant we have. Oh, Lupita can cook, but I can't get along with her. And that maid! Austin will do anything. Father had gotten awfully tired of butlers who wouldn't drive cars and chauffeurs who refused to wait on table. Of course, servants can't be so particular nowadays."

"Was Austin brought up to the profession of butling?" Eleanor said, to prolong the conversation.

"I don't think so. He was in the war when he was quite young, and I suppose had a hard time afterward. He drove a taxi and waited on tables, I know. He wasn't really a trained servant, Father said, but he liked him when he came to see about the position, so he hired him. Norma doesn't like him: she says he sees too much. All servants do. Aunt Georgina sniffs at him. I don't know why: she admits he does his work."

Eleanor wondered it Austin had ever happened on Miss Georgina in the lower part of the house when she was presumably upstairs, asleep. She said:

"Well, you will need efficient help if you clean house according to your aunt's specifications."

"I'll be simply dead by the time we're finished," Beatrice said in nervous irritation. "She even wants the attic put in order: boxes of old things that should be thrown out, but she won't hear to that. Well, Miss Norma isn't going to get out of doing some work this time," she added, tightening her thin lips.

Nor did Norma, though it was at her father's command that she put on a wisp of apron and sullenly obeyed Beatrice's orders, shirking whenever she dared. Eleanor had, and won, her first conflict with Miss Georgina.

"I'm a nurse, not a charlady," she said, refusing to help with the house cleaning. "Aren't we all suffering enough, anyway? Those poor girls have been at the attic all morning, and this room and Mr. Leale's study are the only places that haven't been turned upside down."

"Things should be turned upside down ever so often," Miss Georgina declared. "I suppose that kitchen is deep in dirt, but if we disturbed Lupita to the point of quitting, Al would have a fit."

"She cooks like an angel, and her kitchen is clean enough to pass anyone's inspection."

"Not mine. Well, we'll finish tomorrow and have Sunday to rest, and then we can get away any time after that that Al likes."

Eleanor rather thought that the talked-of trip would not be taken, after all, for Norma and Joseph were not enthusiastic when Leale said firmly that he did not intend to go to any popular winter resort. And on Sunday night he was quite ill.

Eleanor thought that his illness was the result of two helpings of an extraordinary concoction of lobster that was one of Lupita's specialties. But Beatrice became so hysterical in her alarm that Eleanor allowed her to persuade their family doctor to leave his bed, though it was midnight by then.

The doctor was rather disgusted when Eleanor told him what Leale had eaten, said, "Acute indigestion," and warned Leale to be more careful of his diet. For the first time in five years, Norma said, he had breakfast in his own room. He looked, for the rest of that Monday, so miserably ill that Eleanor was amazed when on Tuesday he said at the luncheon table that they would take Friday evening's train to Dayton's Folly.

Beatrice said: "But—Father! You're not well."

"I'm quite all right now. We go on Friday night's train," Leale repeated. "I'll make arrangements so that they will let us off at Rio Linda. You and Georgina had better make lists of things we will want to send ahead. There are no supplies or bedding in the house, but plenty of china and cooking utensils. We will have to take our own silver."

"I'll see to everything, Father, and we can get the things off on tomorrow's train."

"Good. I depend on you, Beatrice. Well, Joseph?"

Joseph's resentful mutter resolved into: "I suppose we're going to this place you've leased? We'll freeze to death. It's a barn, from its pictures."

"I had a furnace installed this fall. I can buy the place so cheaply that I will probably do so after we come back," Leale said equably.

No one made any comment, though all but Beatrice must have been thinking what Joseph and Norma said to Eleanor later: "Plenty of money for anything he wants or anything that will make Aunt Georgina comfortable for a few weeks!"

Dunn said: "Well, then it's ho! for the great open spaces. I suppose we will want heavy boots and woolen shirts, Alfred?"

"Certainly," Leale said rather absently. "Mackinaws or leather jackets—Miss Gannon, I want you to get yourself the proper outdoor things when Norma and Beatrice do and charge them to my account. No, I insist on that. I'll have to try to get a cook from the nearest town: I'm afraid Lupita won't care to go with us.

Lupita did not. She said: "*Madre de Diós, no! A mí no me gusta la nieve!*" When Eleanor repeated this remark to Miss Georgina she sniffed prodigiously.

"I didn't suppose she'd be uprooted from that kitchen. The girl can stay with her; Norma and Beatrice can do everything but the cooking." Miss Georgina sighed. "I've got some bed socks in the bottom drawer of that bureau. You'd better get them out, and there's two or three knitted bed jackets with them."

Eleanor, packing flannels, electric pads, and bed socks, smiled to herself. The old lady did not want to go to Dayton's Folly; like Lupita, she did not like snow. But she would not join forces with the others and try to persuade her brother to give up the trip. Or so Eleanor thought then.

Later, she was not so certain. On Thursday night Leale came in for his usual good-night talk with Miss Georgina. Eleanor went into her own room to finish her packing and was presently aware that

Leale's usual ten minutes had stretched to more than twenty. She did not try to listen, but neither did she stop her ears. So quite plainly she heard Miss Georgina say:

"I think it's a mistake, Al, though I'm willing to do whatever you think best. A lonely place like that, with heavy storms predicted—"

Leale's answer was inaudible. Eleanor closed her suitcase and sat down to wait until he had gone. Presently Miss Georgina's voice came to her again:

"Oh, I see your plan, Al, and perhaps it will work. The surroundings sound—bleak enough, if that's what you want. My dear boy, I know it's a shock to you, but I've always been afraid of something like that." Her next distinguishable words were: "I hope Austin got the right brand of port and sherry from De Rosa's."

Leale said: "I wrote the list myself, and Austin never makes mistakes. Good-night, Georgina."

The next morning Leale introduced a tall, melancholy man to them as a Mr. Pope, who was to be his secretary, as he was going to write a book dealing with his experiences as a lumberman.

III

Eleanor reached for her cup and drank cold coffee. "My throat is dry from talking," she said. "Now,

Mr. Pope, it's your turn. You may tell the rest. I know I haven't told you anything important."

Pope opened his eyes and stared at her owlishly. "Oh yes, you have, Miss Gannon, though perhaps you don't realize it."

"I wanted Rocky to try to understand these people, as far as he can from learning what I know of them. And I don't know as much as I thought I did when I began."

"I get the—would you call 'em 'antagonisms'?" Rocky said. "Couldn't help feelin' they was there, but I couldn't know what all was behind them. It looks like— But I reckon we'd better hear what Mr. Pope has to say."

Pope folded his long hands on the table. He said: "I happened to be in San Francisco."

A wanderer himself, Rocky recognized Pope's casual tone as that of a fellow vagabond. Pope, he felt, had "happened to be" in many places during his lifetime. And after an instant the man confirmed this, with a diffident smile.

"I suppose you two are curious, but I needn't say too much about myself. Thirty-nine, unmarried, possessor of an income that keeps me from starving. I am not," he said emphatically, "a detective, though I did do some intelligence work at one time. I write special features for newspapers now and then. Call me a journalist—though I am not.

"Paul Taylor is Leale's lawyer. Taylor knew my grandfather years ago. My maternal grandfather, that is. He was an army officer and stationed in San Francisco at one time. My father was Irish," he added reluctantly, answering the friendly curiosity in the two young faces opposite him. "A soldier of fortune, if you like—very Richard Harding Davis.

"Last Wednesday Taylor was visited by Leale, and Leale wanted to know if he could recommend a private detective who was not objectionable and was capable of the utmost discretion. He did not at all like the idea of employing a detective, but he could think of no one else who would suit his needs. Taylor recommended me.

"I am," Pope said plaintively, "the least bloodthirsty of men, yet chance has thrown me into more than one murder case. It's my own fault, of course, that I don't run away while I still can, but I'm incapable of minding my own business. Well, I really have none. But Taylor knows of my—experiences, and I went to Leale because what Taylor told me of the family interested me.

"Leale, by the way, would not tell Taylor why he wanted my services. I saw Leale in his study Wednesday night. Austin let me in, but I did not see anyone else."

Leale studied Pope for some minutes before he spoke. Finally, picking up a paperweight of polished redwood, to shift it from one hand to the other, he said:

"Mr. Pope, what I have to confide in you is a hard thing for any man to have to say. Someone in my immediate family wishes me dead.

"I don't understand why that should be!" Leale said, suddenly and pathetically angry. "I've been a good brother and a good father, and I've repaid an old debt to a friend a hundred times."

He let the paperweight fall to the desk and after an instant went on quietly:

"It's true that I did have to neglect my family somewhat until lately. I started out early in life to make a fortune. I married young: a good woman and a devoted wife, though she was not of a— happy disposition. My daughter Beatrice is—too much like her. She died when Beatrice was five, and in a year I married again.

"Foolishly, I will admit, though she was very sweet. By that second wife I had two children, and they are in many ways like her. I am explaining this because the conflicts between these three children have always made things—difficult.

"For nearly twenty-five years, then, I've depended on my sister Georgina to run my household, and while she has been a very devoted sister,

I can see now that perhaps she was not the best person to put in charge of my children. But I had to be away from home so much, and though I did marry again, my wife was incapable of running a house and taking care of Beatrice and our boy. And she died when Norma was born.

"I don't believe Georgina ever tried to win the children's affection, and Norma and Joseph very early learned to deceive her, while Beatrice was made too docile and self-conscious by Georgina's strictness. They were always threatened with my displeasure, so by the time I returned home for good, it seems that it was too late for me to teach the younger ones to love me. With Beatrice it is different, but I'm afraid even she would not love me quite so much if she had not been forced to substitute me for a husband.

"I spoke of repaying an old debt: Because his father loaned me money at a critical time, I've supported Harold Dunn for a good many years. For four years I've allowed him to live here, and he had money from me frequently before that. I have always been rather attached to him, but," Leale said grimly, "last week I learned that he has been introducing my son to different gambling houses."

"Do they know that you know that?" Pope asked.

"No. For once I meant not to act hastily. I see very few people; go downtown very seldom. An old business associate made an incautious remark to me on Saturday, and I got the truth from him. He had it from his son. But I was determined to think well before I spoke to either of them," Leale repeated. "And then—something else happened.

"But first—I suppose that Norma and Joseph would tell you that I am a very harsh father, and God knows what Harold really thinks of me. Well, Mr. Pope, I can't tolerate reckless waste of money, and I do believe in orderly living. I was too severe with Joseph on one occasion, and I won't see Norma throw herself away on a penniless nobody who happens to attract her physically."

Pope said quietly: "You don't want your children to marry, then?"

"Yes! But suitably—not necessarily for money. Joseph is in love with a girl who I feel might make something of him, with my help."

Leale moved restlessly, as if aware of some impersonal disapproval in Pope's glance. And Pope was thinking how impossible it would be to argue against Leale's vision of himself as the patriarchal master of his family: son and daughter, the wife and husband of that son and daughter all living together with their children, under his roof.

Leale said: "Norma knows my wishes, and both she and Joseph know they will never get one penny from me if they go against them. As to Harold, he doesn't know yet what I intend to say to him. He can give up his gambling or get out, and he need not think any more about marrying Norma."

"You hadn't discouraged him in that idea?"

"Not actively. For one thing, I don't think Norma takes him seriously, and I thought, if she did, it might be rather a good thing. He is considerably older than Norma, but I think he could control her."

"With your help," Pope said blandly.

Leale flushed angrily. "Mr. Pope, I feel that you don't approve of my ideas, but they are mine, and I will stick to them. I think I've told you enough of my family. Last Sunday I was so ill that I finally called Beatrice. She became so alarmed, that she woke Miss Gannon, my sister's nurse, and eventually called our doctor.

"He said that I had acute indigestion, and Miss Gannon was convinced that I had eaten too much lobster." Leale smiled frostily. "Nothing like that has ever disagreed with me. I don't know why I became suspicious. No, Mr. Pope, I really do not. I had no reason for my suspicion, but I felt—"

He looked at Pope helplessly. Pope said:

"I can understand that you had some sixth sense that warned you of danger, Mr. Leale." He did not add that by the man's own admissions the atmosphere of this house must be one in which suspicion would grow and thrive.

"At any rate, I remembered that, as everyone knows, there is always a thermos of hot malted milk placed on my bedside table every night. Beatrice almost always attends to that; she did so on Sunday. I go to bed at ten; drink the milk then. But the milk is usually put in my room by eight o'clock. That is two hours, and I do not lock my door. So far as I have been able to discover," Leale said bleakly, "anyone could have poisoned that milk."

"It was poisoned? Arsenic?"

"I suppose that is what it was. I—I read up on the symptoms of arsenical poisoning, and they seemed to—fit. I did not drink the malted milk on Monday. I had it analyzed the next morning. There was nothing wrong with it. But I suppose," Leale's voice was old and tired, "it would be foolish to risk dosing it again so soon, and the thermos had been washed Monday morning before I had had time to think things over."

"But you have no real proof that you were poisoned."

"Mr. Pope, I'm not subject to indigestion. I never felt better in my life—until after I had taken that milk. No, I'm certain— And yet—I'm not," Leale said slowly. "Perhaps you can understand my state of indecision. One instant I feel that my suspicions are insane, and the next—"

"You have a garden?"

"Garden? Oh yes. I haven't attempted to trace the possible source of the arsenic. I suppose there would be plenty in the weed killer the gardener uses and keeps in an unlocked storeroom with his tools. I don't know if Joseph has any in his laboratory."

Pope said, "Laboratory!" and the impassive mask of his face cracked a little. At last he said dryly, "It appears that this house might be a poisoner's paradise," and Leale winced. "There are poisons more efficacious than arsenic, Mr. Leale, though they are usually detected at once. I advise you to see that your son's laboratory is locked, though it's rather late for that precaution."

"I've already issued an indirect warning," Leale said. "I said at the dinner table last night that I would not drink any more malted milk because I had found that it seriously disagreed with me."

Pope stopped, looked at Eleanor. She nodded.

"I'd forgotten that, because I had no idea then— Yes, he did say that, very slowly and deliberately."

"Don't you think," Leale asked, as Pope made no comment, "that it was wise to say that?"

"Perhaps. You have spoken highly of your oldest daughter, but you said that she fixed that milk almost every night."

Leale frowned. "Yes, and everyone knows that, and that is another thing I—don't like. Say that the—the poisoner hoped I would not suspect that anything was wrong. But if I did, how convenient it would be if I should suspect Beatrice."

"Do you mind explaining that statement?"

"I can hardly refuse to do so, having gone so far. The others feel that I favor Beatrice, without realizing that it is because she is never foolish or headstrong. It's equally true that she is jealous of any affection I show them. I allow Beatrice to draw checks on one of my accounts, and the others resent that, but she is the real housekeeper here, and she has never abused the privilege. Besides—"

Leale hesitated, then took a small steel box from a desk drawer and unlocked it. He said:

"A copy of my will is here. I would have said that no one but my sister knows its exact provisions, but I suppose that this box could have been opened if someone planned to do it. It doesn't matter a great deal, perhaps, because everyone does know that Beatrice benefits more by my death than anyone else.

"Her mother had an inheritance of five thousand dollars that she turned over to me, and that money and what Harold's father loaned me gave me my start. So I feel that Beatrice should have more than Norma or Joseph, even if it were not true that money is far safer with her than with them.

"My sister is provided for during her lifetime. Norma and Joseph receive only the income from their inheritance until they are thirty, when it goes to them outright. Harold receives ten thousand outright, and Austin two thousand; our cook the same sum."

"And everyone knows this?"

"In a general way. They know," Leale said slowly, "enough to add to their jealousy of Beatrice. And if anyone has opened this box and read the will—well, it might be worth while to try to cause me to change this will so that it would not be so favorable to Beatrice."

Pope studied a large picture of the *Royal George* that hung on the opposite wall. He said finally:

"It's an unpleasant situation, Mr. Leale. But what can I do for you? What is to be done, unless you tell everyone what has happened as a warning that it would be very unwise for anyone to attempt your death again. And you have no proof that such an attempt was made."

"I'm not entirely convinced that I was intended to die. Oh, I know I said that someone wished me dead. But the dose was not fatal," Leale said quickly.

"And I wonder if perhaps the whole thing is not simply an attempt to turn me against Beatrice."

"That isn't impossible." Pope could not bring himself to say: "And if you altered your will to favor someone else, would he be willing then that you should live?"

But perhaps the same thought came to Leale, for his shoulders sagged a little, and he put his head down on his arms. When he looked up his face was deep lined in decision.

"What I intend is this," he said: "On Friday we are all going to a place that I have leased in the mountains. Presumably for winter sports. We've talked of it for some time, but I had nearly given up the idea. Now—well, I've decided that we will go. I believe that it is a rather isolated place and that we will have more storms."

Pope's voice deepened with the sincerity of his protest: "Mr. Leale, you're a courageous man and a foolish one! If someone did try to kill you and this group is as lacking in—congeniality as you have led me to believe, it would be madness to take them away, herd them together under one roof, miles from anyone else."

"What would you suggest as an alternative?"

"Let your daughter marry as she wishes; give up all responsibility for your son and cousin; break up this household," Pope said bluntly.

For an instant he believed that his first advice to Alfred Leale would be his last. Then the man smiled wryly.

"Not while I live! And few men would have dared suggest that to me. You don't know these people as I do."

"No, and never will. But I can know them as you do not, Mr. Leale."

"Yes—yes, that's it," Leale said, unconscious of being inconsistent. "An outsider— After I'd gone to Taylor, I regretted my action. I tried to get him on the telephone and couldn't. I was not certain when you came if I would talk to you. But I had to talk to someone, Mr. Pope, and I could see that you are—are not the type of man I was afraid Taylor might have to send. I still think it wise to take some outsider with us."

"You think," Pope said, "that isolating this group in unfamiliar surroundings where they cannot escape you or each other will bring things to a head?"

"I think so. And the situation here is impossible. How can I go on, waiting and watching—at last, perhaps, growing careless—" Leale stopped, then: "No, we will go to Dayton's Folly. And when we get there I have several things to say to Joseph and Harold."

"Dayton's Folly?" Pope repeated. Leale lifted his shoulders.

"Leale's Folly, if you prefer," he said bitterly.

IV

"So I let him come to his death," Pope said. "Yet— what could I do? He was determined to come here, and I might have been of some help. Certainly there was nothing I could do for him if I refused to come."

Eleanor said quickly: "You couldn't have stopped him, Mr. Pope. He would have come without you. I thought I understood him fairly well, but now— He wouldn't give up his possessions, would he?"

She had not looked directly at Rocky since Pope had repeated Leale's approval of her. Rocky smiled slowly. Leale would have had a big surprise when he tried to treat his daughter-in-law like the rest of his family. You couldn't blame Eleanor for being burned up when she thought about it—"with my help." It was just as well for her that Leale had died—if it didn't turn out to be Joseph who had killed him.

"One thing I don't understand," he said. "If Leale was so finicky, how come he allowed 'em all that booze?"

"For one thing, I think he had no idea how long we might stay here," Pope said.

"And he had old-fashioned ideas about drinking too," Eleanor said. "Wine for women and illness; a moderate amount of whisky and brandy for men. Exactly as it had been in his father's home. You'll find he brought very little gin. He didn't approve of cocktails. Too modern."

"I get it. And the other thing I can't understand is why he wasn't careful when he got here. Did he get careless, or did he believe everything was all right? He knew ever'body knew he drank all the brandy."

"Yes. I'm afraid only Leale could tell us what his feelings were. His actions—for all the time we were here he would not talk to me—rather exasperated me. However, I did, when he began to fill his flask today, make some gesture of warning. Dunn and Joseph were in here, and I supposed he would not want me to speak plainly. He saw what I meant but only smiled and shook his head.

"I couldn't very well test the stuff by drinking it myself. It had been all right the night before. Oh!" Pope said, his voice suddenly roughened with futile anger, "it was an intolerable situation.

To be told by a man that he thought his life was in danger and yet to be given no help in trying to save it."

"When he didn't tell you any more, seems to me you must've had spells of believing he'd been all wrong," Rocky suggested.

"Yes, and besides that, there were moments when I believed he thought he had been wrong. I am certain now that there was arsenic in that malted milk Sunday night, but we had no proof of that. So it did occur to me that he might be suffering from delusions of persecution."

"He could, couldn't he—a guy like that? But you haven't told us the rest of it," Rocky said. "What happened after that night you first talked to Leale?"

"He paid no attention to my protests; he was bringing his family here whether or not I consented to come with them."

"My sister will be with us," Leale said. "I'd better tell you more about her. She is not really ill, but not long after I retired from business she took up this business of semi-invalidism. The doctors all assure me that there is nothing wrong with her. One of them said that it was simply her method of getting attention; that she likes to be fussed over and deferred to. She knows perfectly well that I know she isn't ill, but she has done so much for me that I am willing to humor her.

"She still superintends the housekeeping: gives orders to Beatrice to carry out. I feel it's her right to do that as long as she wishes. Of course, it is not always easy for Beatrice, and Norma and Joseph are inclined to ridicule Georgina's supposed illness."

"You can scarcely blame them," Pope said mildly.

"She's an old woman and their aunt."

"So I gathered," Pope said. Leale looked at him, frowning, as if he suspected Pope did not consider his statement to have any vital importance. But Pope had hitched himself up out of his chair and was preparing to leave. "When do you want me here, Mr. Leale?"

"We have lunch at one o'clock. You might get here by eleven, though our train does not leave until seven in the evening. I shall introduce you as my secretary."

It was Pope's impression, meeting Leale again, that the man was undecided whether or not to dismiss him at once and go to Dayton's Folly without him. He thought that it must have been true that Leale had felt a desperate need to confide in someone but that now he was sorry he had done so.

No doubt he had spent much of his time since Wednesday night in a one-sided argument against his fears. Yet he could not quite banish them or bring himself to the point of letting Pope go. Instead, he had prepared rough notes for several chapters of a proposed book and insisted on discussing them quite seriously with Pope.

When they went into the dining room, Leale, having introduced Pope as his newly acquired secretary, inquired with painful joviality:

"You didn't know I was turning author, did you? I've been thinking for some time that my experiences are as good material as any you read in the *Saturday Evening Post*."

"You're aiming high for a beginner, Alfred," Dunn said. "But it should be good stuff. Some of the stories you've told me, for instance—"

Beatrice said: "I think that's a wonderful idea,' Father. It would be nice to have a real author in the family." Her drab eyes were derisive for an instant as she glanced at Dunn. "A book like yours would be worth while, too. So many of the things they print are just trash."

She had made the opening that Leale wanted. He said:

"Yes—trash. But some of it is interesting. I rather enjoy detective stories. They are not," he said deliberately, "as far-fetched as you might think. One—reads the newspapers and finds that truth is stranger than fiction. I'm afraid I couldn't write fiction, but if I could—"

"Goodness," Norma said with a nervous little giggle, "you don't mean to say you'd write a mystery story?"

"I believe I could find a plot. For instance, in this house there is Joseph's laboratory with its stock of poisons—I suppose there are poisons there, Joseph? Cyanide, perhaps?"

"Why—y-yes. Yes, of course." Joseph set his glass down hastily, spilling water over the tablecloth. "You—you checked over the list when I bought the stuff."

"Certainly. I don't know a great deal about chemistry, though. But it did occur to me"—Leale helped himself to creamed chicken and reached for a salt shaker—"it did occur to me that your laboratory was better locked. I have the key when you want it."

Joseph muttered: "I haven't felt like working, lately. No one but me ever goes in the place."

"No, but we were discussing its fictional possibilities. Very interesting," Leale said, wiping his lips on a snowy napkin. "Free access to poisons for anyone here. But of course you might argue that no one would be foolish enough to avail himself of that opportunity because then everyone here

would be suspected. On the other hand, a murderer might prefer that it should be that way."

He seemed gravely to consider the possibilities
of his plot. He had issued his second warning, and
everyone went on eating, and presently Norma was
speaking to Eleanor about skis and snowshoes and
had she ever been on either?

"I knew something was wrong," Eleanor said.
"And so did everyone else. At least, Norma and
Joseph said afterward: 'What was eating Father—
talking about poison like that?' And Beatrice said
that she was worried about her father: that she
didn't think he was well. Harold Dunn didn't have
anything to say—to me."

Whatever Leale's secret thoughts, he was well
occupied during the rest of the day, making certain
that every item on his neat lists had been packed
and that everyone had followed his advice regarding clothing. They left the house that evening at
the exact minute set by Leale and with none of the
gay disorder that one would expect to attend the
loading of seven people and numerous suitcases
into two taxis. It was a very sedate group, that
went early to bed on the train, to be awakened by
Leale's orders half an hour earlier than was necessary for them to get off at Rio Linda.

Wharton, the Greenleaf storekeeper, was waiting for them, but there was room only for Miss Georgina, Leale, and the luggage in his car. The others walked: a hard walk and a cold one. The girls had put on galoshes, but they soon plunged over their tops in snow, and Joseph and Dunn were wet to the knees.

"Pope had the right idea, getting into boots when he dressed. I never thought about it," Dunn said. "Old Efficiency forgot to make a note of that."

Beatrice looked at him indignantly, but her teeth were chattering so that dignified speech was impossible. Joseph said:

"I could do with breakfast. Why don't they open that diner earlier?"

"We wouldn't have been allowed to eat on it if it had been open," Norma said. "Waste of money."

She stumbled, and Dunn put his arm quickly about her. Eleanor murmured: "The snow, the snow, the beautiful snow!" She said to Pope: "I worked for a while at a town near here. I heard that people down here can be pretty well snowbound in the winter."

"I don't doubt it. About two feet now," Pope estimated. "That isn't much, but if there is another hard storm—" He frowned.

"Well, we won't be cut off from Greenleaf," Norma said, "if that's any comfort. I suppose most mills are closed down in the winter." She stopped to shake snow out of her overshoes.

Eleanor, as the house just then came into view, studied it critically. "Twins!" she said. Only Pope understood her. "But I thought the cook was to be waiting breakfast for us, and I don't see any smoke coming from the chimneys."

There was no cook, no breakfast, no fires. Miss Georgina, huddled into furs and lined overshoes, received first attention. Austin started a fire in the stove in her bedroom, and Miss Georgina went to bed and said that she wanted to see a doctor.

"This fool trip is starting out well," she remarked to Eleanor. "I want something hot to drink, and you'd better get me a shot of whisky."

Eventually they achieved fires in living room and kitchen, then breakfast. Sarah Powers arrived, unapologetic, and Wharton, who brought her up, took back a message to Dr. Ames, though he warned them that Ames had gone to Humber on a confinement case and might spend the night there. Everyone unpacked and put on heavy clothing. Austin set the dining room in order.

The house on Broadway, a log cabin in the pines—it was all the same to Leale and Miss Georgina. An hour after they had eaten lunch Miss

Georgina had divided the work of the house between Norma and Beatrice and interviewed Sarah
Powers, of whom she said sourly:

"Well, I see that we have another independent
cook, but I suppose we'll have to put up with her."

As for Leale, he had time to decide that it would
be better if they did not go outdoors that day.
They would want to put their rooms in order and
rest from their trip, and Austin was going to oil all
their boots, because Leale had not thought about
having it done before. But it should be done, and
tomorrow they would try the coasting on the hill.

"It was about that time," Eleanor said, "that
I began to see why Norma said their family parties were tiresome. We should have been tearing
out into the snow and having snow fights and be
damned to oiling our boots. But we were told just
what to do and when to do it. If I had found time,
I'd have gone for a walk just to show my independence. But Mr. Leale did have other reasons for
keeping us in the house yesterday afternoon."

"Yes," Pope said. "He wanted interviews with
Joseph and Dunn—and Norma, though he did not
talk to her until this morning. I can guess what
he said to the men, though I doubt that either of
them will want to repeat his conversation with

Leale. I admit that I watched to see how they looked afterward. Whatever he said to Dunn had evidently been an unpleasant surprise. Joseph was very much upset; I wouldn't say that he was angry."

"He wasn't angry: he was puzzled," Eleanor said quickly. "He said to me: 'Well, the old man found out about our gambling. I might have known he would.' Then he said: 'But there's something behind all this, and I don't know what it is. Unless he—' But then he wouldn't tell me what he was going to say: what he meant by 'unless.'"

"And you have no idea what he might have meant?" Pope said.

Eleanor said, "No, I haven't," very quickly, and Pope went on:

"Leale hadn't told me he was going to talk to Norma. Perhaps the interview had no significance."

Eleanor hesitated. "I don't know. Norma didn't tell me anything, but Miss Georgina and I know she was crying while he was talking to her, and Miss Georgina will tell you that she was—"

"Oh, I know that without her telling me. Miss Norma cries rather loudly for a small person. But I wondered," Pope said, "if she always took reprimands so sweetly. She was very much the devoted daughter all the rest of the day. I had rather thought she was the sort who would sulk."

"I don't know. She—yes, she does sulk, sometimes. But she—she was sometimes very sweet to Mr. Leale when she wanted something. Or she might act that way simply to vex Beatrice."

"Well," Rocky said, "was that all that happened—just a nice little family party? It must've been excitin'. Mr. Pope, why do you think he let you come along? Didn't he talk to you at all?"

"I told you he approved of my going out to the guest cabin to sleep. In the evening, he discussed his book." Pope grimaced. "Well, I will admit that nearly everyone in this world thinks that he could write a book. He seemed quite taken with the idea. The book," Pope said mournfully, "would have been an astonishingly dull one."

"There's one reason why Mr. Leale might have been willing for you to come with us, even if he did think he was too hasty in his suspicions," Eleanor said, "and that is because he liked you."

A faint red showed under Pope's leathery skin. "Why—thank you, Miss Gannon. Perhaps—he did rather like to talk to me."

"I can understand that part of it all right, and him thinkin' he might try to write a book. He sounds like the kind of guy who would. But—I'm not scared of much of anything but I don't like the idea of someone tryin' to drop poison in my coffee. My idea," Rocky said candidly, "would be to play safe; cut and run. Of course, Leale wouldn't, it bein' his family that he suspected and him bein' so determined not to ever let 'em get away from him. I ain't so sure, Mr. Pope, that he was right about that arsenic."

"He died by poison!" Eleanor said.

"Yeah—and didn't he maybe put the notion into someone's head with all his talking?"

Eleanor stared at him. "Well!" she said at last. Pope's long fingers beat a tattoo on the table, then:

"Mr. Allan, I'm blushing," he said. "I don't know why that did not occur to me. That laboratory could have been opened by any ordinary passkey. There wasn't a Yale lock on the door."

Rocky said: "I'm the one that's blushin'. I wasn't tryin' to be brilliant, and it doesn't matter, anyway. I think I got things pretty straight now. Not that I suppose I'll ever really understand people like these. There's just one thing more, though: I said I'd run away if I thought someone was tryin' to poison me, but if I couldn't do that—well, if I couldn't prove who was going to do it, but just had to wait and watch— I wouldn't, that's all."

"You mean," Pope said, "that you'd become fatalistic?"

"I guess that's a word for it. You see," Rocky said slowly, "it's mighty hard to believe you're ever going to die. A fellow like Leale would find it pretty hard to believe anyone'd have the nerve to kill him, once he was over his first scare. And at the same time, he might have a 'what is to be, will be' sort of attitude."

"I think you're quite right," Pope said. "I think he had argued away most of his fear and regained his customary feeling of omnipotence—on the surface. And underneath I think he felt: 'What's the use?' Because, if he caught his would-be murderer, the family structure he had cherished would still be destroyed. As to drinking brandy from that decanter, though he ordinarily was the only one who drank brandy, still, someone else might suddenly decide to take some, so perhaps he thought the stuff must be all right.

"This morning Leale did at least refer to our first conversation. He said: 'I've put you off, but I'll talk to you this evening. You needn't have come so far as my first reason for asking you is concerned, but I'm very glad you're here, and I want you to consider yourself really my secretary.'"

"And that might mean," Eleanor said, "either that he knew whom he had to fear or that he'd decided he was mistaken about the entire business."

V

Rocky glanced at the clock on the sideboard. "It's ten o'clock; we've been talking 'most two hours. I can't see that we're much farther along, either. You said that considering motives might help, Mr. Pope, but ever'body had a motive for gettin' rid of the old man. Except his sister, I suppose. And she takes it calmly enough."

"The calm before a storm, perhaps. I don't know," Eleanor said, "but I believe she is thinking things over. She is not emotional; I think she'd always take death calmly. She'd nothing to gain by Mr. Leale's death; in fact, she loses by it, because he always saw that she had everything she wanted."

"It's Beatrice Leale who really gains most," Rocky said. "She'd make a swell murderer, far's looking the part is concerned, and he had so much confidence in her that he wouldn't ever suspect her."

"Yes, I know." Eleanor frowned. "She's so distinctly unlovable that—well, give her a break."

"I wasn't thinking of arrestin' anyone. I wouldn't have the nerve to pick out any one of them. I'm hoping the sheriff will get here tomorrow—but not expectin' it. Humber hasn't called me back, so I guess I'll call her. And Ames must be pretty tired of setting in the living room. I'd like to talk to the old lady, if she's awake."

"She showed no signs of going to sleep when I left her," Eleanor said. "But I don't know if she will talk to you."

Rocky picked up the steel box he had put on the floor beside his chair. "We haven't looked this over, yet. I reckon I won't go to bed for a while, but Ames will want to. I suppose he'll sleep in the cabin?"

"Yes. I'll show him where it is," Pope said. "I hope Austin has started a fire."

"And I'll see if Miss Georgina is awake." Eleanor hesitated for an instant at the door. Rocky looked at her curiously, but she shook her head. "No—I've nothing more to tell you," she said and left them.

Ames had the living room to himself, and he looked at Pope and Rocky rather resentfully.

"Hospitable household, this. Dunn left me an hour ago and wouldn't talk when he was here. The boy looked in, decided to go to bed and said he guessed Mr. Pope would show me where to sleep."

"Sorry," Pope said. "We didn't realize it was so late. I'll take you to the guest cabin now, if you like."

"Oh, no hurry. I was just grouching," Ames said frankly. "I'm tired: had a hell of a time getting back from Humber last night, and then two trips here, today—I don't like being stuck here, and I don't think it will stop snowing tonight. There will be no coroner here tomorrow, Allan."

Rocky frowned, picked up a log, and threw it on the fire. "Six goes through Brookdale at six, if she's on time. But she won't be. Anywhere from two to eight hours late, most likely. So it would be all right, probably, if we could get word to him by tomorrow morning."

"If!" Ames said with his slightly sardonic smile: a smile that somehow suited his square face and determined mouth; his quick, incisive voice. "What about the westbound train? You could send a message."

"Getting the sheriff here ain't quite important enough for me to wave a red lantern in front of Seven," said Rocky, the railroader. "It comes through at 3 A.M., anyway. Doesn't stop at Greenleaf on the winter schedule, either."

"As I very well know. It's the devil of a job arranging for them to stop for me when I have to get down to the city," Ames said. "And that blasted phone service! I'm cut off from Merton after the mill closes, and they kicked like hell about giving me a line to Humber."

"I didn't know you'd got one," Rocky said. "You aren't on this line?"

"No, this is a private line, and so is mine, now. I can ring Humber from the hospital, so you could get me in that roundabout way. I forgot to tell them that. I'll be going back to Greenleaf in the morning. They have some snowshoes I can use. Well, do you want to show me where I sleep, Pope?"

Rocky followed them into the hall and stopped at the telephone. He was still ringing, yanking savagely at the old-fashioned crank, when Pope came back.

"No good," Rocky said. "Our line to Humber's gone out now. Nice, ain't it?" He went to the front door, threw it open, and the wind whipped snow into his face. The carpet was white-powdered before he managed to close the door.

"It's drifting like hell, and that's bad. Say, where's Austin? I just thought of something."

"I suppose he is in his room. I haven't seen him since he cleared the table."

"How'd he get upstairs without us seeing him?"

"By that back stairway." Pope sighed and seemed to brood unhappily over this fact of a back stairway.

"Well, I suppose there'd have to be one if old Dayton intended this place for a hotel. I remember Sarah mentioning it, now."

"I don't like houses with back stairways. I spent some time in one, once. But you wanted Austin?"

"Yeah. I'll find him."

Austin was in his shirt sleeves but had not gone to bed. He said apologetically:

"I didn't want to disturb you in the dining room, sir. I was just going down to see if you needed more wood. I built a fire in the stove in the guest cabin."

"I'll tend to the fire in the living room," Rocky said. "What I want to know is if there's any lamps in this house."

"Lamps? Oh, you mean kerosene lamps. I believe I did see two old ones in one of the kitchen closets. But there are just the two of them, sir."

"Any candles where you can lay your hands on them?"

"Yes, I packed two dozen candles. Mr. Leale"— Austin smiled briefly—"forgot to include them in his lists, but I had some idea that lighting systems in the mountains might be rather primitive."

"Oh, there's nothing wrong with the 'lectricity ord'narily," Rocky said. "But I just took a look at the weather, and it reminded me that, last big storm we had, the power did go off for quite a while. Ames has got a flashlight."

"So have I, sir. Two of them."

"Well, you'd better keep one and give me the other. And get those candles so I can give some to Miss Gannon case the lights should go off. I don't see any use waking up the others. They probably won't be needin' any lights if the power does go off in the night."

Austin looked out of the window rather apprehensively. "I don't know anything about the mountains, but I don't like this."

"Shows good judgment that you don't. Say, Austin, that whisky you said you had—"

"Yes, sir. Did you want it?"

"No, but don't let Dunn or Leale sop it up. We might need it."

"I understand, sir," Austin said.

Rocky thought he probably did: understand that he didn't mind seeing what cutting Dunn off from his regular supply would do to him. He displayed the steel box that he was carrying.

"Did Mr. Leale take this thing with him when he went on trips? I should've thought he'd leave it in a bank or safe."

"Mr. Leale didn't leave home very often: not while I was with him—them. Sometimes I packed for him, and sometimes he attended to it himself, but I don't think he was in the habit of carrying that box with him, sir."

"I just wondered. What do you think of this business, Austin?—leaving out the 'sir.'"

"Oh—" Austin's smile made him look younger and very likable—"well, they weren't a happy family. You've never been a servant, so you have no idea how indiscreet people are in their talk—when servants are around, I mean. They seem to think," he said rather bitterly, "that we don't exist. Of course, a well-trained servant acts as if he doesn't. None of these people except Miss Beatrice and Miss Georgina are sorry that Mr. Leale is dead. Of course, they are frightened."

"That's what the old lady said. Did they call you in when Mr. Leale was sick?"

"A week ago Sunday—today, you mean? Yes, Miss Beatrice called me, but there was nothing much I could do. Why, you mean—"

"Well, we don't know anything at all, but Leale thought there was something suspicious about it. Did you?"

"Why no, not then. I can see now— He had eaten a great deal of lobster, though I never knew that to upset him before. I suppose—that malted milk?"

"Well, that's what he thought did it."

"Sunday night—I took the thermos to his room. I almost always did, after Miss Beatrice had prepared the milk. If she didn't do that, I usually did. Eight o'clock, that was. Mr. Leale went to bed at ten."

"We got all that. But did you see anyone upstairs that evening between eight and ten?"

"I wasn't upstairs after eight o'clock. My room was downstairs, you see, and the maid—Rosa—turned down the beds."

"Oh. Well, that does a lot of good, with her and the cook in the city. Anyway, Leale may just have eaten too much lobster. We'd better get those candles. Let's go down the back stairs. I want to get it located."

Eleanor was in the hall, talking to Pope, when Rocky and Austin came back from the kitchen with the candles and several boxes of matches.

"What are those for? Oh, heavens, I never thought about the possibility of the lights going off. Miss Georgina says she'll talk to you, Rocky—if you'll make it short and snappy."

"I'll make it short, and she'll make it snappy," Rocky muttered. "You go on to bed, Austin. We'll tend to things down here."

Miss Georgina was a pale face peering out from a heap of down comforters, bright afghans, and pastel blankets. Rocky said: "Whew!" involuntarily, looking at the glowing stove.

"I suppose it does seem hot to you. I can't seem to get warm," Miss Georgina said. "Maybe that's not just on account of the weather. Have you gone through that yet?" She looked acquisitively at the box under Rocky's arm.

"No, ma'am. We haven't got around to it. I wondered if you could give us some idea what ought to be in it and why your brother bothered to carry it up here with him."

"He kept duplicates of some papers in it so he wouldn't have to go to his safe deposit box at the bank for them. I suppose there's a copy of his will in it. I don't know why he brought it with him. Maybe he thought we might be here quite a while and he thought he'd be sure to have anything he might want to refer to."

"Such as?" Pope said.

"I'm sure I don't know."

"Well, but didn't he take you into his confidence?"

"He did not, Mr. Allan. Not regarding business matters. Woman's place is in the home; be a good provider but don't tell 'em how you do the providing."

"What I meant was that he did tell you why he was comin' up here," Rocky said.

"Oh!" Miss Georgina looked sharply at Eleanor. "No, I know you didn't listen to anything you couldn't hear without straining your ears. It doesn't matter. Al had a bright idea of coming up here where everyone could have plenty of peace and quiet to think things over. He'd found Harold had been leading Joseph astray and had an ultimatum or two to pronounce. He'd found out Norma didn't keep some promise she made him not to see a man she wants to marry, too. I could've told him Norma never kept her word in her life. Well, I thought it was a fool idea—"

"Wait a minute," Rocky said. "Didn't he say anything about thinkin' someone had tried to poison him Sunday night?"

The old lady didn't waste any time acting surprised or horrified. She didn't say anything at all for a minute or two, but you could tell that she was thinking back, step by step. Only of course you couldn't tell everything she might be thinking. She said, "So-o!" and that word meant a lot. "Al didn't tell me about that. I thought he was keeping something back. Sunday night— How did he think he was poisoned? Not at the dinner table?"

"No, ma'am. The malted milk he drank every night."

"Oh, of course. Hm-m!" Miss Georgina's eyes narrowed. "Between the time Austin brought that to his room and the time he went to bed everyone here was upstairs for a while. Beatrice fixed the milk, I suppose? Norma and Joseph and Harold came in to see me for a few minutes, at different

times. I don't know how soon they went downstairs after they left me. Beatrice read to me for a
while. Well, all that doesn't do you any good."

"I'm afraid it don't." Rocky looked toward Pope
for help. Pope murmured:

"The decanters—"

"Oh yes. Look, Miss Leale—you were in the
house all afternoon. Well, sometime between about
four and five-fifteen someone must've washed out
that brandy decanter. Wouldn't you hear anyone
who came in the front door and went to the dining room?"

"I suppose I would. But what was to prevent
their using the back stairs?"

Rocky had to stop to think before he could answer that, and Pope said:

"Nothing, while Mrs. Powers was in her bedroom, between three-thirty and four. Joseph and
Beatrice came into the house about four o'clock."

"Yes, that's right. I can testify Miss Gannon
didn't go into the dining room while she was with
me. Joseph went upstairs—he always did have
weak kidneys. He came down the front stairs—"

"Yes, I saw that," Eleanor said, "because I was
waiting for him."

"But he could have gone into the dining room
by the back stairs, through the kitchen, if he had

time. And gone back up and come down the front stairs again, I mean. Same thing applies to Harold," Miss Georgina said. "I heard him come in and go out again; I know his way of walking. It's my opinion neither of 'em had time to do all that traipsing around. Beatrice went into the dining room, as soon as she got her things off, to get me some port. Maybe she washed the decanter then. I don't know, but I do know she was gone for just a minute or two."

Rocky felt as if the old lady were thinking about something else all the time she was talking to them; as if she were, for some reason, amused at their questions. She said:

"I heard Austin come through the hall twice: quick trips, both of them. Eleanor brought Norma in after—it happened. She was having hysterics all over the place, and of course she bawled out what had happened. Beatrice rushed out, and then Eleanor had two yelling females on her hands. I guess she took Norma up to her room, then."

"Yes, and shoved her on the bed and told her to quiet down."

"Which she probably did. What's the use of hysterics without an audience? Then Eleanor brought Beatrice in here, and we heard Harold sneak in, out to the kitchen. I suppose ten or fifteen minutes passed before I sent Eleanor for those decanters." Miss Georgina yawned and lay back on her pillows. "I'm tired, and this isn't getting you anywhere."

"I guess it isn't, but could you," Rocky said politely, "suggest anything we can do that will get us somewheres? Because the way it looks now, the sheriff ain't going to get here tomorrow."

"I don't suppose that matters much," Miss Georgina said calmly.

"No, but poisoners have a bad habit of repeating themselves, Miss Georgina," Pope said gravely.

You had to hand it to the old lady, Rocky thought. She didn't turn white and start to shiver like any of the younger ones would have. She said:

"Oh, I've thought about that, Mr. Pope. I trust Eleanor and the cook, and Eleanor will see that my food comes directly from the kitchen." She threw back the bedcovers to show a bottle lying beside her. "I've got that port here. I know it's all right, now, and I'll want the rest of it. So go on about your business and let me sleep."

"I guess one of us will be in the house all night," Rocky said. "That guest cabin is too far away. We'll be in the livin' room if you want anything."

"Nothing but to be left in peace for a while, young man." But before they reached the door

Miss Georgina called them back. "I'll tell you one thing: just a hint. Yesterday Alfred and I were talking about holographic wills. Make the most of that."

PART III
"SOUNDLESS FOOTSTEPS"

Rocky said: "All these 'herewiths' and 'herebys' mix me up. You take a look at this thing and see if it looks to you the same as Leale said his will was."

"Leale told me only its general provisions," Pope said, studying the carbon copy of Leale's will. "But this seems all right. An annuity of fifteen thousand a year to his sister, ten thousand outright to Dunn, two thousand each to Austin and Lupita Gonzales, and the remainder of the estate to be divided, one half to Beatrice and the other half to be shared between Norma and Joseph. Beatrice and Miss Georgina to be executors, and Norma and Joseph are not to have control of their principal until they are thirty."

"Seems to me if you don't have horse sense by the time you're twenty-five there's not much hope you'll get it by the time you're thirty. Well, that's all the will there is," Rocky said, turning over the papers. He inspected the lock of the box. "I wonder if someone did get at this box. We left it up in Leale's room for about two hours. I s'pose someone could've got into that room?"

"I imagine so. For all I know, the keys to the other bedroom doors may fit his."

"Of course he may never have got around to writing another will. This is just like a book. They always kill 'em just before they get around to changing their wills. Do you think that's what happened?"

"I don't know. What else is in the box?"

"It may interest you; it don't me." Rocky moved closer to Pope on the chesterfield in front of the fireplace. He put the box between them. "Help yourself. There ain't so much here. He was always makin' lists, wasn't he?"

"Yes, he had that habit. These are lists of securities; nothing helpful. An inventory of the household furnishings; a summary of the household expenses for the last year and other data for making out an income tax report. And these are the notes he had made for three chapters of his proposed book. You're not paying any attention to me, Allan."

"Hunh? No, I wasn't," Rocky admitted. "I told Austin not to let Joseph or Dunn have any of his whisky, but I was just thinkin' I bet Dunn's got a lot more than he told us he had. He'd have a private supply."

"What makes you think that?"

"I've seen a lot of diff'rent kinds of drunks in my life," Rocky said, grinning. "Dunn's the kind who's never sober and hardly ever drunk. That's how he fooled Leale. I'll bet he drank a lot in his room. But he needs his liquor reg'lar, and I want to see how he'll act when he has to drink water for a change. I guess I'll clean his room out, first chance I get."

Pope said: "Well I'm beginning to have an increasing respect for you, Mr. Allan!"

"Rocky'll do, if you don't mind. I don't think Joseph's the same kind of drinker as Dunn, so going without probably won't have any effect on him. He doesn't seem to be a bad sort of guy," Rocky said morosely. "But he's too damn good-looking."

There was a queer little quirk to Pope's lips as he looked at Rocky. He said: "Well, Miss Gannon will have to be the judge of that. Here are the letters I took from Leale's pockets. You'd better look them over."

"All right. Did Leale have a habit of scribbling on papers or blotters when he was thinking?"

"I don't know. A great many people do that, however. Why?"

"Oh, one of these memos of his—I think it's a list of securities—has two Latin words kind of scrawled on it. See."

"Lightly written and half erased—'*Flagrante delicto,*'" Pope read.

"That means something like being caught in the act, doesn't it?"

"Yes. I wonder—"

Rocky waited for him to go on, and when he said nothing more, turned to the letters.

"Only four of 'em, but I suppose an orderly guy like Leale never kept letters in his pockets very long," he said. "Some fellows always have a wad of them in their pants. I noticed Dunn does. Bills, I'll bet.

"None of these seem to be important," he reported presently. "There's one from a fellow over in Lassen County: kind of a gossipy letter about how bad the lumber business is. Must've been an old friend of Leale's. And a letter from Wharton at Greenleaf, sayin' he's got them a cook. The other two are letters about some extra special sale of suits and shirts. Anything more in that box?"

"Some records of a few stock speculations. This seems to have been as much of a catch-all as a man like Leale would need. And this letter—"

"It's been torn across. That's funny." Rocky read it rapidly: the formal heading—"MR. ALFRED LEALE, DEAR SIR:"—then:

"*I am purposely not giving you my address and will not mail this where I now have a position that pays moderately well, because from what Norma has told me of your last tirade against me, I would not put it past you to injure me with my employers, if possible.*

"*Although Norma will not want me to tell you this, I saw her during my last vacation in the city. Naturally she wishes to avoid friction with you as far as possible. But she told me that you were very happy at having dug up the fact that I have been married and divorced. She knew that but did not bother to tell you so; again I say, naturally. My first marriage was a foolish one and we agreed to a divorce and I really cannot see that the affair is any business of yours.*

"*I was forced to agree that Norma and I would not marry at once, because I was financially unable to marry a girl like her. But I may as well tell you that I intend to marry her and that you had better not try to force her into any other marriage: the kind you want her to make, that will give you some son-in-law who will look on you as God. I sometimes think men like you should be painlessly removed from earth in middle age.*

"Naturally it'd stop just where it was interestin'," Rocky complained. "Typewritten, and we miss out on the signature. Look, Pope—why do you think this thing's torn? Why'd he save just that much of it?"

Pope frowned. "That is what I was wondering. Did he mean to keep this? It was at the bottom of the box, inside another folded paper. I can imagine that this letter would make him very angry."

"It's not torn the way it would be if somebody had grabbed onto the other end so that it pulled apart. The torn edge isn't ragged enough."

"That's true. I wonder if he didn't start to tear it into pieces himself and was for some reason interrupted before he had done more than tear it in half."

"That's the way you go about tearing up a letter," Rocky said eagerly. "First you tear it across, then the two halves into quarters. It's funny that just happened to get in there, but it could've happened that way. You know, I was wonderin'—I was looking at Beatrice Leale when we told the old lady we were going to look this box over ourselves. I kind of thought she looked glad we were going to."

"I agree with you: she did."

"Well—why?"

"Because she knew that we would find this in the box. Certainly she hates her half sister. But Norma was of the opinion that Beatrice did not know of this man she wishes to marry. So unless

Leale had taken Beatrice into her confidence and shown her this letter—which I seriously doubt—she would not know he had kept it."

"And you don't think he meant to keep it. And if someone has been into this box and that some-one is Beatrice, she'd know we'd only find half a letter here, not signed—and what good does that do us?"

"No good at all, I'm afraid. From the way Miss Georgina spoke, I don't think even she knows the man's name, and in any case, he is working in the southern part of the state. Yet Beatrice was anxious for us to look over the contents of this box before her aunt could see them. She must have hoped that we would find something that would incriminate someone here."

"Seems like it, because she knew enough about her father's will to know that when we'd read it over it would show us that she stood to gain more by his death than anyone else. I wonder if she had the same idea as the old lady?"

"You mean, that Leale intended writing a new will and that we would find it in this box?"

"That's it. She may've thought he disinherited somebody and that we'd get an idea from that, who killed him. That'd mean somebody has been into this box. I'd like to know if anyone has."

"So would I," Pope said wearily.

"Why don't you lie down on this couch? I'll take a chair and set up for a while," Rocky offered. "Somehow, I don't feel like it's safe for everybody to go to sleep. Only before you do, I wish you'd tell me what we'd ought to ask people in the mornin'."

"I suppose you will have to ask Norma, Joseph and Dunn about their interviews with Leale. They'll lie to you, of course."

"Yeah, I imagine they will. If any of 'em knows anything about the others, they're scared to tell it for fear someone'll get mad and start telling on them. They hate each other's guts, but they're sticking together, so far. Only I don't know about the old lady. Do you think she's thinking things over?"

"I do." Pope yawned soundlessly, twisted about, trying to fit his length into the chesterfield, and finally solved the problem by drawing his bony knees up toward his chin. "Yes, Miss Georgina is thinking. I wish I were," he said, and went to sleep.

Rocky dragged a large overstuffed chair to the fire and turned off all the lights but that of a shaded lamp on the nearest table. He wished, as Pope snored gently, that he had someone to talk to. It was dull, just sitting here and trying not to go to sleep. The wind sighed around the corners of the house and blew snow with a harsh sound against the windowpanes.

No. Seven, Rocky thought, might start down the canyon, coming from the East, but it was doubtful how far she'd get. As for Six, coming up the canyon— He shrugged. If he was awake at three o'clock in the morning, he'd listen for Seven. There was a curve in the track just past the Rio Linda station, a curve where every engineer used the whistle.

Presently he put another log on the fire, without waking Pope, and wondered if he should open the door into the hall. But now that the furnace was cold, the rush of icy air from the hall was unpleasant. Rocky compromised by leaving the door as little ajar as possible.

He meditated on such matters as clean shirts and having to borrow a razor from someone in the morning. There was no use thinking any more about the dead man in the room upstairs: if Pope felt it was a pretty hopeless proposition, what could he do? But something worried him. What it was, he couldn't remember, but he felt that he had forgotten to do something that should have been done.

He found himself thinking about Eleanor and Joseph Leale and then, because that was unpleasant, considering the matter of those decanters again. It must have been Dunn or Norma who washed the brandy decanter after Leale died. But how did either of them do it without using the front stairs to get to a bathroom when Sarah Powers was in the kitchen?

Of course, they were leaving Austin out of it; taking for granted he had told the truth. But he couldn't have washed that decanter until after four o'clock, and Sarah was in the kitchen by then. And he'd have no reason for doing it unless he knew the brandy was poisoned, in which case he could have done it earlier in the afternoon.

"I don't think he did—or poisoned the brandy himself," Rocky muttered. "Not for two thousand dollars. He don't seem to've had any reason to hate Leale. He had a job while Leale was alive, while the old lady don't seem to like him much."

Pope stirred and gurgled in his sleep; "just like his throat was being cut," Rocky thought, disgusted with himself because he jumped at the sound. But there was something about this house—

Then he started again, but this time it was because the telephone bell was ringing. A faint and jerky tinkle it was, and when he got to the telephone two or three minutes passed before he could hear anything but a shrill singing of wires. Then the sheriff said distantly:

"Rocky? Jake Thompson—Maudie tells me there's trouble at Dayton's Folly. Murder? Is that right? Yeah—well, kid, I'll get there when I can and bring the cor'ner. But we can't make it in a car tomorrow, not even with a tractor. And they say there's a bad slide down at Barton. If that's so, Six won't get in anywhere near on time. You'll just have to hang on, kid, until we—"

The earpiece exploded in Rocky's ear. He said, "God damn!" and held it away from him. "Jake! Jake, are you there? Listen—" He was ready to hang up when Jake Thompson's asthmatic drawl came to his ears again.

"Lissen, Rocky—you there? Well, Humber's had a helluva time getting you. We found out her wire was out of order and then she couldn't—"

Rocky said, "Hello! Hello!" but the wire was dead this time. Not that it mattered much: there was nothing the sheriff could tell him that would help them any. He'd more or less expected they'd have trouble at Barton. Lucky if Six got through in the next twenty-four hours.

Pope was sitting up, blinking sleepily at the fire. "Was that the telephone, or was I dreaming?"

"It was the phone—and it wasn't. Reckon it's out for good now." Rocky repeated Thompson's message, and Pope nodded.

"I've had my nap out," he said. "And I'm good for several hours now. Your turn, Rocky."

"I ain't sleepy. Hope that telephone didn't wake anyone up. The old lady or Eleanor, maybe. It didn't ring very loud."

Pope did not go back to sleep, but Rocky found it impossible to make him talk. He sat and stared at the fire in utter immobility, until Rocky grew drowsy, watching him. He slumped down in his chair and slept, waking suddenly to a room that was dark except for the faint glow of the fire. For an instant he thought Pope had gone; then he caught the light sound of his breathing and whispered:

"Did you turn the lights out?"

Pope's hand touched his arm, and he said, close to his ear:

"The lights went off some time ago. The storm hasn't died down at all. I suppose the power has gone off. Didn't you have a flashlight?"

"In my coat pocket. I hung it over the back of a chair."

"Which chair? I don't want to stumble into any furniture."

"I think I can find it. Why don't you want to make any noise? Something wrong?"

"Perhaps it is only the wind," Pope muttered. "But I feel as if someone is down here—"

"Sneakin' around, you mean? Where?"

"I don't know—now. I thought I heard someone in the hall, and I've been listening since then, but I haven't heard any definite sound."

"It's hard to. This place creaks and groans a lot. Want me to get that flashlight?"

"You might try. Didn't you keep any candles?"

"Didn't think we'd need 'em. I left some extras on the sideboard in the dining room."

Pope said: "We'd better have one for some kind of light in here. You don't want to run down that flashlight battery. I think we should go the rounds, anyway, to be on the safe side."

"O.K. I think I can locate that chair."

The chair on which he had hung his coat should have been directly back of the chesterfield, but it was dark there, and a table was the first thing to materialize: a table that dug a sharp corner into Rocky's thigh. He muttered profanely and felt with outstretched hands for the chair; finally located it and got the flashlight from his coat pocket. He managed to avoid the table, getting back to the dim shape that was Pope.

"Hear me bump into that thing? Think anyone else did?"

"I don't think so. And I doubt if there is much to be gained by trying to move silently, but I think we can move more quietly if you put on that light."

Eleanor's and Miss Georgina's doors were closed; the dining room was silent and deserted. Rocky got a long tallow candle from the sideboard, and they went on to the kitchen.

"Better be quiet here and not wake Sarah up," he whispered. "She'd be hopping mad."

Pope said politely: "Did we disturb you, Mrs. Powers?"

Sarah Powers, an overstuffed pillow of pink flannel, was looking at them wrathfully from her bedroom door.

"I didn't say nothing the first time you come sneakin' around in here, but now you got to come back again, just when I'm going to sleep, it's a little too much," she said.

"But Mrs. Powers, this is the first time we've been in here," Pope said.

"Oh!" Her eyes squinted up into their surrounding rolls of fat. "Well, I'd swear someone was in here not so long ago. Well, I couldn't swear to that part of it because it's hard to tell time when you're dozing. I'm pretty sure I heard someone come through here, though."

"From the back stairs or the dining room?"

"Couldn't say, Mr. Pope. The door to the back stairs squeaks and so does the dining-room door. Might've been either. That was what I thought I heard—a door squeakin'. Then someone moving, very soft. My door was open a bit. So then I got up and closed it—and locked it," Sarah said defiantly. "I was nervous, but when I got back into bed again it come to me that it probably was just you two. I heard you say you was going to stay in the house tonight. This here floor is so tracked up by wet boots that you couldn't pick out a footprint on it now."

"We won't disturb you again, Mrs. Powers. Go back to bed, but lock your door," Pope said.

"I'll do that. Rocky Allan, ain't you never seen a woman in a nightgown before?"

"Plenty of 'em, but never one just like that," Rocky said, grinning. "I thought it was a tent."

Sarah's little eyes twinkled, though her mouth was severe. "I'll bet that kind of woman don't wear my kind of nightgown, if any," she retorted. "No need to stare like that. Mr. Pope's a gentleman manages to act like I was all dressed out in my Sunday best. Goodnight."

"Kid curlers too," Rocky said solemnly. "Where to, now?"

"I suppose we can go up the back stairs and down the front," Pope said gloomily. "We don't know who was here, or why."

"Or if Sarah was just imaginin' things," Rocky said in a discreet undertone. "These stairs ain't carpeted; awful hard not to make some noise, walkin' on them."

They reached the top of the back stairway. The upper hall was quiet and dark. Rocky murmured:

"This is an awful waste of time. Why didn't we go to bed? We might as well have— Son of a bitch!"

"I take it that something's troubling you?" Pope said.

"I been trying to remember something I should've done, ever since dinner time. Got it, now. You got that key to Leale's bedroom? No, I guess I kept it. Wait a minute."

He did not look toward the bed but went straight to the bureau, jerked open a top drawer. He said:

"Well, it's gone. Would you mind kickin' me where it'll do most good?"

"What is gone?"

"Leale's gun. It was in here, 'long with an un-opened box of ca'tridges. Box is opened now; some of 'em gone—and the gun. I meant," Rocky said humbly, "to take charge of that gun. Then I got to looking at that steel box and the things you took out of Leale's pockets, and it clean slipped my mind."

"There's no help for it now," Pope said, but the lines about his mouth deepened. "Tomorrow we had better search the bedrooms to try to find who took the gun. I'm afraid it would cause a good deal of unpleasantness if we did that now."

"Prob'ly be just like stirrin' up a hornet's nest," Rocky agreed. "I don't see much use lockin' this door, but I will. We'll want to look at the keys to the other bedrooms tomorrow. Find something?"

Pope looked at a small piece of hard-packed snow that he had picked up from the carpet. "There was more than this, but it melted."

"So what?" Rocky said, unimpressed. "We all tracked plenty of snow in here. This hall's cold. I never did any experimenting 'long that line, but I reckon a piece of snow that'd been packed down hard by your shoes would last a long time." He added: "Your evidence is turnin' to water."

Pope wiped his hands on his handkerchief and followed Rocky down the front stairs. But now Eleanor's door was open, and the faintest beam of candlelight showed from her room. She came to the door, smiling at them drowsily. No pink flannel for her: some kind of green robe and her hair loose. Rocky tried to keep from staring at her and wished he had never ridden out of Merton with Dick Barnes. She said:

"If you two boy scouts would go to bed, Miss Georgina would like to sleep."

"Did we wake her up? I'm sorry," Rocky said. "I thought we were movin' pretty quiet."

Miss Georgina said clearly: "Young man, my hearing is excellent and Alfred's room is directly above this one. For heaven's sake, go to sleep! I'll take a tablet, Eleanor, and that cook will have to give me a late breakfast."

Eleanor smiled at them again and closed the door.

"Boy scouts, hunh?" Rocky said. "And not such good ones. Well, you can set in that chair if you like." He stretched himself out on the chester-field. "Better stick some more wood on the fire and light your little candle. I'm goin' to sleep."

II

Rocky caroled:

> "Oh, she's my darling, my daisy,
> She's cock-eyed, she's crazy,
> She's humpbacked, bow-legged, and she's
> blind—"

He stopped to test Pope's razor: an old-fash-ioned ivory-handled thing. He'd probably cut himself all to hell with it, but he didn't care about borrowing from Dunn or Joseph. He rubbed lath-er into his face and resumed his song:

"And they say her teeth are false,
'Cause they rattle when she walks;
She's my cock-eyed consumptive Mary
Brown."

It must have been, Rocky calculated, about two o'clock when he and Pope had gone back into the living room. So he'd had about four hours' sleep until the noise Austin made, moving about in the cellar, starting the furnace fire, had wakened him. Pope looked rather haggard but admitted that he had finally drowsed off in his chair. He went into the kitchen to make coffee, but by that time Sarah Powers was beginning her day.

"Can't sleep after six. I'll make you two 'n' Austin some coffee. There's doughnuts here. Better just take a snack now. I suppose I can have breakfast at eight. Anyone that don't want it then can take it cold."

While they waited for the coffee, Rocky stepped outside, stared at a white drifted world, and whistled.

"Must be five foot in some places," he said. "Looks like Ames' car will have to stay where it is till some of this melts."

"Do you think the storm is over?" Pope said, behind him.

Rocky sniffed, head up, like a hunting dog. "For a while. But you notice it's getting colder?" He grinned slowly. "This bunch has been yapping about the cold, but it's fairly warm when it's snowin'. When it stops, you usually get three days of real cold. They'll have to watch the water pipes or they'll get froze up tight tonight. Wonder if Ames is awake?"

"I'll see." Pope plunged into snow over his high boots, stopped to ask: "Will he be able to make it back to Greenleaf, do you think?"

"On snowshoes, if he knows how to handle 'em. I don't think Seven went through last night."

"No? Why?"

"I would've heard the engineer whistlin' on the curve down by the river. Oh, yes, I hear things like that: subconsciously, I guess. I imagine they're holding Seven at Merton till they get things cleared up down at Barton. You can tell Ames that so he won't think about tryin' to stop Seven."

Austin had come upstairs, and he and Rocky were drinking coffee at the kitchen table before Pope came back, a brown flannel shirt over his arm and his razor in his hand.

"There is no hot water in the cabin, so I brought these in here. Do you think you can carry a kettle of water out to Dr. Ames, Austin? And a spare safety razor, if you have one."

"Yes sir, I have. I brought one in case one of the gentlemen forgot his."

"Is that shirt for me?" Rocky said doubtfully.

"Yes. You very obviously can't borrow from anyone else. I think you can wear this, because," Pope said sadly, "if I buy a shirt small enough to fit my shoulders it is never large enough to make connections with my trousers."

Austin was already filling an enameled pitcher from the teakettle. Rocky said:

"I'll build up the fire in the front room. Must have it nice 'n' warm for these little hothouse plants."

Austin smiled. "That's very good of you, sir— Mr. Allan. When the furnace has been going a little longer there will be plenty of hot water in the bathrooms."

Rocky investigated the drug cabinet now and decided that Leale must have allotted this bathroom to the men. One shelf of highly scented hair tonic and after-shaving lotion and powders he decided must belong to Dunn; the expensive lavender accessories to Joseph. And the plain bay rum—to which he helped himself—would have been Leale's. Dunn must use that little brush on his mustache—and that reminded him that he still intended to look Dunn's room over and take charge of any liquor he might find there.

He hadn't heard anyone moving around, but someone had already been in here to shave and had not bothered to clean out the washbowl. Probably Norma and Beatrice would want breakfast in bed. More work for Eleanor.

Rocky hummed:

> *"Lyin' in jail with my face to the wall,*
> *An' a red-headed woman was the cause of*
> *it all—"*

—and then looked thoughtfully at the drug cabinet again.

There were iodine, cotton, adhesive tape, and a bottle of aspirin on the lower shelf; nothing else. He didn't suppose there would be any poisons lying around in plain sight, but he wondered now where the cyanide had been hidden until someone was ready to use it. While he knew very little about the stuff, he did know that you wouldn't need very much of it. Just a very small packet or bottle that you could carry on you. No use searching anyone now, of course.

He got into Pope's flannel shirt, moved his shoulders cautiously, and decided that it would do. Someone rapped on the door, and Pope said:

"Breakfast is ready, Rocky. Austin isn't ringing the gong because Miss Georgina is still asleep."

"Be right with you. Here's your razor—" Rocky stopped, listening. Norma's door was slightly open, and Eleanor was saying:

"I am not going to bring your breakfast up here. If Beatrice can go down, so can you."

Rocky grinned. "That's telling her," he muttered. "Is Dunn downstairs?"

"Yes, he and Joseph just went down."

"Well, seems like at least one person's going to be late to breakfast, so it won't matter if we are."

"We?"

"You can be witness to what I do in here, just in case." Rocky opened the door to Dunn's room. "I guess we can wait till later to test out those keys?" He looked at the disordered bed and held up a silk pajama jacket. "Baby blue!"

Pope's face wrinkled into a smile. "Don't be too severe with Mr. Dunn's effeminate tastes, Rocky."

"Oh, I had a pair of silk pajamas once. Felt nice, next to your skin, but I'd rather sleep raw. Only—baby blue!" Rocky pulled up the mattress and disclosed three full quart bottles of whisky, seals unbroken. "They always hide it there and never expect you'll find it. Funny! Look in his suitcases, will you?"

"Nothing here."

"He must have his flask on him, and I'll leave this pint he's got in his bureau drawer so he may not get wise for a while. Bottle's most empty, anyway. Question is, what shall I do with the stuff?"

"Smuggle it down to Mrs. Powers and let her hide it in her bedroom."

"Good idea. She'll hang on to it. You don't see any gun, do you? Didn't think you would." Rocky looked cautiously into the hall. "The coast is clear. We'd better sneak down the back way."

Sarah nodded wisely at Rocky's request. "I knew that fellow was a boozer. Had a cousin like that. I'll keep the stuff till you find a better place for it. And for pity's sake, get in to your breakfast!"

No one had taken the chair at the head of the table. No one had sat there last night, but there had been plenty of room, then. Rocky had to sit uncomfortably close to Pope at the foot of the table. He wondered how the others would act if he took Leale's place. But Beatrice sat at the right of that empty chair and kept looking at it. Rocky decided to stay beside Pope.

Eleanor was opposite Beatrice with Joseph beside her. You couldn't hear what he was saying to her, but he didn't look quite so jittery this morning. His hands were steady, and he had a new air of self-assurance. Perhaps he'd had time to realize that he was "Mr. Leale" now. The income from his share of Leale's estate would make him independent, and he had only six years or so to wait to get his hands on the whole thing. And maybe he'd decided he didn't have any reason to be afraid of Dunn, now. Eleanor's influence, more than likely.

Dunn's face looked pastier than usual: he'd get full credit for his thirty-six or -seven years this morning. He was already wanting another drink. He pushed his plate away and lighted a cigarette, then glanced toward Beatrice and hesitated. So Leale hadn't liked them to smoke at the table? Beatrice's mouth was tight; Dunn started to douse the cigarette in his coffee cup, and Norma said clearly:

"Light one for me, will you, Hal?"

Dunn said, "This is my last one, Norma," and inhaled slowly.

Beatrice went on looking at her father's chair and Rocky fumbled in his pockets and got out a crumpled package of cigarettes.

"Can you smoke this kind?"

"Of course. Thank you so much. It's nicer to smoke right after a meal than to wait until everyone is through and you can leave the table. Don't you think so?"

"I never gave it much thought, ma'am," Rocky said soberly. "But I reckon you're right."

She was cute as six bits: no getting around that. Beatrice had on some kind of dark dress with a white collar, but Norma was wearing blue velvet

VIRGINIA RATH

pajamas, and her pale yellow curls were held back with a ribbon, the way little girls wore their hair sometimes. She didn't look like she had lost any sleep or needed to have her breakfast in bed. She said suddenly, as if she knew what he was thinking:

"Family meals are perfectly ghastly, under the circumstances. I didn't want to come down at all."

"What are you going to do when there aren't enough servants?" Dunn said irritably. "Not enough to pack trays up and down stairs. I couldn't sleep last night. Tried having my windows open, and the snow blew in so that I had to shut them. It was cold enough even then, and stuffy. Besides— which one of you was wandering around the halls last night?"

No one answered, until finally Pope said:

"At what time, Mr. Dunn? Mr. Allan and I went over the house at about a quarter of two. Did you hear us?"

"No, I must have been dozing by then. Oh well, it was probably my imagination, but two times I thought I heard someone. I tried to see what time it was, but those damned lights had gone off by then."

"They're still off," Joseph said. "I didn't hear anything, Hal. It must have been the wind you heard; it makes some funny noises."

"It wasn't just the wind," Beatrice said precisely. "Someone—someone went into—Father's room."

"What? Oh—nonsense, Bea! That door was locked. Anyway," Joseph said, "how could you see anything?"

"That was the trouble: I couldn't see. Who it was, I mean. But there was someone, after the power had gone off. I'd—" Beatrice flushed unbecomingly—"I went to the bathroom. I was only half awake; I felt stupid—" she glanced accusingly toward Ames—"I suppose it was the tablets I was—given. When I got to the door of my room again I felt as if there was someone there."

"In your room?" Norma said with a derisive smile.

"No, in the hall or somewhere near me. I couldn't see much, it was so dark. But even in the dark, you can make out—moving shadows. And the door to Father's room swung open, very slowly."

"So what?" Dunn said.

"Nothing. I was terrified. And I told you I was half dazed. I simply sank down on my knees inside my own room and closed my eyes and finally I managed to get back to bed."

Dunn laughed. "Not a very convincing story."

"No—no, I don't suppose it is," Beatrice said impersonally. "But I thought Mr. Pope and Mr.

Allan might like to hear it. Didn't you—imagine noises too, Harold?"

"Yes, but nothing definite. I admit it was probably just the house creaking."

Rocky waited for Pope to speak, and when he did not, "Miss Leale's story is kind of interestin'," he said. "Any of you want to admit you took Mr. Leale's gun and some ca'tridges from his room?"

It was plain enough that none of them liked that: the idea that there was a gun somewhere around the house and they didn't know who had it. They looked at each other furtively; then Norma said:

"I suppose we all knew Father would bring his gun with him, if we thought about it at all. But Joseph said you locked his room."

"Yeah, and that's interesting too. We did lock his room, and we ain't got around to seein' what keys fit that door," Rocky said. "Maybe two or three diff'rent ones do."

"They're ordinary old-fashioned locks and keys," Dunn muttered.

"Anyway, we'll want to see about that right away and try to find that gun."

"Search our rooms, you mean?" Dunn said.

"Sure. Any objections?"

It was evident that Dunn did object but didn't dare say so, and he probably wouldn't feel any better, Rocky thought, if he knew that he had nothing to fear from a search, now. Joseph said suddenly:

"What about Aunt Georgina? Taking that gun, I mean?"

"Your aunt? What makes you think she'd take that gun? Be the last one here I'd expect would want it," Rocky said.

Joseph smiled. "You don't know Aunt Georgina. She used to be a crack shot. Father taught her when they were kids. She's not afraid of guns. Norma squeals when you get one within ten feet of her."

"If there was someone in Alfred's room—at the time Beatrice thinks—ten to one it was Cousin Georgina," Dunn said. "You know how she likes to wander around at night."

"Aunt Georgina? You mean she— Oh!" Beatrice said blankly. "You mean, even at home—?"

Again Norma's smile was derisive. "Really, Bea, I don't see how you could have been so dense. How did you think she kept tab on the housekeeping?"

Pope said: "I hope your aunt has the gun. I'd feel that it was safe in her hands"

"Really, Mr. Pope!" But Dunn's indignation was half-hearted. Joseph said thoughtfully:

"Of course, we were all upstairs for a long time before dinner, as you know, Mr. Pope. So I don't need to point out that we—someone could have gotten into that bedroom then."

"We managed to figure that out. But of course," Rocky said blandly, "you were all just lyin' down all the time. There might've been something else someone wanted to get at in that room before we looked it over. Your father's strongbox, I mean."

"That's right, he did bring that with him. Well, but did he keep anything important in that?" Joseph asked. "He had a safe deposit box at the bank."

"Oh, nothing so very important. A lot of lists of things—" Rocky helped himself to ham and eggs. "And a copy of his will."

"The old one? He hadn't changed—" Dunn stopped, biting at his mustache.

Rocky drawled: "Did he threaten to change his will?"

"No! That is—"

"Don't be silly, Hal," Norma said sweetly. "Of course he threatened to change it. He did, once; decided that Joe and I weren't to be trusted with our principal until we were thirty."

"That's the way it is now. What did he say to you yesterday mornin'?"

"To me, Mr. Allan?"

"You don't have to tell him that, Norma," Joseph said quickly.

"Oh, but I don't mind." Norma turned toward Rocky a look that was all sweet candor. "You and Mr. Pope know that all of us quarreled with my father. Our interview yesterday wasn't anything unusual. A lecture on my frivolous habits and wasted life. Made me so mad that I cried. He didn't need to drag us all up here to tell me that again. But he didn't threaten to disinherit me, if that's what you mean. Goodness, how could he? He wasn't that mean, when he'd brought me up not knowing how to earn my own living."

Rocky hesitated and decided to ask her privately if Leale had not mentioned the absent George during that interview. He wished Pope would help him out; take charge of things. But the man sat there dipping toast into his coffee, looking as if he were half asleep. Yet Rocky felt that Pope would cut him short if he said the wrong thing, so he went on doggedly:

"Your dad seems to've brought all of you up here to talk to you. Did he say he was going to change his will when he was talkin' to you, Mr. Dunn?"

"No!" Dunn said quickly. "I was always to have ten thousand from him. I think he had figured out that was about what I should have to pay off some money my father loaned him once; with interest and deducting all he'd already given me."

Rocky thought of another question he would postpone: whether Leale had told Dunn he might as well give up the idea of marrying Norma. Pope had said Leale meant to tell him that. Rocky asked instead:

"What did he have to say to you, then?"

Dunn looked at Eleanor; then toward Pope. "I suppose you did—hear all about the little audiences His Royal Highness held. He'd found out I did a little gambling now and then and that Joe had been with me at times. He didn't like my leading his little boy astray."

Joseph's fair skin reddened. He said evenly: "That's the truth; Father spoke to me about the same thing. He said he was thinking of putting me to work. Well—" he very carefully did not look at Eleanor—"I can think of worse things than that."

"Since when all this craving for honest labor, Joe?" Dunn asked jeeringly. Norma said:

"Father didn't threaten to put you to work, did he, Hal? I suppose he wouldn't attempt the impossible."

Now, if they would only get to squabbling among themselves, he and Pope might get a little information, Rocky thought. But Joseph snapped:

"Cut it out!"

Dunn looked surprised, then sulky, but he didn't say anything, and Norma only smiled. So that was that: they'd told him as much as they thought they had to, and it didn't amount to anything. Beatrice sat and sipped black coffee, as if she had not heard a word that had been said since they had spoken of Miss Georgina's habit of wandering about the house at night.

Probably she knew plenty about all the others, but Rocky did not intend to try to talk to her. Not alone, at least, and Pope could ask the questions. Meanwhile, there was the old lady— And Ames, who had been looking politely bored for some time, was saying:

"If you'll loan me a pair of your snowshoes I'll try to make it back to Greenleaf. I suppose there's no chance of getting my car out, Allan?"

"Oh, I reckon we could dig it out, but you couldn't get it through the rest of the snow, and it'll be froze up, anyway."

"Cheering! Well, I must get back to Greenleaf. I have a patient or two there, and you don't need me here."

"Aren't you going to see my aunt before you go?" Beatrice said.

"Do you think it's necessary? Oh, I suppose I had better. But I can't wait much longer."

"I think she should be awake by now," Eleanor said, rising. "I'll go in and see. She was sound asleep when I came in here, but I think she will want her breakfast a little earlier than usual this morning."

Austin, putting fresh coffee on the table, asked: "Do you want me to come in and build up her fire, Miss Gannon?"

"I'll call you if she is awake. I'll be back in an instant, Dr. Ames."

Dunn got up and stood looking out the windows. "And what do we do today? I suppose the sleuthing goes on? Ames was telling us that there's very little chance the sheriff will get here today. What in heaven's name are you fussing around in here for, Austin?"

"Sorry, sir," Austin said pleasantly. "I was looking to see if that carving knife is in here. Mrs. Powers wanted it this morning and couldn't find it. It's the only really sharp knife in the house."

Pope put his cup down slowly. He repeated, "'The only sharp knife—'" before Eleanor screamed.

III

She didn't scream again, but you could see the muscles of her throat tighten as she fought against doing it. Her face was so white that her hair looked redder than ever. Rocky caught her by the shoulders, and then she dared to let go of the door to Miss Georgina's bedroom. She said:

"Don't let Norma and Beatrice come in! She looked as if she was asleep, but she was so still. You couldn't see anything until you lifted the covers. They're—not white any longer. I didn't know such an old person could bleed so much."

"Skip it!" Rocky said sharply. "Come away from here and let Pope and Ames get in." He led her away from the door. "Snap out of it, honey. I don't want to have to rub snow in your face."

Joseph said hotly: "Don't talk to her like that! After what she's just seen— Sit down, Eleanor, and I'll get you a glass of water."

Eleanor tightened her hands about Rocky's arm. "No—no, I don't want to sit down. Not for a minute or two. I'll be all right. I don't like hysterical women."

It would be just as well if Norma heard that. But she hadn't made any fuss, Rocky realized now. Dunn had stopped her at the dining-room door; he had his arm around her, and she was crying a little, but not loudly. He didn't see Beatrice at all, but in an instant they all heard her. She had started to laugh, and it was like little pieces of broken glass flying through the air. Eleanor whirled around and let go Rocky's arm.

"I'd better go to her."

"You had not! Go down to that front door and open it and get some fresh air. Let her sister take care of her."

"I'll go," Joseph said. "I'll—she's stopped, now—"

Norma had run back into the dining room, Dunn behind her. Rocky hesitated, looking from Eleanor to the closed bedroom door. Pope and Ames were in there, and it looked like he was shirking if he didn't go in too. Eleanor was standing straight and steady now, and there was a murmur of soothing voices from the dining room. Beatrice Leale had stopped even the moaning that had followed her laughter. Austin came into the hall with a whisky glass in his hand.

"Miss Beatrice is all right now, sir. I got her some of that whisky from my room. And I thought Miss Gannon—"

"Thanks, Austin." Rocky took the glass to Eleanor. "Here you are. This is all right: Austin's private stock. Now, can you go on down to the others while I go in the bedroom?"

"Yes—yes, of course, Rocky. And I've kept you too long now, looking after me. But she—she was killed while I slept with just a door between us—"

"And while Pope and I slept right across the hall."

Pope, coming out to them, said: "Yes, while we slept." There was a whitish look about his mouth. "The door between your rooms was closed, Miss Gannon?"

"Yes. She never wanted me to leave the door between our rooms open. She said she liked to be to herself after she went to bed. I suppose—back in the city—that was so I wouldn't hear her when she didn't stay in bed."

"Undoubtedly. And perhaps her reason was the same here. I rather thought—"

"You thought she went upstairs last night?" Rocky said. "Did she have that gun?"

"If she did, it was taken from her. Of course she knew everyone here. And she must have been deceived by her murderer. I mean that she could not have been unduly alarmed by the person who killed her. I think that she raised herself a little on her pillows before she was—struck. But she fell back against them, and then her body was eased down in bed and the covers drawn over her—I'm sorry, Miss Gannon."

"That's all right," Eleanor said steadily. "I was going to tell you that after I spoke to you, about two o'clock, I put more wood in her stove. It must have been very warm in there, and she was wearing a knitted bed jacket, so probably she did not have the covers completely over her. That would make it easier for—for—"

"Yes, it was a remarkably clean blow. She must have died instantly. The knife is there; the handle wiped clean. I suppose that is why it was with-drawn. If she had only been afraid!" Pope said. "She should have been: we warned her."

"But she wouldn't take these—these people seri-ously," Eleanor said. "And it was poison she was warned against: Perhaps she thought a poisoner wouldn't use another weapon. They don't usually, do they?"

"Not usually. Well, she knew something, and perhaps she meant to tell it to us today. I've been in your room, Miss Gannon, and when I stood with the door open I could just see Miss Georgi-na's head."

"That's all I saw. I opened the door very care-fully before I went in to breakfast. I didn't want to wake her. She was lying on her side with her face away from me and the covers up around her chin. I thought she was asleep."

"Certainly you would." Pope turned to Ames as he came out; he had washed his hands, but there was a stain on his cuff. "Miss Gannon says she built up the fire at two o'clock. About how long do you think it would be before it went out, child?"

"Oh—nearly two hours. I closed down the dampers. And the room would be warm for an hour or so after that."

Ames frowned. "Well, allowing for all that heat in the room—I'm only guessing when I say she was probably killed between three and five. Who started to have hysterics a minute ago? Beatrice Leale? I'd better go in and see her."

Rocky closed the front door, took a turn about the hall and came back to Pope and Eleanor.

"I been thinkin'—I know we ain't supposed to change anything like that—" he nodded toward Miss Georgina's bedroom—"until the cor'ner gets here, But these folks are going screwy if this keeps up. I don't mind them losin' their nerve—some. But there's no use us plannin' to sleep in that cabin: it's too far away from this house. One of us had better be upstairs tonight. I'll take the responsibility with the cor'ner of moving—them out to that cabin."

Pope nodded. "I think that would be a wise idea, Rocky."

"The cor'ner may raise hell, but we can't have a house full of rooms that people tiptoe past. Eleanor, you go in the dining room and send Austin out to help us. Make those people stay in there till we come."

He squared his shoulders and turned toward Miss Georgina's room. "This ain't a job I'm crazy about. Let's get it over."

Sarah Powers was stolidly washing dishes when the three of them came into the kitchen some twenty minutes later. Austin wiped his forehead on a kitchen towel and sat down with a sigh. They had gone out the front door, and breaking a path in the snowdrifts around the side of the house had been his task. Rocky said:

"I can do with a drink. Where'd you put that stuff, Sarah?"

"It's under my pillow, right now. Ain't made my bed up yet, and no one's been in my room."

Rocky brought out one of Dunn's quart bottles of whisky. He was disgusted because he found suddenly that he was nervous about using the stuff. Maybe Dunn had planned to substitute it for some of the other bottles. Then he saw that this was a different brand from that in the sideboard. The neck of the bottle was covered with lead foil, and it had a cork instead of a cap that screwed on.

He poured a stiff drink and said, "It's just whisky," to Pope's little smile. "Take a shot, you two. Everybody still in the dining room, Sarah?"

"Just settin' around. I run in there when that oldest girl started gettin' highsterical, but she come out of it."

"They might as well go into the living room and be comfortable. It was just that I didn't want 'em to be around the hall to see what we were doing. I reckon Ames will be wantin' to go, too. Then what?"

"Oh," Pope said wearily, "I suppose we must search the rooms and see about those keys."

"If you let a pot simmer long enough, it fin'lly comes to a boil," Sarah said suddenly.

Pope looked at her, one eyebrow crookedly up-raised. "That does seem to be our best method of procedure."

"The pot seems to've boiled over last night," Rocky, said tactlessly. "The sheriff's going to gnaw on me plenty about this. And I don't feel so hot, thinking I was asleep when it happened, but I reckon he—the sheriff—would've slept sounder than I did."

"'*The soundless footsteps on the grass—*'" Pope said absently. "Well, I thought I was only dozing, so you needn't feel badly. Someone moved very quietly."

"Must have. Austin, you might as well go in and tell those folks they don't have to stay in the dining room any longer."

"Yes, Mr. Allan. But about that knife—it belonged to the carving set that we brought with us, and I put it in the top drawer of the dining-room sideboard. Mrs. Powers used it last night to carve the roast."

"Because there ain't one decent knife in the stuff that was already here in the kitchen," Sarah said. "I washed the thing, and Austin took it with the other silverware back to the dining room. This morning I wanted it to slice some ham with, and he said he couldn't find it in the dining room. I guess he thought I took it out of there and mislaid it."

"I did think you might have done that," Austin said mildly. "But I helped you look the kitchen over for it, and we didn't find it."

"I thought that ham at breakfast looked like it had been just kind of chewed to pieces," Rocky said. "So the knife was in the dining room and someone got it out of there? I was wondering if you wouldn't have heard anyone gettin' it from the kitchen."

Sarah nodded. "I might have heard something rattle if it had been in this drawer with the rest of the utensils. And again, I might not."

"Well, we'll go up the back way and look over the bedrooms. You can tell 'em what we're do-ing, Austin, and then can come up and watch, if they want to." Rocky opened the stair door, then turned to say: "Someone's got to move downstairs tonight. Could you do that so Miss Gannon can take your room? One of us can take Leale's."

"I'll move my things as soon as you've searched my room," Austin said.

Rocky looked after him as he went into the dining room and lowered his voice. "What do you think of him, Sarah?"

"I ain't used to workin' with a man in the kitchen, but he's handy and obligin'," Sarah said grudgingly.

"That's what I thought. Did you ever," Rocky asked as he and Pope went up the back stairway, "know one man to kill another for two thousand dollars?"

"For far less than that. But Austin, so far as we know, was certain of a position while Leale was alive. And from what Miss Gannon was told about him, he probably had a rather hard time of it after he left the army; a hard enough time that he would value that position. Now that the household will be broken up, I suppose he is out of work."

"Yeah. What happens to the old lady's share of Leale's money, now?"

Pope sat down on Austin's bed. "It will revert to the estate and be divided among the other heirs, I suppose. Of course she was only to have a life interest but she might have lived a long time. They don't have to wait, now. And Beatrice is the only remaining executor."

"Nice for Beatrice."

"Perhaps," Pope said, frowning. "Offhand, one would certainly say that she benefits greatly from both deaths. But—well, when her father was alive she was more courteously treated by the others—"

"Than she was at breakfast this mornin'? She's got money, but from all I've heard about her, she won't enjoy it much. Leale gave her all she wanted, anyway, and now she'll probably be left sole alone. There ain't anything interestin' here. Is there anything under that mattress?"

"The springs. Austin hasn't a gun? Too bad. I can't shoot straight; I always shut my eyes when I pull the trigger. But I wish that we had a gun."

"If I'd known what all was going to happen after I left Merton I'd have strapped a couple on my hip. I wonder if Ames has one? But he wouldn't want to come back here. Well, there's nothing here but clothes and things. Austin didn't bother to lug along his private papers, if he has any."

"I'm afraid no one else did that. You'd better try these keys on Leale's door, one by one, or you'll get them mixed."

"They do all look alike. Austin's don't fit Leale's door," Rocky reported presently. "Let's see Norma's, will you? No, it's too big for the lock."

Pope patiently trotted from door to door, collecting keys and returning them to the proper locks.

"There's just one that fits," Rocky said finally. "This last one you gave me—"

"Harold Dunn's."

"Ain't that nice? You got the ones from the bathrooms and those connectin' doors?"

"All of them. Try this key, Rocky."

"It fits. Where'd it come from?"

"Miss Georgina's bedroom door."

"Oh!" Rocky sat back on his heels. "Why do you think she came up here last night?"

Pope said: "Of course someone came into and left the lower hall around four o'clock and I did not hear him. Or sometime between three and five, according to Ames. It's questionable if I did hear someone in that hall around one-thirty. I thought I did, and Miss Georgina was the only one who would have found it most convenient to use the front stairway. The back stairs would have been safest for anyone up here, and I wouldn't have heard anyone who went down that way."

"Unless one of 'em came into the front part of the house, and I don't see why they would—then. The old lady was alive at two. If she had that gun, why didn't she use it?"

"If someone entered her room, bent over her bed, speaking to her in some way that kept her from being alarmed—"

"After that it was too late. I get it. She was an old tartar all right, but she had guts," Rocky said. "I reckon I'll have to ask Eleanor if she thinks the old lady was out of her room last night. How about interviewin' Beatrice Leale?"

"If you like," Pope said unenthusiastically. "What do you intend to ask her?"

"I don't. I intend you to ask the questions."

"Oh. We'll get nowhere with her."

"I don't suppose so. But—what the hell! If she knows anything, she'd ought to talk, for her own good. Because I suppose it's occurred to you, same as me, that she might be the next to go? That half of Leale's estate that she gets might come in very handy to Norma and Joseph. Is that Ames leaving? I want to talk to him."

In the lower hall Ames was putting on his gloves while he said to Eleanor:

"If she can't sleep, you know what to give her. You have everything you need. If I were you, I'd guard my supplies carefully."

"I will, though I haven't anything—dangerous. Dr. Ames thinks he must go, Rocky."

"I suppose you do, though I'd like to have you around. I wanted to ask if you have a gun over at your place."

"Yes, I have; two of them." Ames frowned. "It's too bad I didn't bring one with me. It might be a handy thing for you to have. But I don't see how I can come back here tonight. God only knows how long it will take me to get to Greenleaf."

"It'll be plenty hard going. If they have another pair of snowshoes, I might be able to make it over there and back this afternoon. If the snow wasn't so soft, I could make it on skis. Well, you'd better get going. It's near to ten o'clock."

"If you don't get into Greenleaf I'll try to come back here tomorrow morning," Ames promised. "And I'll see if I can raise Humber and find out how things are down the line; get in touch with Brookdale if I can."

IV

Eleanor said: "I hope you won't go away this afternoon, Rocky. It would take a long time to get to Greenleaf; you might not get back."

"The afternoons are pretty short, but I think I could make it. You'd have Pope here."

"I have a good deal of confidence in Mr. Pope, but I'd rather have you here, too."

"I s'pose in case someone needs to be socked on the jaw?" Rocky suggested. "I'm pretty dumb about this business."

"You know as much about it as I do."

"Sure about that?"

Eleanor nodded, but she didn't look at him. "If I know anything I haven't told—it isn't important," she said finally. "I—I have to draw the line somewhere, and guessing isn't knowing."

"Sometimes it amounts to the same thing. Come upstairs, will you? There was something Pope wanted to ask you."

Pope was in Norma's room. Rocky wondered how anyone could have scattered so many clothes about in just two days, and Eleanor laughed.

"That child! She thinks I'll clean this up for her, but she's sadly mistaken. Except for these woolen things." She hung Norma's outdoor clothes on a chair near the register and put her small boots beside them. "She would take them off damp and leave them to mildew before she'd touch them." She tossed an armful of silk and lace onto the bed to clear a chair. "What did you want to ask me, Mr. Pope?"

"Did I want to ask you something? Oh yes. Didn't you think Miss Georgina had been out of her room early this morning, some time before she spoke to us?"

"Yes, I did. Not that I had any real reason to think so. I'd been sound asleep and didn't hear her, but when she did call me to tell you two to be quiet she looked—oh, there was a satisfied sort of twinkle in her eyes. She looked that way when she thought she had been very clever. But I don't know where she went or why. She might have wanted to—look at her brother, alone. Or could there have been something she wanted in Mr. Leale's room, that you hadn't found?"

"Perhaps," Pope said, mechanically straightening perfume bottles and expensive toilet articles on the crowded bureau top. "There isn't anything incriminating here, Rocky."

"We might as well get through with the rest of these rooms. I was wondering—"

"I'll go downstairs now," Eleanor said as he hesitated.

"It's no secret. It's—well, there was a good deal of blood on those sheets. You said the knife handle had probably been wiped clean on them. Doesn't that mean that someone had to clean his hands, too?"

"I should think so," Pope said slowly. "I'd thought about that. You couldn't tell, four or five hours later, if someone's stained hands had been wiped on the sheets."

Eleanor looked rather sick, but she said: "Of course, there is a lavatory in that room. But there were no lights, and I might have heard the water running. The faucets were apt to grumble when they were turned on. Everyone knew that, because Miss Georgina complained about it, and Austin tried to fix them but couldn't."

"There aren't any washstands in these rooms, and it'd be risky washing up in the kitchen," Rocky said. "That leaves the bathrooms up here. Did Leale make any arrangements about them?"

"What do you mean? Oh, he did assign one to the men and one to the women. He would," Eleanor said. "That's what you meant?"

"Yeah. I guess Joseph and Dunn had shaved before either Pope or I went in the one on the other side of the hall. It was in good order: lots of towels, and some of them had been used. I think I'd have noticed if any of 'em had been stained."

"There's nothing out of the way in our bathroom. The faucets there are all right," Eleanor said. "If I had to—wash my hands and didn't want anyone to hear water running, I'd hold my hands close to the faucet to smother the sound. Even so, all that would have to be done in the dark."

"'*Retire we to our chamber. A little water clears us of this deed . . .*'" Rocky muttered; then grinned deprecatingly. "Things like that stick in my mind sometimes. No one had any candles, but there's matches in all the rooms. I suppose for cigarettes. There must've been a few matches struck during that cleanin' up process. No one'd dare to take a chance doing a good enough job completely in the dark. But there weren't any burnt matches lyin' around. Oh, hell! what's the use?"

"Sometimes I wonder what is the use in trying to find out who has done all this," Eleanor said.

Rocky wondered if she was thinking protectively of Joseph Leale, but she went on: "Then I think—aside from the danger that someone else may be killed—if it isn't cleared up, all our lives we will be suspicious of each other. For instance, Norma and Joseph—they are very fond of each other, but neither one of them can trust implicitly in the other's protestations of innocence."

"Would you?" Pope asked.

"No. And while I think Mr. Leale was pretty awful in some ways, I did like Miss Georgina, and both murders were such cowardly ones."

"Don't successful murders have to be?" Rocky said.

"I suppose so. But I do want to know the truth, and that's why I have—told on people, though I know it doesn't seem a very admirable thing to do. It will be better for them in the end, to know the truth."

"I don't know," Rocky said, "what the sheriff'll do with this case. When folks get killed up here it's mostly because they get liquored up, or maybe one Mex sticks a knife in another one's back. By the way, Eleanor, did Austin tell you he's going to move downstairs and you can have his room?"

"No, but that's thoughtful of you, Rocky. I was wondering—I didn't want to be silly, but I didn't see how I could sleep there again. I'll go downstairs and collect my things."

Pope and Rocky followed her into the hall. "Look," Rocky said suddenly, "what becomes of the towels and things?"

"They go into a big hamper in that closet at the end of the hall," Eleanor said. "Down there by Austin's room."

But Rocky had already dragged the big hamper out of the closet and was tossing soiled linen onto the floor. When he turned around there was a limp towel in his big hands.

"This thing's wet," he said triumphantly. "Wet all over, like it'd been washed. And there was a burnt match right by the side of the basket."

"Which proves?" Pope said gently.

"Nothin' important," Rocky said rather irritably. "I'm just stumblin' around in the dark, Mr. Pope. But when the sheriff gets here he's going to want some facts—material ones—and somehow I don't think you care much about those."

Pope smiled sadly. "I'll admit that, Rocky. It's one of my weaknesses that I don't."

"Well, maybe they aren't much use. But I'll hand this towel and match over to the sheriff, and he'll be right pleased with them. Then he'll start pounding away at people, tryin' to find out if they didn't hear someone at this closet or in the bathroom last night—this mornin', I mean. Someone should've heard something, at that. There won't be

any roamin' around done tonight," Rocky promised. "Not if I have to camp down right in the
middle of this hall."

"If you're going to do that, you'd better take
a nap this afternoon," Eleanor said. She went on
downstairs. Rocky said:

"That had all the earmarks of a dirty crack.
Let's see what's in Joseph Leale's room."

Joseph's room was almost as disorderly as Norma's, "though men's things don't make as much mess
as women's," Rocky said. And Joseph had forgotten to remove a small red notebook from the inner
pocket of the mackinaw he had worn the day before.

The book's pages were filled with a number of
unimportant scrawls: *"Dinner at Solari's at 8";*
"Suit fitted, 3 p.m. Tues." There were several pages
of chemical formulas and equations, and at the
very back of the book a page headed: *"Owe to H."*
Rocky totaled the figures quickly and whistled.

"That guy Dunn must be lucky at cards if he
could stake Joseph that heavy. Comes to over five
grand. Which means Mr. Dunn gets fifteen instead of ten thousand, now that the old man's
dead. I wonder if Leale knew how much Joseph
owes Dunn and if he would've paid it?"

Pope said: "I doubt it. Men like Leale, who dis-
approve of gambling, aren't very apt to recognize
the sanctity of an I.O.U. of that kind."

"I wonder if Dunn would've preferred fifteen grand outright, or to live off the old man a while longer. If he really thinks he can marry Norma, he'll be sitting pretty. And Leale intended to tell him he couldn't do that. I guess we're through here."

They had just finished with Beatrice's starkly neat room when Dunn came out of his bedroom, his pasty face flushed. He said:

"I—I suppose you've been in my room already?"

"Sure we have; quite a while ago," Rocky said.

"Well—you didn't find anything?"

"Not a thing. Did you expect we would?"

"N-no." Dunn was looking at both of them closely, but neither was wearing a coat and obviously had no pockets in which quart bottles of whisky could be concealed. "But there's something missing from my room."

"We haven't taken anything—nothing this search," Rocky said. If Dunn didn't catch his slight emphasis on "this," that was all right. "What's missing?"

Dunn hesitated but he was afraid not to answer now. "I had some extra whisky I wasn't telling anyone about. I wonder—"

His eyes were ugly. He was thinking back, trying to remember who could have gone into his room earlier in the morning. He would find out

Pope and Rocky had been upstairs before breakfast, but still he wouldn't be too certain that they
were the only ones who had been there after he
had gone downstairs. He muttered:

"If Joe has been into my things—" and slammed
his bedroom door behind him. Rocky grinned.

"The kettle's beginning to boil some," he said.

PART IV
"HE WASN'T TOO OLD TO MARRY AGAIN"

Rocky gave a final crank to the antique telephone and decided that the line to Humber was still out. And if the trouble was between here and Humber, there wasn't very much chance that the trouble shooter from Brookdale would manage to get past Humber to fix things. There were still no lights; Austin had put candles in the bedrooms, and Sarah had trimmed and filled the old kerosene lamps.

It was only eleven-thirty: still an hour and a half till lunch. Norma and Eleanor were upstairs making beds. He supposed Austin was in the woodshed, and he didn't know where Dunn had gone. Beatrice and Joseph had the living room to themselves, but they hadn't been talking when he looked in a minute ago.

Beatrice was sitting close to the fire, as if she were very cold, staring at the flames, chin in hand, while Joseph played an aimless game of solitaire.

And Pope was, for some reason in Miss Georgina's room.

Rocky jingled the keys in his pocket: the key to the guest cabin, the key to Leale's room—and much good it had done them—the key to the steel strongbox. He had put it back, locked up again, in Leale's room.

He yawned and decided to look around outside. He couldn't stay in the house all day. The sun was shining palely, but there was still a haze of clouds over the mountain tops. Rocky stopped to look at a thermometer hanging on a porch pillar. Only thirty above at almost noon; it was too cold to storm again.

He might as well go take a look at Ames' car, he thought, pushing his way through the drifts of snow in front of the house, unbroken except for the tracks of Ames' snowshoes. Ames was going to have a plenty hard trip, and before he had gained the curve of the road at the top of the hill Rocky had given up his idea of trying to make it to Greenleaf and back that afternoon.

Ames' car was halfway up the hill and a little off the road. Snow had piled up over the fenders and a heavy white blanket lay on the top. Rocky walked around it, whistling softly. It would be a hard job to dig the car out and then you'd never get it up the hill without a tractor to pull it.

Evidently Ames had stopped to investigate, and he must have cussed plenty at what he saw.

Rocky left the car and walked on down the hill until he was in sight of the gated bridge across the stream. He regretted not having worn gloves now; thrust his hands into his pockets and shivered. He had turned to go back to the house when the gate creaked and he faced about to see Ames limping across the bridge.

Rocky said, "Well, I'll be damned," and went to meet him. "What're you doing back here?"

"It's not my own choice," Ames said disgustedly. "Damn! Let me grab hold of your arm—I tripped and fell on my nose a mile or two down the road. Twisted my ankle; wonder I didn't break a leg. I thought I might be able to make it to Greenleaf, but I soon saw I couldn't, and it was a shorter distance to come back here." He looked toward his car and made profane comments. Rocky grinned.

"You don't have very good luck. It must've been pretty hard going under any circumstances."

"It was. I'm sweating like a horse. Well, thank God there is no one seriously ill at Greenleaf, but I wish your friend hadn't been able to find me yesterday."

"I suppose you didn't see anyone down the road?"

"Who would I see? You couldn't even get a horse along that road: the snow's still too soft."

It was a hard pull, climbing the hill through the snow, and Ames was leaning on him heavily. Rocky waited until they reached the front door before he said:

"Have you any objections to sleepin' in Miss Georgina's room?"

"Not if you give me fresh sheets," Ames said callously.

"We just—bundled her up in those bedclothes. Austin's moved into the other room. Shall I call Eleanor to help you with that ankle?"

"It's only a strain. Get me some hot water and I'll bandage it myself. You'll have to help me get this boot off, first, and see if you can find a carpet slipper I can wear."

"Maybe Austin can find you one. I'll ask him."

Rocky opened the door to Miss Georgina's room, saw that Pope had gone, and helped Ames to a chair. He unlaced the man's boot and got it off with one jerk before he went to the kitchen to get hot water.

"I'll find Austin and ask him about a slipper," he said, putting the steaming water on the table. "If I can't help you—"

"I can manage," Ames said irritably. "You'd better tell the cook that I'm here for another night."

Austin had obviously cleared his belongings from the back bedroom, and Eleanor had taken possession of it, but the room was empty. Pope did not seem to be upstairs; perhaps both he and Austin were outside. Rocky started toward the back stairway and stopped. People were talking in Dunn's room across the hall, and he was curious.

It was Dunn and Joseph who were talking, and more than likely they had been at it for quite a while, because they sounded as if they had been arguing and reached the point where they forgot to lower their voices. Joseph said:

"I haven't been in this room before, and I didn't take that whisky! I might have known you were holding out, but even if I had, I wouldn't have taken it. I'm not so sure I'd want to risk drinking it."

"Just what do you mean by that?"

"Oh, not that you might have poisoned the stuff. But someone might—just might—have gotten at it."

"I don't see how, because I buy a better brand than Alfred ever would, and there's lead foil around the neck. You have to tear that off and draw out a cork if you want to meddle with the bottle."

"Oh, I see. Yes, I know your brand. Well, I hadn't been in your room," Joseph said impatiently.

"Why suspect me? That fellow Allan may have taken it. He searched your room."

"I just found out he was up here before breakfast. God damn him! If he—"

"I don't know what you can do about it. I wouldn't want to get into a fight with him. It won't hurt you to lay off the drinking for a while, anyway."

Dunn took a moment or two to say, "What's got into you, Joe?" and his voice was edged. Joseph laughed shortly.

"Listen, Hal, we've always been good friends, and I appreciate what you've done for me. Well, perhaps some people would say you hadn't done me any good, but we won't go into that. The way things were back in the city, I had to break out now and then. But don't try to keep me under your thumb any longer. I admit I've been afraid of you, but that's over. I'll pay what I owe you, and that's the end of it."

"Why shouldn't it be?"

"That's what I want to know. You seem to feel you can make trouble for me if you want to. Oh, you haven't said so, but that's the impression I get."

Dunn said softly: "Couldn't I?"

"How? What could you tell that everyone doesn't know? And I could do some talking myself."

Dunn did not answer this directly. He said: "We've already admitted Alfred didn't like our gambling. I suppose he'd already told his private detective that."

"And perhaps he also told him he'd finally decided you weren't a suitable husband for Norma."

"Did he tell you that, or did Norma?"

"He didn't tell me anything and neither has she. I could guess that for myself. You pulled the wool over his eyes for a good many years."

"And you never managed to. Well, I'm planning on a little talk with Norma."

There was a sound as if Joseph might have moved a few steps closer to his cousin. He said: "You let her alone!"

"The chivalrous brother!" Dunn jeered. "She'd better play ball with me, and so had you. Because I don't think anyone knows how much money you owe me."

"And that you were pressing me for payment? You'll have to argue that you incited me to murder if you're going to say I killed my father because you wanted your money."

"And also because you wanted yours. That wasn't my argument, though. I don't think Alfred found out about your debts because if he had he'd have been red-hot."

"Not only against me," Joseph said coolly. "He wouldn't have liked your staking me any better than my getting in debt to you. And for that reason I don't think you'd ever have told him about it. Another thing, I'm beginning to think your luck in those poker games—and at the roulette wheel—was really phenomenal!"

"Are you suggesting that I—"

"I'm suggesting just what you think I am: that you and the rest of the bunch played me and a lot of others for a sucker. But let that go. I don't think this would particularly impress Pope and Allan. They know I had reason enough to kill my father. Do you think I did?"

"Do you think I did?"

"Skip it. None of us is sure of anything."

Dunn said nastily: "I'm not a chemist."

"My lab was open to anyone, and I know that you were in it the last Sunday we were home."

"I was looking for you, and the place was open to anyone, both before and after that. Did you ever miss anything?"

"I'd been so damned careless keeping check on things that when I finally locked the place I couldn't tell if anything had been taken."

"Convenient! You wouldn't have known I'd been in there if I hadn't told you. I wouldn't tell anyone else if I were you."

"I don't intend to. Good Lord, who started this? If I had any whisky left I'd certainly let you have it, Hal. God knows you need it. Forget it, will you?"

"If you say so, but don't get high and mighty with me, Joe. I had to take that from the old man, but not from you. And you haven't fooled me a bit," Dunn said. "I know you wouldn't kill Alfred just for money, but you had a better reason than that."

"What do you mean?"

'What about that girl? The one I settled with for you; found an obliging doctor and so on. Isabel, wasn't it? She could have caused you a lot of trouble, Joe, but she didn't. And there wasn't any real reason why you shouldn't have married her except that you were afraid of the old man."

Joseph's voice was suddenly uncertain. "I know. I was afraid to tell him I should marry her. You know what funny notions he had about things like that. I didn't want to marry her, but she was the kind of girl he approved of, except for—"

"Except for the fact that she found you irresistible. Well, I never told the old man about her, but you know as well as I do that someone did."

"I don't! I didn't know that! But I begin to see now what he may have meant—"

"By what?"

"Something he said. Never mind. That brother of Isabel's—he was a louse and I think he was suspicious. He might have tried to make something out of it."

Dunn laughed. "You know more about it than I do. Not only that, but a more important face, to you—"

Someone was coming up the back stairs, and Dunn must have been able to hear the noise, for he stopped talking. Rocky moved swiftly away from where he had been standing, close to the door, and silently down the hall. When he met Austin he was near Leale's bedroom door. He thought the man looked at him rather curiously before he said:

"I just came in from outside, and Dr. Ames said you were looking for me. I think he could wear one of Mr. Leale's slippers, if you'll let me into this room."

"Sure. Have you seen Pope anywhere around?"

"He was outside for a while, but he's in the dining room now, sorting out that liquor. He said that he thought it would be safe to use some of the wine, if necessary. The bottles that are fixed like that whisky of Mr. Dunn's. Unfortunately I'd already taken the lead foil off some of the bottles and uncorked one or two."

Austin waited, leather slippers in hand, until Rocky had locked the door again. Then:

"Mr. Dunn has already tried to buy that whisky from me," he said. "I told him I used all of it this morning."

"How long do you give him?"

Austin smiled. "I don't know. But I do know that he's a steady drinker and that his nerves aren't any too good."

"That's what I figured. There's a thing I've been meaning to ask you: Wasn't there an off chance someone besides Leale might've drunk some of that brandy?"

Austin said: "I've thought about that, too. I suppose you're thinking that there was a risk that someone besides Mr. Leale would be killed? Well, as long as there was plenty of everything else, the chance wasn't so great. But while Miss Beatrice drinks very little, she would drink brandy when she takes anything of that sort."

"Oh! No one bothered to mention that."

"I'm afraid they wouldn't."

"No. I haven't asked you if you heard anyone rambling aroun' this hall last night. I suppose you slept, like everyone else says they did."

"I was very tired," Austin said apologetically. "Really, you cannot hear people walking in this hall if they move very quietly."

"I know that, but I think someone was at that closet with the clothes basket in it, and it's near

your room. Never mind, though. I reckon it would-
n't help much if you'd heard anything there."

II

Rocky finally found Pope outside by the woodshed, methodically smashing bottles against its
wall. "Playin' safe?" he asked.

"I thought I had better destroy this. The other
box is still in the kitchen with the lid tightly
nailed down. I think you had better put it behind
the furnace, though. I left four bottles of wine in
Mrs. Powers' room. I'm quite sure they are safe to
drink."

"Better hide them from Dunn. He's gettin'
jittery. I been listening at doors." Rocky leaned
against the shed and told Pope what had been
said in Dunn's room, while liquor spilled onto the
snow's whiteness. "Joseph Leale was pretty cool;
lot more nerve than I thought he had, till Dunn
started talkin' about this Isabel," he ended. "Do
you think the old man might've made Joseph marry her if he'd known all about the affair?"

"They spoke as if she might have been accept-
able to Leale, except for having thrown her cap
over the windmill," Rocky grinned at the old-fashioned phrase. "I know Leale's standard of morality

for women was very rigid—and not any too elastic where men were concerned."

"Then he might've thought Joseph should marry the girl." Rocky kicked at the snow. "Damn!"

Pope stood erect and wiped his hands on his trousers. "What's the matter, Rocky?"

"I don't like to see Eleanor marry a guy like that. Oh, I've been around—plenty. But I never had anything to do with a woman who didn't know what it was all about. From what they said, I got the notion this girl was just a kid. My friends may be roughnecks, but if they get a girl knocked up they figure on marryin' her. I don't say it always turns out very well, but there it is. Well, I suppose you don't care much about eavesdroppin', but seems to me it's got to be done, if possible."

"Norma and Harold, you mean? Yes," Pope said regretfully, "I'm afraid we will want to overhear their little chat. I'll try to keep an eye on them, in case they elude you. Austin tells me Ames had to come back."

"Yeah, and I'd just as leave have a doctor in the house. By the way, Austin says that if anyone but Leale had drank any brandy, Beatrice would have been the one to do it. There goes the dinner gong—pardon me: I mean lunch. I'm ready for it, though I must say these meals are kind of ordeals."

Austin had placed two chairs at the foot of the table, but he had also laid a place at the head of the table. Rocky hesitated, walked around the table, and said to Beatrice:

"Do you mind if I sit here? It's kind of crowded, sitting by Pope."

"No—no, I don't mind," she said after an instant. "It doesn't matter as long as it's not—someone else."

"Are you feelin' better now?" Rocky said, because her face looked coldly pinched and all her movements were so slow and stiff. "We've got our doctor back. I reckon you don't mind him stayin'? He couldn't make it to Greenleaf."

"That is what Austin was telling me. No, I don't mind." Beatrice looked down the table. "We won't wait for Harold and Joseph," she said as Ames came shuffling in. "I don't know where they are."

When they did appear, Joseph's color was high, and Dunn had a look of sullen malice. But the younger man was still cool enough: he apologized for his lateness, sat down by Eleanor, and talked about the weather. Dunn ate almost nothing, began to smoke before the meal was half done, and grumbled about the food.

"I think it's very good, considering," Eleanor said. "I don't know what Mr. Leale intended to do about getting fresh meats and vegetables."

"Neither do I," Ames said. "Of course, we get a certain—or rather, an uncertain, amount during the winter. You aren't anticipating a food shortage, are you?"

"Oh no, Mrs. Powers says there will be plenty to eat—and we can take it and like it. Her baked ham is delicious."

Eleanor helped herself from the big meat platter, and Dunn said:

"I don't like baked ham. What did you carve it with, Austin?"

Austin was pouring coffee. He filled Ames' cup a little too full. "We used one of the old kitchen knives," he said without emphasis. "Will you have coffee?"

He addressed Dunn, and the omission of his customary "sir" was noticeable. Beatrice had closed her eyes; she said:

"I'd like black coffee, please," and Pope suggested deliberately:

"You'd better make Mr. Dunn's black too, Austin."

Dunn scowled and crushed his cigarette out with unsteady fingers. Norma said quickly:

"Do you often have such bad storms up here in the winter, Mr. Allan? Bad enough to stop the trains, I mean."

"This is the hardest winter we've had for five years. We don't have snowsheds on this road,"

Rocky said. "And just one of the big rotary snow-plows like they have back in the Middle West, where they have to use them a lot. There's one or two places on the line where they're always havin' slides."

He went on talking because someone had to, and Ames helped him out by telling how he had been stuck in the canyon for twelve hours in December.

"With the dining-car supplies running low and rocks rattling down the side of the hill against the cars. And of course all the women would screech at that, and I had my hands full. I made up my mind to stay home until the storms were over," he ended, as Eleanor pushed her chair away from the table.

Everyone left the table but Ames, Pope, and himself, and Rocky sat smoking and debating what to do next. Pope took off his glasses and looked at Rocky with a sympathetic twinkle in his blue eyes.

"Inactivity is very trying to a person of your temperament, I know."

"Well, but what can I do? Talk some more? Ask questions, I mean? I kind of intended we should—"

"If you wouldn't mind waiting?"

"Not if you say to. But what'm I going to do all afternoon? Just sit around on my tail?"

"And wait for Dunn to start seeing pink ele-
phants," Ames suggested.

"I supposed you'd catch on to that. Do you
think he's approachin' the state where he'll talk in
exchange for a drink?"

"Oh, very likely, but suppose he doesn't know
anything?" Ames said.

"All of 'em know something and whatever it is,
I want to hear it. Pope can decide how important it is. I guess I'll go take a nap," Rocky said.
"You'll keep an eye on things, Pope? Do you think
you can manage alone?"

"Oh yes." Pope's look said that he remembered
that he was to watch Norma and Harold. "You go
on, Rocky. Then you can take over, and I'll get
some sleep against tonight."

Like most railroaders, Rocky could sleep at any
time, quickly and well, and wake instantly. When
Pope came into Leale's room an hour later, Rocky
sat up, yawned, and was ready for action.

"Anything doin'?" he asked.

Pope sat down on the bed. "It was really very
easy, mainly because Dunn was so anxious to talk
to Norma that he didn't take very many precautions against being overheard. Beatrice Leale came
up here, and all the rest of us were in the living
room. Joseph and Eleanor and Dr. Ames began

to play bridge and wanted Norma to make the fourth, but she made some excuse about having to go upstairs. Dunn had been whispering to her just before that.

"After she had been gone about five minutes Dunn followed her, and then I eased out of the room. People forget I am around if I don't talk," Pope said plaintively. "A rather humiliating but sometimes very useful thing. They went onto the side porch on the left-hand side of the dining room, and I listened from the dining room, since Dunn forgot to close the door tightly."

Norma said pettishly: "If you have to talk to me, Hal, does it have to be out here in the cold? It's freezing."

"I don't know where else you'd suggest. I doubt if you'll want anyone to overhear what I have to say. We could go to your room, if you like."

"I don't. And I don't like the way you say that, either. You can keep out of my bedroom, at all times!"

"You're a damned little—flirt," Dunn said. "The kind that leads a man on and never comes through. But I'm crazy about you." He slid an arm about her waist. "Are you going to marry me?"

Norma smiled slowly, not trying to move away from him. "What do you think? Why should I marry you? I'm not Beatrice: I don't have to grab at just anything that resembles a man. I've been nice to you because Father seemed to want me to be, and it teased Beatrice. I don't mind your kissing me. Cousins can kiss, anyway, can't they?"

"Third cousins—"

"A third cousin close to my father's age," Norma said cruelly. "Honestly, Hal, you're so conceited that you're funny."

"So that's it, is it?" Dunn's small mustache twitched. "I'm funny! Not as funny as you think, you little slut!"

"Hal! You hurt!" Norma struck his arm aside. "And don't you dare call me names like that! I'll tell Joseph."

"Do that. Listen, my lady," Dunn said calmly. "I've suspected for a long time that there was another man in the picture. I've watched you sneak those typewritten letters out of the mail before Alfred could see them. You didn't think anyone but you two knew about it, and he didn't tell, but I knew there was some special reason for one or two rows you had. I never managed to find out who this fellow is, but I saw you sneaking into the house at four o'clock in the morning last month. If Alfred found out about that he'd have jumped to conclusions at once. The correct conclusion—"

"It wouldn't be—not what you mean! The car broke down."

Dunn laughed. "A car's as good as a hotel room. I suppose Joseph helped you get in: that's why he's worried about you. However, I'm willing to forget that. I want you, and I'll be a reasonable enough husband. I'll probably get tired of you in a year or two, and after that, no questions asked."

"I don't have to marry you. Father said I didn't. Have you told anyone that? He actually forbade my marrying you. That shows what he finally thought of you. So you had reason enough for killing him if you wanted more than your ten thousand, and of course you did."

"Do," Dunn corrected.

"That sounds well, doesn't it? But I suppose they—Mr. Pope and Mr. Allan—know that about you. Just like they probably know about me. So there's no use your telling them."

"Plausible! Of course you're making a play for Allan, just in case. I'd advise you to pay a little more attention to Pope. He's the brains of the outfit."

"How unusual for you to admit that anyone but yourself has any brains," Norma said sweetly. "I don't believe Mr. Allan's as stupid as you'd like to think. And he's so good-looking. I like men who have tanned faces and white teeth. Of course, you wouldn't admit he's handsome, because he makes you look insignificant."

"Put your rough diamond in store clothes and you'd not care so much for his looks!" Dunn stopped; achieved an amused smile. "So you want me to believe you've managed a grand passion for someone? Tell me what he's like."

"He's—" Norma shook her head. "No, I won't tell you one thing. You just want to trick me into talking too much."

"What does he do? He doesn't happen to be a chemist, does he? Or a druggist? Convenient professions."

Norma looked frightened. She said: "He's an engineer. And he has a good position now, and I don't intend to have him dragged into this. Because we won't be snowbound forever."

"And when we aren't the authorities can start inquiries in the city. Some of your friends may have seen you together."

"No, no one ever did," Norma said quickly. "Because he— I'm not going to talk any more about it."

"But you'll not stick it, my dear. You'll talk if you ever have to save your neck that way. And suppose," Dunn said softly, "that I saved Pope and Allan some trouble by telling them a guess of mine? Or that I told them you were out of your room once last night?"

"You couldn't know that unless you were out of yours! But—you said you guessed—"

Dunn smiled unpleasantly. "Think it over, sweet. If you're going to be self-sacrificing, here's your chance. I want to marry you, since I suppose nothing else will do. Oh, for God's sake, don't cry! I'm in no mood for your sniveling."

Norma had been sobbing very effectively into a small handkerchief. She stopped abruptly, tore the handkerchief in two, and stamped her foot.

"You go to hell!" she said. Pope barely managed to get out of the dining room before she rushed through it.

"I think she started to go upstairs," Pope concluded. "Then probably she decided there was safety in numbers, for she went back to the others. I don't know what became of Dunn."

"Was he mad when she told him where to go?"

"I couldn't see his face because I had to dodge out." Pope moved his long legs experimentally. "I'm tied in knots from wedging myself between a door and window. I don't think Dunn was angry at that particular remark, however. That was bravado on her part—and a childish loss of temper."

Rocky said reflectively: "She sure let him know what she thought of him, though. What effect do you suppose that will have on him?"

"I'm afraid it will make him rather vindictive. Vain men are apt to be when their vanity is wounded."

"He's a louse. I don't see much point in his threatening to tell about this guy she's in love with, except to make out a stronger motive for her to kill the old man. S'pose he had seen her sneakin' in at 4 a.m.?"

"He wouldn't have waited so long before punishing her. And if Miss Georgina had seen her, she would have told, at once. But someone else might have withheld the information until recently. 'Flagrante delicto,'" Pope added.

"Hunh? Oh, that's right: what Leale scribbled on that paper. And Norma was cryin' before he got through with her. But I imagine she cries whenever she doesn't want to talk any more."

"I'm certain of that. She cries too prettily."

"Well, I suppose I got to try to get this fellow's name out of her. I don't want to. As she says, it's too bad he has to be dragged into it. But Dunn insinuated this guy might've put her up to poisonin' her father."

"And of course it is quite possible that Dunn is right. But I think you are wasting time trying to make her tell the man's name."

"I shouldn't wonder. But you know the sheriff will try to find it out and think I should have, if

I don't. Like Dunn said: once he gets here, he can start things going from the other end, in the city."

Rocky walked over to the window. He said, his back toward Pope:

"Meanwhile, I wish Eleanor was out of this."

"Eleanor? She's above suspicion, Rocky."

"I know that, and so do you. I don't know that the sheriff and cor'ner will, once they find out about her and Joseph. They may argue a nurse would know about poisons and be handy with a knife. They'll probably question her a lot. That don't matter so much, though. But suppose Joseph happens to be the murderer? That's going to be tough on her, even if she has got nerve enough to want to know the truth."

Pope's voice sounded as if he might be laughing to himself. "There always seems to be—shall we call it love interest?—mixed up with murder cases. I am sentimentally inclined, but I don't like to have my attention distracted too much from more serious matters." He added casually: "Why don't you marry Eleanor yourself?"

"Just like that!" Rocky smiled wryly over his shoulder. "I was tryin' to get around to suggestin' it to her, spite of a remark she made about not thinkin' she'd care to marry a railroader. But she left Merton when she could've had a steady job there, so I kept my mouth shut. Never expected to see her again."

Pope said: "She won't be happy with Joseph Leale. He's weak."

"She could make something out of him, and that seems to be what some women like. Eleanor is kind of bossy, you know. I reckon nurses get into that habit. I can't dislike Joseph, and he's educated and got good manners. I wish I'd stayed home and gone to school like I should have."

"And then you would never have met Eleanor. Advice to the lovelorn by Uncle Theophilus Pope: Make her marry you. She doesn't belong with these people."

"I kind of thought she did. Anyway, I like your nerve. You won't take it that easy when your time comes."

"I'm not expecting ever to marry. Can you think," Pope said rather bitterly, "that any woman would want to marry a face like mine? Don't embarrass yourself by trying to answer that politely. You take over downstairs while I get a little sleep."

III

Eleanor was standing in the front doorway as Rocky came down the stairs. She started when he said: "Getting some fresh air?"

"I didn't hear you coming. Yes, this house is getting stuffy from so much furnace heat, but everyone is complaining of the cold. I'd like to go for a long walk. Couldn't we?"

"Who's we?"

"You and I."

"I'd like to," Rocky said. "But I don't see how I can. Pope is getting him some sleep, and I'm afraid to leave this gang by themselves."

"I suppose you are. Never mind: it will be dark before very long, won't it? I wish that we didn't have to depend on candles and lamps tonight."

"Nervous?"

"Of course I am," Eleanor said crossly. "Jittering! You haven't found that gun, have you?"

"No. Could you suggest any out-of-the-way place it could be in?"

"I'm afraid I can't. I suppose it would be easy enough to hide. Joseph said it was a small gun."

"It is. Are they still playin' cards in there?"

"We began to snap at each other and trump our partner's aces, so we stopped. The others are keeping the fire warm."

"Dunn too?"

"No, I don't know where he is. He didn't come back after he left the room, soon after lunch. Did you take charge of his private stock?"

"I sure as hell did," Rocky said. "I'm going looking for him now."

"And I'm going to take off this uniform. I don't need," Eleanor said sadly, "to wear it any longer."

"Except that you look swell in it. All that white makes your hair look so red."

"What a compliment! Perhaps I'd rather my hair didn't look any redder than is absolutely necessary."

Rocky said gravely: "I meant it for a compliment just the same. When you get upstairs, would you mind lookin' in to see if Beatrice is all right? I don't want to bother her."

"You're worried about her? But of course you would be. I'll look in on her."

Rocky started on down the hall, intending to try to locate Dunn, but before he reached the dining room Norma Leale came out of the living room. She said:

"I've been wanting to talk to you. Isn't there any place in this house where people can talk privately?"

"The side porches?" Rocky suggested.

She looked at him doubtfully. "Oh, wouldn't it be too cold out there? Joseph and Dr. Ames are still in the living room."

"I reckon this will be all right." Rocky held open the dining-room door. "No one will be coming in here for a while. What did you want to talk to me about?"

"I wish you wouldn't be so abrupt. It frightens me," Norma complained. "And Mr. Pope makes me nervous because you can't ever tell what he may be thinking."

She sat down at the table, but in an instant she was up again and walking restlessly about the room. Rocky sat still and watched her.

"Cigarette?" he said finally.

"No—yes, I will. Did my father tell Mr. Pope I'm engaged to a man he didn't want me to marry?"

"Yes, he told him that."

"But not his name?" Rocky shook his head. Norma said: "I didn't think he would."

"But it won't be impossible for the sheriff to find out this man's name if he thinks it's important."

"Why should he think it's important? What does it matter who he is? He wasn't here or ever in the city for a long time."

Rocky shrugged. "Well, I'm not the final judge of that. Maybe it's important and maybe it isn't. The main thing is that people always want to know everything in a murder case."

"They haven't any right to! They drag out things that haven't anything to do with the murder, and it isn't fair. You don't think I killed my father, do you?"

She came closer to him so that he caught the fragrance of some kind of perfume that she wore. It was the sort of perfume that went with the blue pajamas she was still wearing. It was only at first glance that those pajamas made her look like a little girl: a second glance gave you a very good idea how she'd look if she didn't have them on. Rocky said politely:

"No, I can't really think you killed your father. Your looks are all against it. But I've always been told you can't tell a murderer by the way he looks. Who do you think is guilty?"

Norma hesitated. "Of course, I'd say it was Beatrice if it wasn't for one thing. As much as I'd like to, I simply cannot see her killing Father. It wasn't just that she adored him, but she needed him. She'll be alone, now; none of us will bother with her. That is, no more than we have to. If it had been me who was poisoned— But I never drink brandy, so she couldn't have made a mistake. And she wouldn't want to kill Joseph or Harold: just me."

"Hasn't it ever occurred to you that someone might've wanted to kill her? I've been told she drank brandy sometimes."

"Oh! Y-yes, she did, but just once in a great while. That would—make it look bad for me, wouldn't it?"

"I suppose so. You've admitted you don't like her."

"Just the same, she does gain more from Father's death than any of the rest of us," Norma said quickly.

"Sure she does—in money."

Norma looked at him uneasily and threw her half-smoked cigarette into an ash tray. "Well, I didn't intend to discuss Beatrice. Did you—or someone—hear Harold talking to me a little while ago?"

"I didn't. Pope did."

"I was afraid of that. I thought I heard someone leave this room as I left the porch. Well, it doesn't particularly matter. Harold doesn't know anything worth telling. And I'll manage him," Norma said, setting her teeth together. Her mouth did not look at all babyish when she did that, nor her chin quite so soft and round.

"Short of marryin' him, what do you propose to do?" Rocky asked. "While I'll admit he seems pretty crazy about you, he's got his eye on your money too, and he's got to marry you to have a whack at that."

Norma muttered: "Hateful thing! I wouldn't marry him. He could be perfectly awful if he wanted to."

"Then I take it that maybe you know a thing or two about him that's enough to keep him from talkin' about you. Though why you didn't say so to him a while ago—"

"I got angry. No, I don't know anything that's important enough to tell you. But I think Joseph and I together can persuade him to keep his mouth shut. Buy him off, though I'll deny that if you tell anyone I said it. The less any of us talks, the safer we are, but of course certain things have already come out, and we might as well admit those. Oh," she added to Rocky's quizzical look, "I may have a baby face and not be particularly intellectual, but I'm not dumb. For instance, I'm not dumb enough to think it's any use for me to offer you a lot of money."

"Not a bit." Rocky's eyes looked, briefly, more yellow than brown. "An' just what would I do to earn my bribe?"

"But I'm not offering you money! Please don't be mad." She put a soft hand on his shoulder. "But you don't have to tell your sheriff everything, do you? Not something that doesn't matter to anyone but me? And it does matter so much to me."

"You mean you want me not to tell about this fellow you're engaged to? If I didn't, the others would."

"No, they won't. If you don't talk, they won't."

"You're leavin' Pope out of your calculations."

"He's not an official of any kind, and you could persuade him not to talk. It isn't so much just letting people know I was engaged to a man my father didn't want me to marry. But Mr. Pope may have guessed something, being with us all the time, and if he wouldn't tell—they'll never get me to tell anything. And I'd do anything you asked to keep from having his name dragged into this." She tightened her hand on his shoulder as if she liked the feel of the firm muscles under her fingers. "I don't think you understand me," she added, as Rocky did not answer.

"Sister, I understand you perfectly, though you don't put your proposition quite as crudely as some. I was just readjustin' my ideas," Rocky drawled. "I reckon I still had something to learn, an' I just learned it—that what I been used to calling a lady ain't any different from any other kind of woman. Moreover, you rate yourself pretty high, though I admit it would probably be a pleasure to sleep with you."

He caught her hand before she could slap his face again.

"I wouldn't do that," he said pleasantly. "You run along and peddle your groceries. And if you're thinkin' of telling big brother than I insulted you, I wouldn't do that, either."

Norma jerked her wrist from his fingers, said, "You—you—" in a little gasp of rage, and slammed the door into the hall violently.

Rocky muttered, "Whew!" and stood up. Sarah Powers wasn't making any noise in the kitchen, and he wondered if she had been listening. He pulled the door open, and Eleanor stared at him, crimson cheeked.

After an instant she said icily, "Beatrice is quite all right," and tried to get past him into the dining room. Rocky blocked the doorway. He said recklessly:

"People that listen at doors usually get their noses pinched. Just exactly what have I done for you to look at me that way?"

"I don't care to discuss it! Please let me by."

"You sound like someone in a movie now," Rocky said angrily. He stood aside. "If there's anything more unreasonable than a red-headed woman, I'd like to know what it is."

Eleanor's shoulders stiffened, but she did not turn until she reached the door to the hall. Then: "I'm sorry I listened," she said. "just let it go at that."

Sarah Powers was evidently in her bedroom, and Rocky thought he heard her give a little snort of laughter as he kicked the kitchen door open. Austin was sitting on the chopping block in the woodshed, smoking.

"A.P.O.?" Rocky said. "What'd Leale get such big logs for? They take a lot of splitting for the kitchen stove."

"They certainly do." Austin looked at his reddened palms. "I think I've spent at least half the day out here."

"I wouldn't doubt it." Rocky picked up the ax: woodchopping was a good prescription for the way he felt. "Sit over there on one of the other logs. What I came out for was to see if Dunn is anywhere aroun'. You seen him?"

"When I came out here, about an hour ago, he was walking over toward the road."

"Toward that coasting hill, you mean? You can see it from outside here, can't you? Well, I guess the exercise won't hurt him. What'd you do if you had something you wanted to burn?" Rocky asked abruptly.

Austin looked rather blank. "Something I wanted to burn? You mean, without anyone knowing it? Depends on what it was, but I could easily use the furnace. There are plenty of fires downstairs. I suppose you couldn't tell me what this article is?"

"Probably just a little piece of paper. You could light a thing like that with a match, though, and then get rid of the ashes in the toilet or throw 'em out a window."

Rocky stopped to put another log on the chopping block; halved and quartered it. "If you had ever seen Norma Leale sneaking into the house at four in the morning, would you have let Leale know it?"

"I would not," Austin said emphatically. "Even if I had cared to tell—and I wouldn't have—I'd have kept my mouth shut. Mr. Leale would have resented my talking even if my story had been proved true."

"Well, I won't ask you if you did see her, then. Would the old lady have told?"

"Oh, of course. She was the only one he would listen to. Keeping my place in a household like that involved a nice use of discretion," Austin said frankly. "Though it was Mr. Leale who had hired me and could fire me, I wasn't above helping Joseph Leale and Dunn when I could, and glad enough to take a five- or ten-dollar tip for it."

"I don't blame you. You've had some education, haven't you?"

"Some. I was in college when I was overcome with patriotic fervor and joined the army," Austin said dryly. "While I was making the world safe for democracy, the uncle who'd looked after me died, penniless. Well, you soon get into the habit of saying 'sir.'" He watched Rocky enviously. "You get more of that done in fifteen minutes than I do in an hour."

"I'm a better woodchopper than a detective. Lots of practice too. I never was actually on the bum, but I've split plenty wood for a meal. I have to favor this left shoulder, though. I think that ought to last till tomorrow, with what you've already split. I'll take some in to Sarah. It'll begin to get dark pretty soon, and I got to wake up Pope and locate Dunn."

Sarah Powers said: "It's about time. Is Austin bringin' some more in?" She turned up the wick of the kerosene lamp she had just lighted. "I wanted to see how this thing works. I found a bunch more candles when you need 'em. After dinner you can have one of these lamps."

"Have you seen Dunn lately?"

"He come through here a while ago and went upstairs the back way. You'd better find another place to put that booze," Sarah said grimly. "I don't want to be murdered in my bed if he finds out where it is."

"I'll take it upstairs pretty soon," Rocky promised.

He went up the back stairway, stopped to listen at Dunn's door until he thought he heard the man moving about in his room. Pope was just sitting up, yawning tremendously. Rocky looked at him severely.

"Do you know something you're not telling?" he said.

"That's indefinite," Pope objected. "I keep my guesses to myself. I don't think I know anything I haven't told you. Why?"

"Norma Leale's worried about her boy friend. She seems to think we may know who he is, and she wants us to kind of forget to tell the sheriff."

"She needn't be so worried. I don't know who he is."

Rocky looked at Pope suspiciously, catching his faint emphasis on the word, "know."

"Well, she didn't have anything to fear from me, that way, but I didn't bother to tell her so. Let her worry. I'd almost forgotten that will proposition for a while. If Leale did write another will and someone did take it from that box, do you think it's been destroyed?"

"That's hard to tell. It would be an easy thing to destroy, but suppose that such a will was unfavorable to more than one person—"

Rocky grinned. "Call 'em X, Y, and Z, why don't you?"

"Very well. X has the will, and it is unfavorable to him but equally so to Y and Z. If I were X I would hesitate to destroy the will because it would give me a useful hold over Y and Z."

"Blackmail, hunh? Not necessarily for money; sort of 'you scratch my back and I'll scratch yours,' proposition. Well, and even if X found out the new will left him fixed as well as the old one, he might hold on to it because it disinherited Y or Z or both. There's a lot of int'resting possibil- ities when you start thinkin' them out. It's—what time?"

"Five minutes after four."

"And dinner ain't till seven. Too long, if you ask me. Why don't they have it at a decent hour? You comin' downstairs?"

Pope said: "I might as well." Then: "What's that?"

Rocky was already halfway across the room. "Lock up: the key's in the door. Sounds to me like some kind of row downstairs."

IV

The living-room door was open, and Austin was saying urgently:

"I tell you I haven't seen anything of that whis- ky, and we used what I had this morning."

Joseph's voice was strained. "Of course he isn't hiding the stuff from you, Hal. For God's sake, be reasonable. I know you're all to pieces, but why don't you talk to Allan—"

Rocky could look into the living room now. Dunn was shot to pieces and no mistake: his eyes were crazy and his upper lip jerked. Norma had gotten behind Ames, who was regarding Dunn with an impersonally professional look. He said:

"Yes, talk to Allan, and if he thinks your whisky isn't safe to drink, I can give you something else to tide you over."

"But, for heaven's sake, don't make a scene," Joseph said. "After all, the rest of us have had to get along without liquor."

"How do I know that's so? By God, I want that whisky and I'm going to have it!" Dunn looked wildly about the circle; moved toward Eleanor, who was standing behind Beatrice's chair. "How do I know one of you two didn't steal it? One of you—"

Rocky drawled amiably: "I didn't exactly steal it, Dunn. I just took charge of it for the time being. Any objections?" He felt that Pope was standing behind him now and moved a step or two into the room. "You'd have sopped it up by now if I'd left it where it was."

"All right. I don't ask for all of it," Dunn said, his voice shaking. "But it's my property; you hadn't any right to take it. No one could poison it."

"No one did; not one bottle, anyway. I tried it out," Rocky said provokingly. "As a favor to you. I'd cert'nly hate to see you pass out on us sudden. Why, this is just a beginning. You had a drink or two this mornin'—"

He stopped, staring at the small black gun that appeared suddenly in Dunn's hand. He felt, for an instant, very foolish and a little frightened. The fellow's hands were shaking so that there was no telling where a bullet would go if he fired the gun, and he might even pull the trigger without intending to. His hope that the gun was unloaded was ended with Dunn's:

"This thing is loaded! And I'm going to have that whisky! Wherever it is, go get it for me—no, tell Austin and let him get it. You can stay here."

Rocky shrugged. "Oh, if you want it that bad. Run along an' tell Sarah we want a bottle of whisky, Austin."

Austin looked at him doubtfully; then raised his eyebrows and started toward the door. To get by Dunn he had almost to brush against him and for one instant Dunn's eyes wavered. In that second Rocky leaped forward, head and shoulders low. A bullet sang past him, and wood splintered somewhere, but he got his hands on Dunn's wrists before the man could fire again.

He said, "Drop it!" tightening his fingers. Dunn gasped, and the gun thudded to the floor. Rocky swung him about, arms pinioned, behind him, and looked toward Pope, who was just rising from his knees. He said:

"I figured you'd have sense enough to duck. Grab that gun, will you? And never mind about the whisky, Austin."

Dunn said: "But I've got to have it! I tell you, I've got to have it." He was whimpering now. Ames said:

"Don't you think you're carrying this too far, Allan? He needs a drink."

"I never said he didn't, and maybe he'll get one when I'm through talkin' to him. You get that whisky, Austin. Maybe he'd like to look at it."

Norma cried: "Oh, you're—you're cruel!"

"Don't let your sympathetic nature run away with you, Miss Leale," Pope said. "It was just a minute ago that Mr. Dunn was waving a loaded gun around rather wildly. In fact, that bullet passed about two inches over my head. Perhaps Mr. Dunn would like to tell us where he got this gun."

Beatrice said, without looking up: "You thought someone might have taken it from Aunt Georgina, didn't you?"

Dunn tried to twist about so that he could see her face and failed. His lips drew back from his pointed teeth.

"All right," he said. "I didn't get that from her room; I got it from Alfred's. You've intended all

along to make me talk, but the joke's going to
be on you, Allan! Because you're crazy about that
damned, red-headed slut—"

Rocky struck him across the mouth and sent
him reeling onto the chesterfield. Eleanor said:

"Please, Rocky! That's enough. I don't want you
to—not for me."

"Just as you say." Rocky looked down at Dunn,
his eyes yellow. "Stop shivering! I'm not going to
hit you again. Go on with what you've got to say."

Dunn wiped his lips. "All right, we'll leave per-
sonalities out of it. You'd better look at Joseph
too—all of them, for that matter. I suppose everyone's tried to give you the idea the old man was
willing for Joe to marry—Miss Gannon. Well,
maybe he was, once. But he thought better of it.
He decided that Joe had other claims on him, and
then that he wasn't too old to marry again himself."

Dunn began to chuckle; then to laugh hysterically. "You've got to hand it to the old boy. Keep
his family in order by giving them a young stepmother; maybe have two or three kids to inherit
his money."

He lay back on the chesterfield, shaking with
laughter. Rocky took the glass and bottle of whisky that Austin offered; poured a very moderate
drink.

"Take this," he said curtly. "And go on."

"But he's making all this up! He's raving; he's in no condition to know what he's saying—"

"Better give Joe a drink, too," Dunn said. "He doth protest too much. If the old man didn't come right out and tell you his plans, you were beginning to guess them after your last interview with him."

Norma said: "I don't believe it. It's—it's impossible! Beatrice, you don't believe him, do you? Eleanor—"

Eleanor was standing very straight, staring at Dunn. Her lips were white, and a muscle quivered in her cheek. She said:

"Let's hear what else Mr. Dunn has to say."

"Oh, nothing much on that subject." Dunn looked avidly at the bottle in Rocky's hands. "You'll have to get the truth of that out of the rest of them. Give Joseph a little third degree; ask him about Isabel. Ask Miss Gannon a few questions if you can bring yourself to do it."

Eleanor let go the back of Beatrice's chair and walked toward the door. "I'm ready to talk to Mr. Pope and Mr. Allan whenever they wish," she said. "The rest of you might like to know that your father never mentioned marriage to me. I'll ask you to excuse me. And I wish," she added, turning briefly in the doorway, "that I'd never heard the name of Leale!"

Joseph made a movement to follow her, but Pope said: "Better not. We want to talk to you, you know."

"Then let me go," Norma said. Rocky liked her for that; she must really care something about Eleanor. "Even if Father was such an old fool that he thought— Well, even if he was, Eleanor wouldn't have listened to him."

"No, she wouldn't," Beatrice said unexpectedly. "I can't believe what Harold says. Of course Father had a right to marry again." She rubbed her forehead fretfully. "But he never said anything to me about it. And Aunt Georgina wouldn't have liked it."

"Good reason why he didn't say anything to either of you," Dunn said, still looking at the bottle of whisky. "Of course, all of you'd say you hadn't any idea what he meant to do, because you've got sense enough to see what it would mean to you."

"But if Eleanor wouldn't marry him—and she wouldn't have—" Norma began.

"There are plenty of women who would, once he'd got the idea into his head."

Joseph said spiritlessly: "It would have made some difference to you too if it had been Eleanor. You know she detests you."

"You're wasting our time with these accusations and counter accusations," Pope said with sudden and unusual impatience. "You'd better stay here for a while, Miss Leale. Suppose we leave your— information for a few minutes, Mr. Dunn, and deal with your actions. When and where did you get that gun?"

"Where I told you: in Alfred's room." Dunn moistened his lips. "You can't try to pin Cousin Georgina's murder on me because I have that gun. You haven't any proof she ever had it, though she might have gone looking for it. I found out my key fitted Alfred's door, and I got into his room some time before Ames arrived. Around six-thirty, that would be. The rest of you were in your rooms, but you didn't hear me."

"Were you in such a state of alarm that you thought a gun was necessary to your safety?" Pope said.

"Well, I thought it would be a good thing to have."

"Why? What do you know that would make you dangerous to anyone?"

"Nothing—nothing at all. I just didn't like the situation."

Pope said mildly: "Suppose you look through his pockets, Rocky. I'd like to know if he took anything besides the gun from Leale's room."

"With pleasure." Rocky jerked Dunn to his feet. He thought it would be very nice if Dunn were carrying cyanide around with him, or even if he had the will Leale might have written. But the only thing in Dunn's pockets that interested Pope was a thick roll of twenty-dollar bills.

"Five hundred dollars. Are you in the habit of carrying so much money with you, Dunn?"

"Of course he isn't," Joseph said. "He told me he was broke before we came up here. That's Father's money. He always carried a large amount, in twenties."

"That is what I thought. I saw this roll of bills when he paid our driver, the day we arrived. The money wasn't in his pockets when he died. Where did you get it, Dunn?"

Dunn sat down and put his head between his hands. "You've got to give me another drink."

"Give him a good stiff one, Rocky," Pope said. "He's gone too far now not to go on talking. All right, Dunn."

"I did go into Alfred's room for that money. I happened to think that it was probably there, and I needed it. It was in the suit he'd worn on the train. Suppose someone missed it: anyone might have taken it. Then I looked around, as long as I'd bothered to go in. I couldn't open that strong-box, though I supposed the key to it was in his pockets. But I couldn't bring myself to look for it. When I looked through the bureau I saw the gun and I thought it might come in handy, so I took it. That's all."

"Well, it's enough, isn't it?" Joseph muttered. "Change a thing or two in the way you've told it and it might be—plenty."

"That's all—about me," Dunn retorted. "We haven't begun on you, yet. I don't know how much Pope and Allan know."

"More than you think, I imagine. For instance," Pope said, "that Mr. Leale owes you money and that you want to be paid. That his father had decided you were not to be encouraged even in your idea of marrying Miss Norma. That you have been threatening both her and her brother."

"Threatening? You mean, suggesting I could tell a few things they'd rather I didn't. Well, I'll leave it to you to find out who Norma's—boy friend is. I don't know, anyway. But I'd like to know where she was last night when I wanted to talk to her."

"Would you? Don't be indelicate, Hal," Norma said sweetly. "In the bathroom, very likely."

"You see? You'll get nothing from her or any of the other women, Beatrice included. She'd like you to believe she'd have just loved a nice step-mamma."

"I would have hated it," Beatrice said evenly. "But Father wasn't ever actually unfair, was he? If the rest of you were afraid of him, it was for other reasons." She rubbed her forehead again. "I haven't anything to tell, really. And my head aches. You know Father never consulted me about really serious things. I mean, when they concerned the rest of you. He didn't tell me about Joseph or Norma. But Aunt Georgina must have known."

"Undoubtedly she knew—far too much," Pope agreed. "Now Mr. Leale, do you wish to explain Mr. Dunn's insinuations?"

Joseph put his hands on the back of a chair as if he wished to brace himself. "I suppose I'd better, because I don't—didn't know all he seems to think I did. I thought all along he was willing for me to marry Eleanor. Why, I thought he wanted me to."

Rocky lighted a cigarette. He didn't care about hearing this, and Dunn knew it, damn him. The whisky he'd drunk had restored some of his confidence.

"All I was worried about was whether Eleanor would ever marry me or not," Joseph said, without looking at Rocky. "He certainly liked her. It never entered my head he might want to marry her himself. Not even when he—

"Well, there'd been a girl—I suppose I have to explain that—this Isabel Harold spoke of. I admit we were—pretty friendly, and if she hadn't been a good sport it might have made trouble for me. But we broke off, and as far as I knew, Father didn't know anything about it. Or any of her family. Her father and mother were nice, but she had a brother who didn't like me, and perhaps he found out about our—affair and wrote or went to see my father."

Austin said: "What did this man look like, sir?"

"Why, he was a thickset fellow, very dark. Black eyes and hair and a rather large nose. He—he always looked like his hair needed cutting in back, it was so bushy."

Austin nodded. "I noticed that. He came to see Mr. Leale on Monday afternoon, the day after Mr. Leale had been ill. He insisted that I let him in, and Mr. Leale heard us arguing and said he would talk to him. That was late afternoon, when everyone else was either out of the house or upstairs."

"He'd never miss a chance of collecting a few dollars," Joseph said bitterly. "But I don't imagine he got any money out of my father. I don't suppose he had very much, if any, proof to give him. Isabel wouldn't have talked; she probably didn't know Sam was going to my father. Well, Father didn't bother me, talking about it, until we got up here. Then we had this interview.

"First he touched on my gambling and Harold's bad influence over me. But if he knew I owed Harold more than just a few dollars, he didn't say so. I said if he'd just find something for me to do I'd try to amount to something. Christ, what kind of life was that, stuck around that house and treated like a six-year-old! It made me mad, thinking about it; I said more than I usually dared to: that I'd rather earn a decent living for myself and cut loose from his apron strings.

"He just looked at me and said: 'I intend that you shall, but perhaps not exactly as you have planned. I have always recognized my obligations, and I intend that you shall fulfill yours.'

"That," Joseph said, "was what I couldn't understand until now. Oh, of course I thought about Isabel, but I didn't really think he could know about her. I thought perhaps he was referring to my obligation to him. I don't think he intended to explain then. If he really wanted to marry Eleanor he'd have waited until he was sure of her."

"He was vain, then?" Pope said, half to himself.

"Vain?" Dunn laughed. "Did he fool you? Of course he was vain, and all of us were part of his vanity."

Joseph said: "I guess Hal's right. He'd been successful in life, and no one had ever opposed him and come out winner. Well, he would have waited, anyway, and then told us his plans and all the plans he'd made for us. He probably wanted me to worry, too. But if he was going to explain, he didn't have time just then, because the dinner gong sounded. He didn't try to talk to me again."

He looked at Pope haggardly. "I'll take that drink now, if you don't mind."

Rocky said: "Help yourself. Is that all, Pope?"

"If there's nothing you want to ask. Then suppose you escort Mr. Dunn to his room and lock him in."

"Lock— Are you placing me under arrest?" Dunn demanded, sitting erect.

"Oh no, and I don't suppose there's really any need to put you under lock and key. You can't get away. But it will keep you out of mischief," Pope said pleasantly. "If you want a reason for our action, remind yourself that you were in possession of five hundred dollars that doesn't belong to you."

Dunn shrugged. "Just as you say. It's a good disciplinary measure. No handcuffs? Did our stalwart deputy go off without his handcuffs?"

"I don't reckon I'll need any." Rocky picked up the bottle of whisky, and handed it to Dunn. "This is yours: you earned it."

Norma laughed, and Dunn's face reddened unhealthily. He and Rocky were halfway up the stairs before he spoke again.

"I'll admit you're a lot smarter than I thought you were, Allan. Not subtle, of course, but essentially practical. Only you were a bit too smart for your own peace of mind, weren't you? Oh, you won't hit me—now. There are advantages in being smaller than you."

"No, I couldn't hit you unless I was pretty mad," Rocky said. "But I might kick you to hell and gone up the rest of these steps. I can explain why, if that's too—subtle for you, Mr. Dunn. Pleasant dreams," he added, and closed and locked the door.

Eleanor's door was shut, but she was walking about her room. Rocky knocked lightly; then more loudly. "Can I came in?"

No answer, unless you took a sound like a chair being kicked out of the way for one. Rocky said again: "Can I come in?" He thought, Well, what the hell? and thrust the door open.

PART V
"WATER, WATER EVERYWHERE—"

Eleanor had been crying, and not in Norma's artistic fashion. She said: "Go away, will you? I don't want to talk to you! Go away."

She turned toward the window, her slender shoulders shaking. There were only two things you could do with a woman who was crying—kiss her or slap her. Rocky strode across the room and caught her in his arms.

"Forget it," he said, kissing her wet eyelids. "Damn the Leales, if you say so, but you're through with them."

"Am I?" Eleanor said tremulously.

"You're going to marry me, aren't you?"

"Now that you've asked me to. I—I began to think you wouldn't."

"You know all you ever had to do was whistle and I'd come runnin'."

"N-not exactly that," Eleanor murmured. When finally he let her go, she looked at him, smiling, trembling a little. "I've been cold inside all day long until now. Except," she admitted, "when I heard Norma talking to you. I was angry enough then."

"Redhead!" Rocky kissed her mouth; gently, this time. "It's nice you don't use any lipstick. Honey, I wish I had a good command of language otherwise than just profane. There's a lot of things I'd like to say to you, but they wouldn't sound right the way I'd say 'em. You won't mind, will you?"

He thought that of course she would laugh, but she didn't. She said: "No, I won't mind. Just kiss me and call me red-headed. Rocky, I'm not going to speak about Norma again except to say I was angry with her—not you."

"Then why wouldn't you talk to me?" Rocky said reasonably.

"Because I was afraid to. I mean, afraid I'd say—something about her. No, I'm not going to tell you what it was."

"I see you're not. Let it go, then."

"It isn't really important, you see. At least, I don't think it is. I'd probably be sorry if I did tell."

"Well, since you brought up the subject yourself, do you think she's really crazy about this fellow? George, wasn't that his name? You think she's really determined she's going to marry him?"

"Yes, I do. That is, marry him, or no one else, though she wouldn't have been willing to sacrifice her comfort to marry him."

"I wonder what he'd think of her methods of tryin' to keep his name out of this?"

"Norma probably once read a book in which the fair young heroine sacrifices her virtue to save the man she loves. She hasn't any of what we still call morals. But she wouldn't try to buy Harold Dunn off that way, because he doesn't appeal to her. 'No trespassing on private property' signs don't mean anything to Norma, either."

"You hadn't posted any signs."

Eleanor looked at him scornfully. "Oh, you wouldn't know. No man would, but Norma did. I suppose I'd better stop saying nasty things about Norma and get down to the case of Eleanor Gannon."

"It isn't a case, and you don't have to— Yes, I suppose you do," Rocky said reluctantly. "I wonder if Pope— Maybe that's him now. Come in."

Pope said diffidently: "I thought, since you didn't come back—"

"I was just goin' after you. We been talking about—other things. We're going to get married," Rocky said.

"I am very glad to have you off my mind and very glad too that you are going to be married,"

Pope said with his infrequent smile. "Each of you will keep the other in order, you know. And if I interrupted—"

"No, I was just going to tell Rocky what there is to tell. Sit down, both of you," Eleanor said, reaching for a cigarette. "I don't like this."

Pope sat down, wearily and somewhat like a very thin puppet being lowered by invisible wires. Rocky's shoulders obscured the gray-white dusk outside as he leaned against the window sill. The candles Eleanor lighted wept tallow tears into their saucers. She stooped to light her cigarette from one of them, repeated:

"I don't like this. It's humiliating."

"My dear child, why?" Pope said.

"Oh, that a man like Mr. Leale should think I'd marry him for his money."

"It is just conceivable that he thought his money was not his only attraction."

Eleanor gave Pope a startled look. "You know, I thought of that, but it didn't seem possible. Still, he was not too old, and good-looking enough. But first I'd better tell you why I didn't speak of my suspicions to either of you. It was because I'd convinced myself that one or two remarks and incidents that had puzzled me were nothing but imagination and vanity on my part.

"Last night, when we had finished talking, I did stop for an instant and start to say something about it. But it would have sounded so ridiculous to say, 'I think Mr. Leale was considering marrying me.' I'm sure he didn't have any such idea at first. When he'd talk to me and ask me things about myself, I thought he was just making certain that I was worthy of Joseph."

Rocky muttered profanely. "Yes, you would think that." Eleanor said:

"But you know what his ideas were. Anyway, I think he did approve of me, but I don't know when it was he began to think of me for himself instead of his son. Or did he have a change of heart?"

"I think so," Pope said. "It's hard to tell when, but don't you think it was after his illness?"

"Yes, I do. Of course, I acted the ministering angel to him then. And that illness did make him decide on extreme measures: we know that. Nice, isn't it, to have been one of his extreme measures? Well, one evening—I can't tell you exactly when it was, but I think Wednesday—I was looking at the newspaper, and he pointed out an item about a fifty-year-old man who'd just married a girl of twenty-five.

"He said, 'Did I think that man was foolish?' I wasn't interested enough to answer very seriously;

besides, he himself was over fifty, and I didn't
know what he thought about it. So I only said I
supposed it would all depend on the parties concerned. He thought that it would; that a marriage
like that would work out all right if the man were
hardy and young in spirit and the girl mature and
sensible."

Eleanor shrugged impatiently. "I don't see,
now, how I could have been so blind, particularly
as Harold Dunn overheard us and gave me one of
those malicious looks of his. Well, that was the
first thing. He talked to me a good deal after that,
but I still supposed he was just getting acquainted with his future daughter-in-law. Sometimes I
wanted to tell him I wasn't at all certain I cared to
marry his son. As to his remarks about marriages
between youth and gilded age, he might have been
thinking about some other woman. But I can't
find out that there were any whom he ever saw.

"But there's not much more to tell you. Once he
talked of the advantages of money, especially when
people had had an early training that made them
know its value. I suppose he meant me, as well as
himself. And he was very—solicitous, wanting me
to ride up here the day we came, when everyone
but himself and Miss Georgina was walking.

"The last thing was that he said to me very
abruptly, the day he—yesterday—that a compara-
tively young man like himself should build a new

life when he found the old one unsatisfactory, and that he should find new objects of affection when those on whom he had fastened his affections disappointed him. You know the way he talked."

"Conceited old bastard," Rocky said. "I believe Dunn understood him better than the rest of 'em."

"Did Mr. Dunn say he was conceited? That's rather funny, coming from him, but he probably did understand Mr. Leale," Eleanor said, "or he couldn't have deceived him for so long. Mr. Dunn was the only one who noticed Mr. Leale's gallant attentions. It seems as if he was always listening to our conversations."

"And you don't think," Pope said, "that anyone else did notice?"

"Did you?"

"Well, yes," Pope said humbly. "But the idea of thinking you might marry him seemed as preposterous to me as it does to Rocky. I hadn't thought Leale quite so vain. I should have known that anyone who wants to be Deity to his family must be vain. Of course, his remark that with his help you might make something of Joseph was ambiguous when one thought it over. I was worried about it, child, but I kept arguing as you did—that he was only trying to become acquainted with his future daughter-in-law. I didn't know, then, that there was anyone else, and I—trembled for you."

Eleanor said, with a placating look toward Rocky: "Oh, Joseph isn't that bad."

"He's very likable and a good match. I think Rocky hasn't told you all our conversation after you left us."

"He didn't tell me anything about it. Oh—Mr. Dunn did mention a girl's name. Well, I knew there had been one. I suppose the affair was more serious than Joseph wanted me to know?"

"I think it was. At any rate, Leale learned of that affair, and I think he intended that Joseph should—"

"Do right by little Nell?" Eleanor said with forced flippancy.

Rocky left the window and went over to her. "You don't want to blame him too much, honey. Joseph, I mean. Lots of fellows get themselves into a jackpot."

"I don't like evasion. If I'd loved him, that wouldn't have made any difference. Oh, perhaps it would have if I'd known all the facts. I don't know."

Pope said "Well, we need only consider it because of the fact that it undoubtedly inclined Leale to be more severe with Joseph and to block his marriage with you. Now, you think that no one—not even Miss Georgina—guessed anything of this?"

"Except for Harold Dunn. There's always a possibility that Miss Georgina guessed, but I don't
think so. Whenever we three were together Mr.
Leale treated me in a very businesslike manner.
I don't think he wanted Miss Georgina to know
anything. Norma might have read the signs correctly if she hadn't been so self-engrossed. Joseph
wouldn't, unless he had more to go on than I think
he had. As for Beatrice—I don't know. But I don't
think so. She seemed quite resigned to accepting
me as a step sister-in-law. Do you—do you think
this is very important?"

"On the surface it seems so, though only when
taken in conjunction with everything else that
happened. Undoubtedly the danger that their father might marry again would strengthen all the
previous motives his children—and Dunn—had
for getting rid of him."

"It makes a stronger case against Beatrice,"
Rocky said. "We've kept saying his money wasn't
enough motive, but she wouldn't like bein' set
aside for a stepmother. I don't think, though, that
she'd have lost everything by that. She said herself
that Leale wasn't unfair."

"No, I think he would still have remembered
his obligations to her. And of course," Pope said,
"there is always the fact that anyone who knew
Eleanor could be certain she would not marry

Leale. Against that we have the possibility that, as Dunn suggested, once Leale had considered marriage, he would find a woman who would marry him, so that danger would not be averted simply because Eleanor refused him."

"And so far as I'm concerned, Mr. Dunn has not a very good opinion of me, and he knows I despise him," Eleanor said. "And I wouldn't even be certain that—that Joseph might not think that I'd marry his father. What—what did he say about that?"

"He insists that he had no idea his father thought of marrying again, but he admits he was uneasy because Leale had given him a hint that he had some change of plans for Joseph in mind. Well," Pope said, "we have Mr. Dunn safely locked up. That was good work on your part, Rocky; getting that gun away from him."

"I was scared," Rocky said candidly. "His hands were so shaky, there was no telling when or what he might shoot. I kind of overreached myself on that proposition, but I hadn't an idea he had that gun. Kind of hard on you: you were the only one in his line of fire. Are you going to keep him locked up?"

"Of course, we don't have to. He can't escape. It's rather comforting, though, to know where one person is. There will be no charge against him because he took that money, but it won't do any harm to let him remain in solitude for a while. I suppose he might as well have dinner downstairs if he wants to."

"Well, I doubt if he can get tight on what whisky was left in that bottle," Rocky said. "What kept you downstairs?"

"Oh, I thought you might want to talk to Eleanor—alone."

"And they say women are matchmakers," Eleanor remarked.

"I have a strong maternal instinct. None of them had a great deal to say after you left, Rocky. Austin went back to the kitchen, and Ames finally excused himself. Norma and Joseph would not talk freely before me, or Beatrice. So I brought up the subject of a possible holographic will."

"You did? Why?" Rocky said.

"Oh, I thought I—should. It worried them a good deal."

"Which was the reason you mentioned it, I imagine. Do you really think," Eleanor said, "that he did write another will?"

"Yes, I believe he did. He was not inclined to postpone a thing that he thought should be done. He did take time to think things over, but he said that he had made up his mind what his course of action would be before he came up here. It seems that it almost certainly involved some change in his will. While he—as we think—managed nearly to convince himself that he would not be killed, there must have been enough doubt in his mind to make him guard against that."

"Then someone got into that steel box. If he didn't happen to look into it yesterday, the will might have been taken before he died," Eleanor said. "That is, by one who was reasonably certain that he would die."

"And if it wasn't taken before he died, everyone had a chance at his room between about five-thirty and seven," Rocky said. "Except when Dunn was in here, if he wasn't the one that took it. If it was taken while he was out on the hill—well, Joseph and Norma and Dunn were upstairs. Beatrice wasn't, according to the old lady. They could do what they liked up here. An' Austin had plenty of chance at the room." He sighed. "It all sounds very nice. Maybe the sheriff'll like to hear it, but I'm damned if I can see where he's going to get a case against anyone."

"Would he be apt to arrest Mr. Dunn?" Eleanor asked.

"Well, he might hold him for threatenin' an officer of the law or because he thought Dunn was his best bet. But Jake Thompson ain't the kind who goes aroun' arresting people to be doing something. This'll be a nuisance to him. He'll probably want to know why the hell Leale had to come up here to get killed. I feel kind of that way myself."

Pope said thoughtfully: "Of course, we do know some things, but I'm afraid they wouldn't impress your sheriff."

"What do we know that's any help?"

"Why, certain facts—no, I'm afraid they can't be called facts. But Eleanor's story seemed to me to offer several important suggestions. I meant that my own should do the same."

Rocky shrugged. "I'm dumb. You might write it down for me. Do these suggestions point out the guilty party to you?"

"Not quite. If we could get one definite piece of information to go with our inferences—"

"They're yours, not mine. If we could get that will—providing there was one and it's still in existence—maybe our troubles would be over. It's five-thirty almost," Rocky said, looking at Eleanor's wristwatch. "I'm going down and tell Sarah to have dinner when she can get it ready. No use waitin' till seven just to be fash'n'ble. You two can talk things over some more if you think it'll do any good."

II

Sarah Powers said: "I intended hurryin' dinner along a bit. I'd like to get through my work earlier. I hear Mr. Dunn tried to shoot you. Better you than me. I wouldn't've felt safe, sleepin' with that whisky tonight."

"I'll take the rest of it upstairs next time I go. Where's Austin?"

"He just took some more hot water in to the doctor. Said his foot was stiff an' sore, and he still wants to get back to Greenleaf tomorrow if he can. Any idea if the sheriff'll get here tomorrow?"

"You tell me. How long was Six held up the last big storm we had?"

"Three days. That was the spring we had them heavy rains and the bridges washed out, though." She moved a lamp nearer to her work table. "I got to make biscuits. The baker's bread is runnin' low. These lamps ought to be filled again if you use one of 'em in the livin' room tonight. I can't find the coal oil. I wish Austin would quit tidyin' up after me."

Rocky had been investigating the immense wood-box behind the stove. He said:

"I'll get you another load or two of wood. Austin has plenty else to do."

He stopped at the door of the woodshed, looking up at the sky's frosty brilliance. They didn't need to worry about snow for another twenty-four hours, at least. It would be plenty cold tonight; must be close to zero already. He thought he would go around to the front porch and take a look at the thermometer when he had taken Sarah a load of wood.

But for several minutes he stood where he was, looking toward the coasting hill on one side, the corner of the kitchen on the other. What the hell was it that had popped into his head for an instant as he looked toward that hill? The idea was gone, now, before he had had time to think it out.

He shook his head disgustedly and went into the darkness of the woodshed. Halfway to the house, his arms piled high with wood, he stopped again, sniffing. Funny smell— Then he had hurled the wood from him, and his heavy boots kicked up a spray of hard snow as he ran for the kitchen door. He wrenched it open, shouted to Sarah:

"Fire! In the cabin! Get me some help."

He thought he heard her drop a pan of biscuits she was holding, but he knew he could count on her. Thick smoke was curling through the cracks about the guest cabin's windows and door. The place was locked; it took time to find the key in his pockets, and his hands were stiff with cold. But he got the door open finally and for an instant stood choking with the smoke that rushed into his face.

Opening the door had been a mistake; fresh air
fanned flames that had made little headway in the
tightly closed cabin. The heavy, oily odor of kerosene hung over the room, but it could not have
been used very liberally or there would have been
more fire. Then he saw that a blanket was beginning to burn on one of the bunks; the blanket they
had spread over Leale's body. There were blankets
in the other bunk, too; they had wrapped them
about Miss Georgina. They were burning, too.

Rocky put his hands over his eyes and got
through the fire that was between him and the
bunks: a fire of wadded newspapers and small
pieces of wood, laid in a trail to the mounded
blankets. He stamped on it savagely and destroyed
the worst of it, but the blankets were a different
matter. It was on them that the kerosene had been
used; they were saturated with the stuff.

He beat at the blankets with his hands; began
with a sick feeling to try to tear them loose. But
footsteps were pounding the snow outside, and
Austin said:

"Let me in there! I have a fire extinguisher."

"Hop to it." Rocky kicked at the smoldering
remains of the fire on the floor and watched Pope
and Ames running up the walk. He said:

"Don't need you, after all, thanks to Austin.
This paper and kindling's damp, and there wasn't

enough air in here for it to get a good start right away. Once it reached the blankets it'd go like hell fire. The bunks have got coal oil all over 'em."

"But—good God! What—did some fool think he could help matters by destroying the bodies?" Ames said. "There's no other reason—"

"None at all," Pope said. "Very foolish, of course. Just the sort of thing that— Better let Dr. Ames look at those hands, Rocky."

"I feel sick," Rocky said abruptly. He went to the door, glad of the night's sharp cold. "I was just startin' to tear those blankets off, and they were wrapped pretty tight. Did you get it all out, Austin?"

"I think it's quite safe now. Only the outer blankets were burned."

"Well, straighten things up, will you? And let's go. Unless," Rocky said to Pope, "you want to look over the evidence."

"No, I've seen enough." Pope picked up a ten-gallon kerosene container that had been left by the door. "There might be fingerprints on this if we ever have an opportunity to use such evidence. Rocky, I don't like the look of your hands."

"And I don't like the feel of 'em," Rocky said grimly. "That damned oil got on them, and it burns clean through. Ames will fix me up. Another procession seems to be comin' along."

Beatrice had stopped in the doorway, holding her woolen robe tightly about her. Joseph said:

"What happened? Mrs. Powers said the guest cabin was on fire. How—"

"Pope will tell you all about it. Let us by," Ames said. "Allan burned his hands rather badly. Miss Gannon, is there any more whisky available? Then suppose you get it."

Eleanor turned and went back into the house without saying anything. "The guest cabin on fire? You mean where you put the—them—" Norma began to shiver. Ames said:

"Don't do that! I haven't any time for you right now. Get Miss Gannon to give you a drink. My bag is in my room, Allan. Come in there."

As he sat down, Rocky caught a glimpse of his own face in a mirror: a smoke-streaked mask with a greenish look about the mouth. "Christ, I certainly did collect a lot of soot in a few minutes. That was a damned fool stunt, anyway."

"Trying to burn down that cabin? Yes, because you can always identify— In here, Miss Gannon."

"I had to stop to give Norma a drink," Eleanor said. "Here, Rocky." She held the glass to his lips. "Oh, darling, your hands!" She bent down and kissed him. Rocky said:

"You got your face all dirty, honey. Where were you all when Sarah yelled?"

"We were—I'll tell you later."

She put cool fingers over his forehead as Ames began smearing some sort of salve on the lumps of fire that were his hands. Rocky dug his teeth into his lower lip and closed his eyes. Ames said:

"This will help, but the pain will have to wear itself out. I'd better give you a hypo."

"There's nothin' I'd like better, but mo'phine makes me sleepy, and I cain't leave Pope to handle this mess by himself after what's just happened. We got another night ahead of us."

Ames shrugged. "Just as you say. I know it's damned unpleasant, but it won't last forever. They aren't as deeply burned as I thought. Anyway, I've done all I can, so I'll see if I'm needed elsewhere."

"W-would you like to swear, Rocky?" Eleanor said, when the doctor had gone. "I've been around, you know."

"Hell, no! It isn't the kind of thing that swearin' helps any. Wipe my face off, will you, honey? Sweat in my eyes— That's nice," he added, as she drew his head back against her breast. "Sort of— distracts my attention."

Eleanor laughed rather shakily. "I won't ask why."

"No, because you know damn well. Havin' no hands would be an awful disadvantage. If you'd bend down a little, I could kiss that little hollow in your throat and distract my attention some more."

Joseph Leale said: "I—I beg your pardon—"

Rocky twisted about to stare at him. He must have opened the door very quietly and been standing there for an instant or two before he spoke. Eleanor did not move; she said:

"Yes?" looking at Joseph steadily.

"I wanted to ask if Allan was all right." Joseph stopped, and Rocky was sorry for him. His fair, handsome face looked white and pinched; his eyes beaten. He said: "You—and Allan—"

"Yes. It hadn't anything to do with what happened this afternoon. No, I'd rather get it over, and with you here, Rocky."

Rocky muttered, "O.K.," and looked at Joseph's polished shoes. It didn't seem quite fair to watch his face.

"I did try to think I could marry you, Joseph. I'm sorry for that, if you really care—a great deal. But you see," Eleanor said, "I'd run away from Rocky once. I made up my mind I wasn't going to marry you, this morning—"

"Th-this morning? But—"

"Oh, not because your aunt was killed. Because you wanted to get me a glass of water and hold my hand while I had hysterics. You'd never demand very much of me, Joseph. Rocky knows me better. Even if he didn't, it wouldn't make any difference."

Joseph said slowly: "No—no, I don't suppose it would," and turned and walked blindly past Pope as the latter came into the room. Pope looked after him and shook his head.

"Romeo versus Mercutio," he murmured. "Do you feel better now, Rocky?"

"Some. Enough better that I'd rather talk. What you been doing?"

"I went through the routine movements. Took a flashlight and examined the paths, but we have all been on them, and it's impossible to tell who went out to the cabin. Impossible for one no more expert at those things than I am, at least. When do you think that fire was lighted, Rocky?"

"I talked to Sarah about five minutes, and it was about five more before I saw the smoke. I'd think it had been lighted about fifteen or twenty minutes before I discovered it. Of course, you can't tell, because that place was all closed up, and the paper and kindling was pretty damp. It wasn't a very good job, either, the way the fire was laid."

"Mrs. Powers says no one came through the kitchen to go outside, except you, for at least an hour. Of course, the one who set the fire would not. He could have gone out the front door and around the house or out the dining room and the porch on the left side. Dunn broke a path there this afternoon and that would be the quickest way to get to the cabin. Mrs. Powers doesn't know when that kerosene was taken; she last saw it this morning."

"Well, where was everyone? We can count Dunn out."

"Beatrice and Norma say they went upstairs soon after I did. Ames was in here, and that left Joseph alone in the living room. I'd just reached the lower hall when Mrs. Powers gave the alarm. Austin was coming from this room, and he snatched that fire extinguisher from the hall closet and ran ahead of us."

"Good for Austin." Rocky got up and began to walk about the room. "Well, it was a rotten job: kind of fire a woman would build. And whoever did it didn't have guts enough to touch a light to those blankets, though all of the coal oil was saved for them. I reckon they picked this partic'lar time because it's almost dark and they didn't suppose anyone would be goin' outside. When it got a good start it would be too late, though I doubt if the whole cabin would've burned, with all that snow and ice on the roof." He moved closer to Pope, sniffing. "Do you smell of coal oil?"

"I suppose I do, from carrying that container. You do."

"I know. That's why I can't tell about anyone else. Someone else should have that smell on 'em.

Austin, of course. Ames didn't get near to the fire. Wait a minute—"

Rocky stood still, staring at the floor. That was where he had looked while Eleanor was talking to Joseph Leale.

"When did Joseph take off his boots and put on a pair of Oxfords—polished ones?" Rocky asked.

"Since I left him in the living room. He had on high boots then."

"He may only have changed for dinner," Eleanor said without conviction.

"Perhaps. Or he may have splashed kerosene on the boots. I'll take a look at them." But Pope stopped at the door, spoke to someone in the hall, and came back. "Austin will try to find them and bring them here. I think we'd better talk to Joseph."

"I s'pose so. But you got to do the talking," Rocky said. "I don't want to. Not right after— But I reckon you'd better find him and see what he says, unless you want to wait until Austin brings those boots."

Before Pope could answer they heard Joseph saying from somewhere near the stairway: "Austin! What are you doing with those? They're mine, aren't they? Look here, I won't have—"

"Mr. Pope asked me to bring them to him. I wouldn't do that, sir! I'd regret—having to force you to let me by."

Norma began, "Austin—please!" but Joseph said wearily:

"It's no good, Sis. We might as well go in and talk to them."

The boots that Austin silently handed over to Pope were damp with snow and splashed in a place or two with kerosene. Pope said: "Well?"

"Oh, I set the fire, if that's what you mean. What kind of crime is that?" Joseph said defiantly.

"A very clumsy one. What did you think you'd gain by it?" Pope asked.

"I've read about bodies being destroyed. You have to produce a body to prove a murder, haven't you? I thought it wouldn't hurt—them, and it might help us out. Oh, I see now that it was a crazy idea. It was the first thing that came into my head, and there were some extra keys to the cabin, so I could get into it."

"Yes, it was a very foolish idea," Pope agreed. "Because you had very little chance of destroying those bodies past identification, even without our evidence that they were put into the guest cabin."

"For God's sake, don't talk about it! It was all I could do to bring myself to light that fire on the floor. If I hadn't had to do something—"

"Why did you?"

"Because—oh, you know what kind of a mess we're in. And getting deeper every hour, with your help," Joseph said bitterly. "I'm going crazy if this doesn't come to an end pretty soon!"

Norma slipped her hand into his. "He really did it on my account. I was frightened." She wasn't lying about that; she was frightened now. "I'd been talking to him before Harold came back into the living room with that gun. I said I—I didn't see how things were going to end and could we *do* something. Joseph said he'd try to think of some way to get us out of it. I didn't know he'd do anything like this."

Pope said gently: "And why were you so suddenly frightened, Miss Leale?"

"It wasn't sudden. Anyone would be frightened—"

Ames appeared in the doorway. He said: "Pardon me, but may I interrupt you to put my bag in here?"

"You don't need to be so polite—John," Norma said. "You've heard most of these—inquisitions, and a little more won't hurt."

Rocky sat down suddenly. For an instant he was nauseated with pain. Ames looked at him sharply, and Eleanor said:

"Please, Rocky, won't you at least lie down for a while? You can't help here."

"The hell I can't! I'm trying to think of something," Rocky muttered. "It just came to me. Wait a minute."

He had it now: Eleanor repeating something Norma had said, something like, "Father knows because—George told him"—Norma getting behind Ames when Dunn was threatening them in the living room—Ames running down the path to the guest cabin—

"You've kind of forgotten to limp, Dr. Ames," Rocky said.

He heard Eleanor catch her breath, and Pope turned to look at him and then smiled slowly. Pope had guessed, and so had Eleanor, if she hadn't really known. Dunn had had the right idea too. Hadn't Ames spoken of being in the city in December? And it had been that month that Dunn had seen Norma sneaking into the house early one morning.

"I reckon," he added, "that if you started to say 'John' and wanted to change real quick, 'George' would be about as good a name as any to keep the first sound."

"Do you mean that you think—Dr. Ames and I— That's ridiculous," Norma said shrilly. "I've hardly spoken a dozen words to him!"

"That is just the trouble: you overdid it," Pope said. "If you will pardon my saying so, you're inclined to be—flirtatious. You hadn't any reason to dislike Dr. Ames, but you've ignored him very pointedly. Besides, who told you his name is John?"

"I—someone told me! Eleanor or Mr. Allan—"

Ames said coolly: "You're wasting time, Norma. I told you we should have told the truth in the beginning. Yes, I'm your mysterious George, though I didn't know that she referred to me by that name."

III

Rocky closed his eyes and listened to Pope saying: "Suppose you tell us all about it, Dr. Ames."

"I don't know what you want to know. Norma and I met at one of these casual cocktail parties where even the hostess knows only half of the guests. Meeting in that way, her family and friends didn't have to know about me. I'd been practicing—starving, I should say—in Stockton and was looking for a position on the order of this one at Greenleaf.

"We went on seeing each other; became engaged. I insisted on meeting Leale. From all that Norma told me of him, I thought it as well that we should have an understanding. Besides, he could have made our marriage easy if he had wanted to. He didn't. We took an instant dislike to each other, and our first interview was our last—"

"Not quite your last, Dr. Ames," Pope said.

Ames gave him a startled look. "That's right. Well, I told Leale there seemed nothing for us to do but wait until I'd seen how well my new job turned out. I didn't tell him where I was going. I believe that later on Norma told him I had a position in the southern part of the state."

"I thought it would be safer," Norma said. "Because when I came up here last summer—"

"Yes, Norma was near here with some friends last summer. I'd been in Greenleaf since early spring. I'd no idea she was going to try to get her father to buy this place, but once he had, there was nothing I could do but hope he'd not come up here very soon."

"It seemed such a wonderful idea at the time," Norma said forlornly. "But of course I was frightened, afterward. Father leased the place without coming up to look at it, but every time he had a letter from one of the men who was tending to the repairs I was so afraid they'd mention John's name. Then when he did decide to come here, I could guess that Aunt Georgina might want to see a doctor."

"But I don't think Leale heard my name until I came here. He just told Wharton to send up the company doctor from Greenleaf. I was afraid that would happen and tried to put it off by going to

Humber and staying all night. He didn't see me until I came out of the old lady's room, and then he stared at me as if he couldn't believe his eyes. After that he took me into the dining room for an interview.

"Of course, I lied about what he said to me, but it wasn't as bad as I expected. His dignity was offended because Norma had deceived him, but there wasn't much he could charge me with, as I told him. My job was in Greenleaf, and if he chose to come up here he couldn't expect me to clear out on that account."

"Did he refer to a letter you'd written him?" Pope said.

"Letter? Oh!" Ames frowned. "I can't remember exactly what I said in that letter, but I have a feeling I didn't express myself too—tactfully."

"'I sometimes think men like you should be painlessly removed from earth in middle age,'" Pope quoted.

"Yes, I wrote that. For God's sake, don't cry, Norma! So he kept that letter? But I signed it, so you must have known all along—"

"I think that it was an accident that the letter wasn't destroyed," Pope said. "The sheet with your signature was missing."

Ames smiled ruefully. "So I needn't have admitted I wrote it? However, my admission still stands.

Norma would write me about the two admirable young business men Leale thought would make good husbands for her, or that he might accept Dunn as a substitute, to keep his family under his thumb. One night I got to thinking things over and sat down and wrote that letter and sent it to a friend in the city to mail. For one thing, Leale was still harping on my having been divorced. I hadn't tried to hide the fact, not knowing his 'until death do us part' notions.

"But to get back to yesterday morning: He didn't say much; didn't refer to that letter. He seemed to have a lot on his mind. He finally said that he rather expected circumstances to be changed so far as his family was concerned and that the change might affect Norma and me. Make what you can of that; I'm not certain of his meaning."

"What do you think he meant, Miss Leale?" Pope said

"He didn't say that to me; not exactly that." Norma had stopped crying when Ames told her to. "Of course, first he gave me a long lecture on being such a deceitful daughter: not letting him know John was up here. I told him I'd tried to get him to go to Tahoe. When he finished with that he was not so bad. Really he wasn't! It was the first part of our interview that made me mad, not the last, though I don't expect you to believe that.

"He talked—well, just as John says. I didn't know what he meant, but I hoped it was that he wouldn't oppose our marriage. Would give me an allowance, I mean. He wanted to know if I really was determined not to marry anyone but John. Oh yes, and he told me that Harold was—out! Well, I told him that I supposed he might make me marry someone else if he kept at it for a year or two but that I'd probably disgrace him if he did. What he'd call disgrace—"

Rocky said, to spare Pope the trouble of framing the question tactfully: "Did he say anything to make you think he knew you'd been out all night with Ames last time he was in the city?"

"He did not! I wasn't—" Norma stopped and looked at Ames as he shook his head. "He didn't say anything about that," she finished sullenly.

"S'pose he had known?" Rocky persisted.

"If I couldn't have convinced him we had car trouble: he'd probably have thrown me out of the house," Norma said recklessly. "He would have been angry enough to know I had seen John at all. That is, he would have been at the time. You don't let me finish what I'm saying. Father said: 'Well, you may want to marry Ames, after all.' Those are his exact words, because I've puzzled over them enough. Why did he say it just that way? Because his tone wasn't—unkind."

"He might have meant any one of several things," Pope said unsatisfactorily. "But—did you come into the house last night after you'd gone to the guest cabin, Dr. Ames? Or did Miss Leale go out to the cabin to see you?"

"What makes you think either one of those things happened?" Ames said warily.

"Oh, I'm sure one or the other must have. Miss Leale was missing from her room before two o'clock. We don't know what you may have been doing. No one was with you in the cabin: you could come and go as you wished."

"Through the snow without leaving tracks, and through the kitchen without disturbing Mrs. Powers?"

"Someone did disturb her: probably at about the time Miss Leale was out of her room."

"Well, as a matter of fact, I did—"

"Don't say you came in here! Don't you see what that would mean—to him?" Norma cried. "Aunt Georgina—I went out to the cabin, Mr. Pope. I had to talk to John; I hadn't had a chance to see him alone and get him to agree that we were to go on acting as if we didn't know each other. I thought I was very careful. I put on my boots and outdoor clothes—"

"Yes, and they were too damp this morning, if they hadn't been worn outside again, in a storm."

"Oh—that was it. I cleaned my boots very carefully, and while I suppose I must have left tracks on the kitchen floor, I'd noticed that evening that it was already all tracked up."

"It didn't occur to me at that time that someone might have gone outside to the cabin," Pope said. "So we didn't look at the outside paths, as we should have. The back stairway was dirty from wet boots too. I do think you carried a few bits of hard snow to the upper hall with you. Just one thing more and I'm done. Were you alone in the dining room yesterday, Ames?"

Ames hesitated, looking toward Austin. "I'd better stick to telling the truth, I suppose. I was starting to leave after talking to Leale when Sarah Powers asked me to come in and prescribe for her rheumatism." He grimaced. "Damn her rheumatism! I told her, as usual, that she'd probably be better if she didn't eat so much fried stuff. Well, of course I had to go out through the dining room, and there was no one there. Austin met me as I went out through the hall, and you can have Sarah's testimony for the asking. So there you are: motive and opportunity."

Rocky said: "You didn't really sprain your ankle, did you?"

"Oh, I gave it a twist, but I could have gone on to Greenleaf. I'd promised Norma I'd find some excuse for staying here tonight, though I didn't know what earthly good I'd be to her. But I didn't like to leave her in this—this—"

"Madhouse," Joseph said.

Ames gave him an unfavorable look. "If you want to be melodramatic—yes. I suppose Norma told you all her troubles, and so I'm partly to blame for your—incendiary activities. I'm sorry."

"Doesn't matter." Joseph turned to Pope. "Are you going to lock me in my room? Because I'd like to go upstairs. I don't think I want any dinner."

"Oh, I don't think we need to lock you up," Pope said mildly. "I'll let Dunn out if he wants to come down to dinner."

Austin cleared his throat. "And if you don't need me, sir? I imagine Mrs. Powers wants help. She was rather provoked because she dropped the biscuits and they got kicked around the floor when we rushed through the kitchen."

Norma giggled hysterically. "Well, I'm going upstairs too. I don't want anything to eat."

"Of course you do," Ames said. "Try washing your face in cold water." But he smiled and touched her yellow curls gently. "If you tell fibs after we're married, I'll beat hell out of you," he promised. "Run along. What about you, Allan?"

"Me? Oh, it's wearin' off, like you said, though I'd begun to think you were a little optimistic. I'll go upstairs till dinner is ready, so's you can have your room."

Eleanor and Pope followed him upstairs. "If you'll go to sleep—if you can—I'll see that you get something to eat later on," Eleanor said.

"All right." Rocky put his bandaged hands out in an awkward gesture, and she laughed and kissed him. "You're sweet: do you know it?" He added, grinning: "Don't you forget to wash your face in cold water. It needs it.

"I'm beginnin' to feel like something besides a pair of hands," he said to Pope, sitting down on Leale's bed. "Why didn't you put me wise? Seems like everyone else knew."

"About Ames? You knew as much as I did." Pope lighted an evil-smelling pipe. "Would you like a cigarette? I can hold it for you."

"Stick it between my fingers: the tips ain't bandaged. Well, I just took Ames for granted as being one of the natives, like me. I can see, now, that when you put everything together it began to be kind of suspicious. Like her speakin' about this place to Leale and then not wantin' to come here. Anyhow, I should've known if she said he was in the south, he'd be up north." Rocky chuckled. "I'm glad I haven't the job of breaking her of tellin' fibs. I suppose we've got one more suspect for the sheriff?"

"I suppose so. Motive and opportunity, as he admitted."

"But if someone really did try to poison Leale back in the city, Ames and Norma'd have to be in cahoots. Well, I suppose they would be, anyway. Whether Ames had anything to do with it or not, I'd say he had nerve enough to see a double murder through."

"Yes," Pope said slowly, "he has steady nerves and probably a great indifference to death."

"And it beats hell what some guys will do for a pretty little tart like Norma Leale. Though she did stand up for Joseph. There's another thing Ames didn't mention, though he said something about it in his letter. Leale might've had influence to use against Ames at Greenleaf, if he wanted to. Ames said he'd starved, once, tryin' to get a start."

"All those things have to be considered, certainly. If Ames did come into the house last night, he left no distinguishable tracks. There were too many people tramping about the house with wet boots, bringing snow with them. We should have examined the path to the guest cabin."

"We should have woke up when Miss Georgina was killed, then. By the time we were awake, any tracks on that path would be covered with fresh snow."

"Yes, and I have never had any great success with footprints or fingerprints, either," Pope said sadly. "I'll take the key and let Dunn out, I think."

"All right. Take this cigarette, will you? And you'd better get the rest of that whisky and wine out of Sarah's room."

Pope nodded and went out. Rocky thought that he would come back in a few minutes, but he did not. It must be getting close to seven o'clock, but the dinner gong hadn't sounded. If Sarah was in a temper because people had stepped on her biscuits, she would probably take her time about making a new batch. But he wasn't particularly interested in food. He lay back on the pillows and thought he might be able to go to sleep. His hands weren't half bad, now.

He raised himself on one elbow and blew out the candle Pope had lighted. No use letting the thing burn; they might run short before the power came on again.

He lay still in the darkness and thought about Eleanor. She wasn't the kind who bargained, so she hadn't said she'd like him to find a better—and safer—occupation than railroading. He wasn't certain he could settle down. But they'd go down to Texas on their honeymoon, he decided.

His father would be glad to see him again, though he was too stiff necked to ask Rocky to

come home. He'd like Eleanor. Just as well to let
her see that his folks were all right. The trip could
be managed: he still had most of Uncle Bill's money, and he couldn't work for a while, anyway.

Perhaps Pope would come down and visit them
some time soon. He liked Pope, and the man was
sort of pathetic. He didn't know exactly why he
thought that, except that it seemed as if Pope must
always be an onlooker and that must get to be a
lonely sort of thing.

He dropped off to sleep then, to wake suddenly
with a guilty feeling that it must be very late. He
thought too that he had heard some sound recently that should have roused him. He began fumbling for the matches he knew were on the bedside
table, but the bandages about his hands destroyed
his sense of touch.

Finally he got up and groped his way across the
room to the door. It was just as dark in the hall;
if there were any lights in the bedroom they were
too faint to be seen under the doors. But someone
was coming upstairs.

Rocky waited until Eleanor appeared, her hair
gleaming in the light of the candle she carried.
She said: "What are you doing in the dark, young
man?"

"I couldn't locate the matches with my hands
all tied up. What time is it, honey?"

"Couldn't locate— Didn't Austin light a candle for you when he came up to see if you were awake?"

"Austin didn't come into the room that I know of. I'd have woke up if he had. When'd you send him up?"

"Why, about half an hour ago. But he isn't back in the kitchen, because I went in there myself before I came up to see if you'd eaten—"

Rocky said, "Give me the candle, and you wait here," but Eleanor shook her head.

"You can't hold it, Rocky. I'll come with you. To the back stairway, you mean?"

"I reckon he would've come up that way."

Rocky went ahead of her down the hall; stopped, looking down the back stairs. Austin was sprawled grotesquely across the last steps, his hair matted and stiffly red.

IV

Ames said: "It won't do any good for you to stay in here; any of you but Miss Gannon." He added: "She can see that I don't kill the patient. I think he'll come out of it before very long. It's only a bad scalp wound, and I don't believe there's much concussion."

In the hall, Rocky looked at Pope and said: "Well?"

"Oh—the usual thing. Everyone out of my sight."

"You can't stick on their tails every minute. I should've been down here to help."

"You needed to rest. Of course, not everyone was out of my sight. Miss Gannon wasn't. Mrs. Powers was late with dinner; Austin reported that she was not in a good humor. I asked him not to ring the gong because I hoped you were sleeping. Dunn came down; everyone but Joseph. We started dinner around seven fifteen, I think, and took about three quarters of an hour for it.

"When we were leaving the dining room, Miss Gannon asked Austin to go upstairs when he had time and see if you were asleep and to take you something to eat if you were awake or to tell her and she would do it. According to Mrs. Powers it must have been about fifteen minutes later that Austin went upstairs. The stairs were dark, for she told him to close the stair door in the kitchen because of the cold.

"He didn't come back, but Mrs. Powers thought nothing of that. She thought she heard something fall, but she was in her bedroom at the time and wasn't alarmed by the sound.

"Meanwhile Dunn and Beatrice had gone directly upstairs. Dunn is beginning to repent having talked, and no one seemed to wish to talk to him. It was obviously an effort for Beatrice to come to the table at all. The rest of us went into the living room, but Norma was restless and murmured something about Joseph and left us. A few minutes later Ames said that his bag was in his room where anyone could get at it and that he'd better put it in a safer place. He disappeared for ten minutes or so.

"Norma came back and said that Joseph would not talk to her. Then Ames returned. I suppose all of this took up half an hour, but if Austin was struck down as soon as he reached the head of the stairs, Miss Gannon and I are the only ones who can alibi each other."

"You say the thing he was hit with is a door stop?"

"Yes, of petrified wood. I noticed it the day we came, because it was used to prop the front door open while the luggage was being carried in. But it stood in that dark corner by the door, and I haven't noticed it since then."

Rocky looked toward the jagged brown-black lump of wood that Pope had laid on the hall table after he carried Austin downstairs.

"Well, one end makes kind of a good handle for a person to hold on to, but he must've been hit a glancing blow. If they'd hit him square, might have smashed his head in. I suppose that's what was counted on— Well, for crying out loud!"

Wires reddened in the globe above them. The light flickered, became a steady glow, and the telephone began to ring stridently. Rocky said, "Thank God for small mercies," fumbling at the telephone receiver. He managed to get it off the hook and balanced it in his hand.

"Hello! Yes, this is Allan."

Humber said: "Just a minute. All right, Mr. Thompson."

"Rocky? How you making it? Anything happened?"

"Plenty. We got two bodies for you 'stead of one." The sheriff made nasal sounds of consternation. "I know it sounds bad, but there it is. We did the best we could."

"'We'? Is there someone there you can trust?"

"Yeah. Leale may've been kind of thoughtless, getting himself killed up here, but he pr'vided a detective." Pope made a gesture of dissent. "He says he ain't, but he'll do until another one comes along."

"Well, that's good. I don't see much use you telling me all about it over the phone. I suppose it'd take quite a while?"

"Hours," Rocky said discouragingly. "What I want to know is when—"

He stopped, listening. From down on the curve by the river, past Rio Linda station, an engine whistled in short, echoing blasts.

"Seven's whistling round the curve here, Jake. Does that mean Six is comin' through?"

"They tell us it is, though we don't know yet what time it'll get in here. Whenever it does, me and the cor'ner will catch it. You can look for us some time tomorrow morning early, I should think. Was the second one poisoned, too?"

"Stabbed. Plenty of variety. We just had another one, hit on the head. Not killed—"

"Holy jumping catfish!" Jake Thompson said piously. "Don't you know anything about who might have done it, Rocky? Enough to give us a start when we get there?"

"You can take your choice of half-a-dozen suspects. An' we got a lot of nice exhibits for you. A flask with some brandy in it, a carvin' knife, and a door stop—"

The sheriff groaned. "That'll do. There ain't been anything like this in the county, ever. But I don't see any use of going on talkin' to you. If Six don't get through, we'll start out with a tractor and snowplows tomorrow and try to make it by the road. Try not to have any more exhibits waiting for us, will you?"

"Well," Rocky said, turning to Pope, "he didn't gnaw on me so much after all. Of course, he wouldn't, with Humber listening in."

Pope said unexpectedly: "My head aches. Be glad you haven't a jig-saw-puzzle mind, Rocky."

"A—what?"

"Oh, it's not a very good descriptive phrase. I make puzzle pieces of a snatch of conversation, an expression on someone's face, an inflection of the voice. And I keep pushing them about, trying to fit them into a pattern. I want to stop, but I can't."

Rocky grinned, but sympathetically. "Did you lose one of your puzzle pieces?"

"I never had it, but I think I've found it now."

"You have! Well, then—"

"It isn't so simple as that," Pope said irritably. "No proof. Accusations are a waste of time. Suppose I make a mistake? After all, you're in charge here."

"Oh, I'll risk it. What are you goin' to do?"

Pope said, "I don't know," and Rocky laughed.

"Well, that's definite. And while you're makin' up your mind, would it be asking too much for you to get some wood and take a look at the furnace? It's getting mighty cold, and the living-room fire was burnin' low the last time I looked in there. I'd do it, but—"

"Nonsense! I'll see to it."

Pope went off down the hall, and Rocky had started to go into the living room when Eleanor came out of Austin's room.

"He's conscious, but he'd better not try to talk for a few minutes."

"Did he say anything when he was comin' to?" Rocky asked.

"Just, 'Something hit me.' Then he said: 'Should have taken that flashlight.' So you see he doesn't know any more than we do. Was that the sheriff on the telephone?"

"Yes. He expects to get here some time tomorrow." Eleanor sighed. "And then I suppose we will have to answer questions all over again. He won't exempt me from suspicion as you and Mr. Pope have."

"He'd better," Rocky said grimly.

"Don't be silly, darling. Why should he? But I hate to have to explain all over again that Mr. Leale didn't state his honorable intentions to me— Yes, Dr. Ames?"

"Austin insists that he is able to talk, though he apparently has nothing important to tell you."

Rocky thought, going into Austin's room, that Pope must not have been very tactful in asking Ames about his movements when he had presumably been looking over his physician's bag. Or perhaps Ames was only worried because Norma could not account for herself. Austin looked up at him from the bed and smiled pallidly.

"I was just telling Dr. Ames that all I can remember is going up that stairway in the dark—pitch dark, because Mrs. Powers asked me to close the kitchen door, and the upper hall was dark. I should have taken a light. I was going slowly, feeling my way, because the steps are steep and—well, that's all."

"You got to the hall, didn't you?"

"I suppose so. No, I think I was on the top step. Then—" Austin grimaced—"stars and explosions and all that sort of thing."

"Who do you think hit you?"

Austin closed his eyes. "How can I tell? I've admitted servants see and hear things. It might have been anyone. The only thing is that I don't know what it is that I know."

"I get you. You mean you know something that someone doesn't want you to tell but you can't tell it because you don't know what it is." Eleanor laughed. "Yes, I guess that ain't much clearer than what Austin said," Rocky admitted. "Well, you might as well go to sleep for a while. I'll tell Pope what you said."

Ames followed them into the hall. "Are you going to trust me to sleep next door to Austin tonight without posting a guard?" he said disagreeably.

"We'll do whatever Pope thinks best about that. Don't try to take your grouch out on me," Rocky drawled. "Whyn't you go in and give some consolation to that bunch in the living room?"

Ames scowled at him and then smiled. "All right; I deserved that. What's the matter with the others? Afraid to go to their rooms?"

"I reckon they are. Now that we have some real lights, maybe they'll feel safer upstairs. But Pope may want to talk to them again. I'll go see."

Pope had evidently brought a load of wood into the kitchen and left it there while he went down to look at the furnace. Rocky sat down to wait for him; he had the kitchen to himself, for Sarah had already shut herself into her bedroom.

Rocky began to think back over the long day until he was standing in front of the woodshed, looking toward the coasting hill and a corner of the kitchen.

For an instant, there, he had been on the verge of solving some problem. The coasting hill on one side, a back corner of the house on the other, and snow everywhere—"Water, water everywhere—"

Rocky leaped to his feet; hurt his hands getting the cellar door open. He shouted:

"Pope! Leave that thing be and come up here! I got something I want to ask you about."

Pope came, with a smear of oil across his lean face. "What is it this time?"

"Oh, no more accidents. Look, now—let's see if I got this right. Sarah went to take a nap yesterday about three-thirty and— Wait, I'll get Sarah."

Sarah grumbled at being disturbed, but put on a skimpy bathrobe over a red flannel petticoat that was not skimpily cut and came out.

"This is important; you can sleep afterward. Yesterday, when you washed the lunch dishes, you didn't wash those decanters—"

"Certainly not," Sarah said scornfully. "After all your talk about them, d'you think I wouldn't have told you if I had?"

"And Austin didn't wash them before you went to your bedroom?"

"No, he didn't." Sarah sighed. "Do I have to go all over that again? Austin said he noticed them with liquor still in 'em at three-thirty or thereabouts. It probably was a bit earlier, because he had gone out to the woodshed before I went to my room."

"That's what I wanted to know. Was he down here in the lower part of the house all the time between lunch and three-thirty?"

"Yes, he was," Sarah said positively.

"And you say you heard him come through with wood once, when you were lying down. If you heard that, you'd have heard anyone come into the kitchen and turn on the water."

"I ain't deaf. And them faucets kind of growls."

Rocky said apologetically to Pope: "This is awful slow work, but if I don't do it this way I'll lose it again. We agreed that when Joseph was in the house he didn't have time to come down and get the decanter and take it upstairs to wash. Or take it anywhere or get it at all, if the old lady was telling the truth about how short a time he was in the house, and I believe she was. And Beatrice says the decanter hadn't been washed after he'd gone outside again.

"So it's a waste of time considering him, if we believe Beatrice Leale. As for her, the old lady said twice that she didn't have time to wash the brandy decanter and that Austin made quick trips both times he came in with wood."

"He did too," Sarah said. "I know that myself."

"Well, Dunn and Norma were in the house later on, but Miss Georgina said they didn't stay long. They couldn't have come down the back way with Sarah in the kitchen, and Miss Georgina said they only came down the front way once."

Pope's left eyebrow slanted upward. "All of which seems to prove that it wasn't washed at all. The decanter, I mean."

"No—wait a minute. Austin brought in his second load of wood and went on out to the woodshed. That right, Sarah? An' I guess that he split some more wood, but he's not very good at it. It'd take him till about five o'clock to get enough. Then he came out and stopped to look at them coasting a minute. It was getting dark, but there was a light on the hill. Because you can see the coasting hill from the woodshed, outside."

Pope said: "Oh!"

"Sure you can. And he'd stand there and see Leale drink and fall down and tell by our actions what was wrong. And he'd think about that brandy decanter. Well, why he wanted to wash it up is beyond me. Because it seems like if he'd poisoned the brandy in the first place he had lots of chances to wash the decanter and fill it again. But he did want to wash it, to destroy evidence.

"He didn't have time to get upstairs to a bathroom, and he couldn't wash it in the kitchen. But he didn't need water with snow everywhere. He could cut round the house to the porch on the left side, get into the dining room, grab the decanter, and go outside and clean it in the snow without Sarah seeing him unless she just happened to be looking out a window. There was time for that before Dunn sent Sarah out."

Pope said, "I think you're right, Rocky," in a tone that was commendation enough. "And of course, if we had looked around the house for tracks in the snow, by the time we thought of that, his tracks were covered because the snow was falling so fast. We were on the walk about six-thirty, but that was tramped up anyway, and I didn't look around."

"It was too dark for much lookin' by then," Rocky said. "Only I don't see why he bothered to do it."

"Oh, I think I can answer that. I think that his hurried trip into the dining room wasn't primarily for that decanter. He told us that he had not put any brandy into that decanter after Leale had drunk from it with no ill effects. I think that he lied and that perhaps there was a half-empty bottle of brandy left and that he went into the dining room to get that and destroy it."

"Pete's sake!—why?"

"Because with that gone we could not prove that the brandy was poisoned in its original bottle unless all the brandy in both boxes of liquor was poisoned, and we know that it was not. He wanted us to believe that the brandy was poisoned in the decanter, because that meant that everyone here had an opportunity to poison it. Including Ames.

Then I think he tried to be a little too clever by cleaning the decanter, drawing our attention to its importance—an importance that didn't exist. But few people can think things out completely and correctly in ten minutes, even when they have nothing to do but think."

"We can't know all this," Rocky objected.

"I do know that when I dug all the empty bottles out of the snow this afternoon there were only two empty brandy bottles where there should have been three."

"Oh! That's something. And you think if we went out and dug in the snow outside the porch we might find the third brandy bottle?"

"Yes."

Sarah said: "Well, I never! If you two know what you're talkin' about, I don't. You through with me? I'm going to get some clothes on."

"I didn't think you'd go back to bed after this, Sarah," Rocky said. She sniffed and flounced back into her bedroom.

"He's protectin' someone, then," Rocky said. "Who is it?"

"If you remember his testimony, he may be protecting himself. Because he supervised the packing of the liquor, and he said he checked over one box and nailed it up, but the other one was open for some time, for Beatrice, Norma, and Dunn to

inspect. But if he had poisoned the brandy himself he would have made the necessary arrangements beforehand, and whatever was done, it is
certain that some action involving the decanter
and a third bottle of brandy was hastily carried
through. He must have suspected that the second
box of liquor had been tampered with: that is, the
one that was last closed and first opened."

"Beatrice, Dunn, or Norma," Rocky repeated.
"And he wouldn't try to protect Dunn. He might
Beatrice. But by destroyin' evidence that the bran-
dy was poisoned in the city, he drags Ames into it.
And he's fairly young and good-lookin' and wasn't
brought up to be a servant."

Pope said, "Yes," very wearily, and then: "We
might as well talk to him at once."

V

Austin said: "I must congratulate both of you."
He did not bother to speak like a servant now.
"Of course I could deny everything you've said,
but you have narrowed times down inconvenient-
ly—for me. And I can't deny destroying that third
bottle of brandy with any great conviction when
I know that you can find it buried in the snow if
you want to dig long enough. Or you can wait for
the snow to melt.

"Besides, Miss Leale—Beatrice Leale—may remember that there was a bottle half full of brandy in the sideboard when she got that port wine for Miss Georgina. I don't know, any more than you do, if that third bottle of brandy was poisoned. But if the brandy was not poisoned after it was put in the decanter, that was the bottle that caused Leale's death.

"I put two pints in the decanter the day we came, and he drank from that without harm. But I did add more brandy to the decanter in the morning, and afterward I tried to remember opening the bottle. You know how you do: go over and over every movement and sometimes you think you've managed to call them back? I thought I remembered that the label on that bottle came off very easily, as if it had not been glued down tightly. But then, a good many of them aren't.

"Well, I told you that I put the last pint of brandy in the decanter before Leale drank that nightcap, and I acted as I did just for the reasons you've guessed. Of course I wanted to drag Ames into it. I hadn't missed those letters that were postmarked Greenleaf. When we got here and Ames appeared, I was able to add two and two. As you say, I was too clever, washing that decanter. But I hadn't time to think it out."

Pope said: "You expected to benefit by your— altruism?"

"Oh, of course," Austin said coolly. "It was not entirely a matter of affection." And to Rocky, in sudden anger: "Don't look at me like that! You probably think you've suffered a few hardships in your life, but you always knew you could go home if you had to. I was a kid and half sick when I got out of the army. I starved and froze; picked cigarette stubs out of the gutter; stood in bread lines and got turned away because the food gave out. Ate off garbage cans and slept in corners until a cop kicked me awake.

"I never forgot it; I never will. After that, a job for a month and nothing for three or four until I finally found myself a house servant and glad to be fed and warm. But I began looking ahead. If Leale died, I had two thousand and was out of a job. But his children would have money. Figure it out for yourself. I wasn't to blame for her being that kind of woman. It's as good a hold as you can have over a woman as I know of."

"Didn't Leale know?" Rocky said.

"Leale never really saw me, except as a perfect servant. If he did know, he didn't speak to me."

"That's pretty hard to believe."

"But I am rather inclined to believe it," Pope said. "*Flagrante delicto*'—that was an indication

of Leale's intention. It perhaps accounts for his
not sending Austin to the guest cabin. Miss Georgina hadn't given him enough evidence: he wanted
to verify her guesses."

"I suppose the old lady might have seen something, the way she prowled around the house,"
Austin muttered. "She never liked me. But you
still haven't any proof. I'm not giving you any—
no more than I had to, to try to save my own skin.
I suppose, at that, if you brought it to court and
proved I washed out that decanter and buried that
brandy bottle, any jury would jump to the conclusion that I'd poisoned the stuff in the first place."

"Fortunately for you, I can't believe that," Pope
said. "We'll get proof, through you. Lie down! At-
tacking you was a bad mistake, you see. It linked
you with—events, and I had been waiting for
something like that. Lie down, Mr. Austin! We'd
better lock him in, Rocky."

Rocky watched Pope put the key in his pocket
and said:

"You do the talking. This is going to be tough
on everybody. Eleanor and Joseph and Ames. Get
it over."

Someone had finally gone out to the kitchen
and brought in enough wood to build up the fire.
Red and yellow flickered in warm shadows across

the room. But it was false warmth: you didn't forget for an instant that the house was circled with
cold; that there was a deeper chill of fear in the
room.

Rocky found himself staring at Norma and
looked away hastily. Yellow curls and blue eyes
and small white hands. They'd splash her pictures
on all the papers, and the sob sisters would write
stories about the "beautiful young defendant."
But Pope was saying:

"Murderers always make mistakes. Trying to put
Austin out of the way was a mistake, Miss Leale.
It called our attention to him and his—activities.
The instinct of self-preservation is very strong,
you know. Austin admits that he knew that one
bottle of brandy was poisoned before we left the
city."

Joseph said harshly: "This is another of his
tricks! You don't have to talk."

"You're right in your last statement, Mr. Leale,"
Pope said. "But—think it over. The law is very
slow; a county jail and a hostile country jury isn't
the same thing as a trial in the city. I'll let you
off that, Miss Leale, for a written confession. You
have only to say good-night and go upstairs—"

Rocky looked at Norma then. She had put her
face in her hands, and Ames had his arm about

her shoulders as if he were trying to keep her from shaking to pieces. She'd never have the guts to do it.

Beatrice Leale said: "Thank you, Mr. Pope. I'm very tired." She was at the door now. Her brown eyes were dead as a muddy pool; then for an instant they flickered as if the pool had been stirred. "It was—rather interesting while it lasted. Goodnight," she said deliberately, and closed the door.

Ames sprang to his feet. "Pope! You can't do that! It's murder!"

"I have been under the impression all along," Pope said precisely, "that we were concerned with murder."

"But I can't let you do that! You told her to kill herself."

"You exaggerate. I appreciate your feelings, Dr. Ames. It's the instinct of your profession. But sit down. I still have that gun in my pocket, and I'll use it, if necessary. That should clear your conscience."

Rocky stumbled across the room and pulled Eleanor to her feet. She locked her hands about his arm, her face hidden against his shoulder. She whispered:

"I still—don't understand."

Rocky muttered: "I thought it was Norma. Don't think about it. Pope's right. We'll get married and go down south where it's warm. Go to Texas and see my dad. You'd like that, wouldn't you?"

Near the door, Pope was something tall carved out of stone. The burning logs snapped and crackled. It seemed impossible that people breathing could make so loud a noise. There was no other until the one from upstairs: a faint sound like someone falling.

PART VI
"JIG-SAW-PUZZLE MIND"

Rocky had found an electric percolator in the dining room, brought it into the living room, and had just decided that the coffee was strong enough when Eleanor came in. She had her green robe on over woolen lounging pajamas; her feet thrust into puffy wool-lined slippers.

Rocky said: "You look cute, honey. Want some coffee? Somehow I have an idea you aren't going to sleep tonight, either."

"I'd like some coffee. You've taken off some of those bandages."

"Just a few, so I could use my hands some."

"You shouldn't have. No, I'm not going to sleep tonight. It's freezing since the furnace fire is out. Norma wanted me to stay with her, and perhaps I should have, but I didn't want to. Where is Mr. Pope?"

"He went in to talk to Austin."

"Oh. He was rather—awful, wasn't he?"

"Pope? I suppose so, but he was right."

"What are you going to say to the sheriff?"

Rocky shrugged. "He'll be damned glad not to have to figure this out for himself or to have to have a trial. I'll just say we let her go upstairs to write this confession and never thought she had any poison on her. No one will say different—even Ames."

Pope came in, sat down, and took off his glasses.

"Coffee? That was a good idea, Rocky. What are you doing down here, Eleanor?"

"I can't sleep, and I prefer your company to that of anyone else. Besides," Eleanor said, getting up to pour the coffee as Rocky frowned and grimaced, trying to handle the heavy pot, "though you sent the others away without explanation after you let them see that confession, I want to know how you knew. I thought you might tell us, to pass the time away."

"Yes, and to excuse yourself for foolin' me," Rocky said.

Pope objected: "There was more than one Miss Leale, but Beatrice had first right to the title. Besides, when we talked to Austin, he did not specify with which one he had been intimate. We mentioned the names of those who were known to have had access to that box of liquor, and he let us think what we wished."

"An' I thought one thing and you thought another and didn't bother to correct me," Rocky said good-naturedly.

"But if I had to choose between the two I would have chosen Norma as the one most likely to be involved with Austin," Eleanor said.

"Do you mind if I begin at the beginning?" Pope said. "I think that it was, for me, the question: 'Why did Leale change his mind about wanting my help, between Wednesday night and Friday morning?' He did, you know. But when he had suspected a plot against Beatrice as well as himself and had been concerned only with the sins of Joseph, Norma, and Dunn, he had given me a good deal of his confidence. He was prepared to deal with them, and if one of them had tried to poison him, he wanted me to help him. Why did he change his mind?

"Well, one could find various answers to that question, but it seemed to me that perhaps he had discovered that a person whom he had left out of his calculations might be concerned in his sweeping reforms. That person would have to be Beatrice. And what happened between the first and second time he talked to me was that his sister had talked to him on Thursday night. And one of the things she said to him was: 'My dear boy,

I know it's a shock to you, but I've always been afraid of something like that.'

"Of course, one jumped at once to the conclusion that she probably had something to tell him that she had discovered in her nightly prowlings. You see why I said Eleanor's story was invaluable? But if that shock had something to do with Norma, Dunn, or Joseph—again I said: Why did he not still want my help?

"Miss Georgina's revelation, then, might have concerned Beatrice, the only one whom he had not complained of to me; the one he'd told me was a dutiful and devoted daughter. It was hard enough for him to tell me about the others; he didn't want to admit she was no better than the rest of them.

"We'll never know if he believed she had tried to poison him with arsenic. Perhaps he argued that he had been mistaken. I think it would have been hard for him to believe that his devoted daughter had tried to kill him, even when he was told she had carried on an intrigue with a servant.

"I think he could hardly believe Miss Georgina; he knew the old lady's weaknesses and meant to have proof of his own before he acted. Of course, if he did catch her, he meant to punish her, and he took precautions in case of his death. But he didn't want me to know about that.

"Remember that he was a very vain man. He'd had one devoted daughter, and he was losing her, if Miss Georgina was right. Perhaps that was one reason he thought of a third marriage: he would not have any scruples about setting Beatrice aside for a third wife. But he hadn't spoken to Beatrice about Austin; he thought her feelings toward himself were the same as ever. So how could he believe he was in any danger from her unless he admitted that her affection had always been a sham?"

Eleanor said: "He would never do that. Besides, we decided, once, what sort of fatalistic attitude he might have developed. Don't you think, with all his interviews with everyone, he must have bolstered up his self-assurance as well? And that with everything he had to think of—his proposed 'new life' included—he may have forgotten that he once felt himself in danger?"

"Yes, that is reasonable. We can't ever know what fluctuating state of mind he went through. And for all he knew, there might have been a plot against Beatrice, as he had first supposed. Well, from everything I was told and forced to believe, Beatrice did sincerely love her father, and even Norma could not say she believed Beatrice killed him. If she had, she also must have suffered a change of heart. That is, if we believed Leale had been poisoned on that Sunday, because at that

time he had not talked to his sister, so it would
not have been fear of him that led Beatrice to try
to kill him.

"What, then? From what I heard of her life, it
had been singularly monotonous. The only thing
worth recording seemed to be that Harold Dunn
had once paid her some attention but that they
hadn't married. And what happened just before
we came up here? Nothing, apparently, but that
the house was thoroughly cleaned. On Saturday
Beatrice and Norma cleaned the attic, where there
was a large accumulation of odds and ends, according to Beatrice herself. And on Sunday someone tried to poison Leale.

"At that point, I admit I gave free rein to my
imagination. But Dunn's brief courtship seemed
to me to have been the only episode in Beatrice's
life that she would have cherished. Then, I had
always wondered at Leale's tolerance of Dunn,
and with that wonder came a second one. Had
Dunn—as well as his father—perhaps done Leale
some favor? Could it be connected with Beatrice?
I tried to convey to you without commenting on
it—because my ideas then were in a very chaotic
state—Leale's hesitation in speaking of his wife.
Do you remember his exact words?"

Rocky said: "I don't know that I do. We ain't
all like you."

"He said: 'I married young: a good woman, a devoted wife, though she was—not of a happy disposition. Beatrice is—too much like her.' Miss Georgina spoke of Beatrice's mother as 'a queer stick.' And later on, speaking of Beatrice's devotion to him, Leale used the words: 'if she had not been forced to substitute me for a husband.' Now, I can see that you youngsters are thinking that Beatrice was unattractive and that no man would want to marry her, but it occurred to me that Dunn would certainly have done so if Leale had wanted him to.

"If Leale had blocked that marriage and Beatrice had discovered it, even some years later— Well, I didn't know then of her relations with Austin, but if I had, I think I could have guessed that she must feel that she was very wicked. I use her own word. So that she would blame her father doubly, not only for having prevented her marriage with Dunn, but for driving her into what she thought of as sin by so doing.

"Of course, one could only guess that Beatrice might have come across some old paper or letter in the attic that had shown her what her father's action had been. And she did find such a letter."

Pope pulled a creased sheet of paper from his pocket and tossed it over to Rocky. Eleanor put down her coffee cup and came to sit beside him in one of the big overstuffed chairs. The letter said simply:

> *My Dear Harold:*
> *We were not able to finish our conversation yesterday because I did not wish to talk before anyone else, but I hope I have made myself clear. I do not wish to discuss the matter further, for reasons you will understand. But I think your marriage to Beatrice would be most unwise. You will not find me ungrateful if you do as I wish and do not refer to the subject again.*
>
> > *Alfred.*

"And Dunn didn't destroy the letter?" Rocky said.

"No. Didn't you remark that he had the habit of carrying wads of old letters about with him? I have talked to him. He said: 'Christ, I'd forgotten all about that. I supposed I'd destroyed the letter.'

"Then he told me that he had intended to marry Beatrice solely for financial reasons. He supposed Leale would favor the marriage, but when he spoke to him about it, Leale acted very oddly. He finally hinted that he did not believe Beatrice should marry. Though he did not actually say that

Beatrice's mother suffered from some mental in-
stability, Dunn gained that impression from what
Leale would say.

"Leale obviously did not want to discuss the
matter any more than necessary, and Dunn admits
he was glad to be let off marrying Beatrice so long
as Leale promised to be generous with him. But
Leale's letter is misleading, as you see. Beatrice
obviously knew of no reason why she should not
marry, and Leale's interference seemed sheer cru-
elty to her.

"Dunn supposes he must have tossed this letter
with others in a box of odds and ends that eventually were taken into the attic. If it hadn't been
for Miss Georgina's system of housekeeping— But
Beatrice did look through the boxes of letters, and
being interested in anything of Dunn's, she read
some of them. Norma Leale says that she did the
same thing but that she did not pay any particular
attention to Beatrice, so that she would not have
seen if Beatrice betrayed herself in any way when
she read this.

"So you see that without anyone's knowing of
it, Beatrice's attitude toward Leale had changed,
and so she was the most likely suspect, after all. If
you argued farther that it was quite possible she
would sense some change in her father's attitude
toward her, she would know that the only thing he

could discover against her was her relations with
Austin. And she would know what Leale's reaction
to that would be and that she needed to act quickly if she was going to save anything for herself.

"She would know too that his informant would
probably be Miss Georgina and even if Miss Georgina did not know Beatrice's initial motive for
killing Leale, she could supply one that would be
just as damning."

"But why didn't Miss Georgina talk?" Eleanor
said.

"Sheer perversity, it seems to me. She wanted
to conduct the investigation herself. She did give
me one hint by her choice of words when she said:
'Beatrice was the only one who ever *did* care for
Alfred.'"

"Well, go on," Rocky said as Pope stopped.

"But that's all. All that matters. Except that
Beatrice was glad to have us look through Leale's
strongbox, and why should she be unless she knew
Ames' letter was there? Of course, it was not necessarily the murderer who opened that box. But
when you linked Austin with the case, that link
solved it."

"Did it?" Rocky said. "How?"

Pope got up to pour himself another cup of
coffee. "Putting it as briefly as possible, the at-
tack on Austin showed that he was involved. Your

argument that he had washed the decanter led to my supposition that he had destroyed that third bottle of brandy. Beatrice had had no opportunity to do so.

"Then you remember that we argued that Austin must have been shielding Norma, Dunn, or Beatrice. I argued for Beatrice, and an intrigue between her and Austin with his hope of marrying a rich woman or being generously paid oil was the only reason I could think of for his trying to hide her guilt. It was only then, of course, that I could assign a reason for Leale's conduct toward me and a second motive for his murder. You thought of Norma because Austin's attempt to drag Ames into it seemed to point to jealousy of Ames on his part."

"Well, now that we've talked it over, I'd like to read what she wrote, again," Rocky said. "Let's see it—and that will."

"I killed my father because I discovered that he had been responsible for destroying my one chance of happiness," Beatrice had written in a precise copybook hand. "I had loved Harold Dunn, and my father kept him from marrying me. The letter I am leaving you with this will explain itself. I found it in a box in the attic when we were cleaning house. That was on Saturday. On Sunday I

tried to kill my father with arsenic, but I didn't
know enough about it, so I failed.

"Afterward, I could see I had acted hastily and
unwisely, so I decided to wait and next time use
a poison that would be sure: cyanide, that I took
from Joseph's laboratory. When my father said we
were coming up here, I thought it a better place
for him to die, where we would not be bothered
with city police. Besides, I knew he was having
difficulties with all the rest of the family, and that
would be convenient.

"You must understand that I hated my father
now, though I hid it from him. I felt he was not
only responsible for taking Harold away from
me—perhaps to give to Norma—but for causing
me to—"

Here, for the first time, Beatrice had hesitated, scratched out several words and finally written
blackly: "sin. Austin had always treated me con-
siderately and when he seemed to find me attractive, though I knew it was wicked, I did not seem
to be myself—the self I had thought I was. He
always spoke of marriage, but I knew that was no
use. It was not very often that we—"

She had paused again, started a new paragraph.

"In fact, it had been such a long time that I
didn't feel I was in any danger of discovery. I did
suspect that Aunt Georgina wandered about the

house at night. Austin thought she did, and I am not as stupid as I was willing to have Norma think. On Wednesday night I had gone to Austin's room on an entirely innocent errand about some of the packing that had to be done. He wanted me to stay—but I didn't. Aunt Georgina saw me and it was rather late.

"I didn't know any of this at the time but I could feel that my father was suspicious of me. I suppose he suspected he hadn't just had indigestion Sunday night but it must have been hard for him to believe that anyone who had adored him as I had would try to kill him. He'd have felt differently about the others. So I thought that there must be more than that; that someone had hinted something to him about Austin and myself.

"I knew what that would mean if he believed it. I'd never cared about money before, but now I'd lost him and everything else, and I wanted that. And when we got up here I could see he was going to try to marry Miss Gannon. I didn't think she'd marry him, but there were a lot of women who would, once he had the idea. However, that really had nothing to do with my determination to kill him, because I'd already poisoned one bottle of brandy. There were only three in the box. It was the smallest one and I saw that Austin opened it first, so I wouldn't have too long to wait.

"I never believed Mr. Pope when he said Austin knew I poisoned that brandy, but I was tired—I felt that sooner or later he would prove I was guilty. Austin didn't know, though he may have guessed.

"I saw Austin put some of the last bottle of brandy in the decanter, and I was quite certain my father would be dead by evening. So before we went out on the hill to coast, I looked over his strongbox. I'd prepared for that by getting an extra key from his bedroom in the city. I found this will he'd written and took it. I left that part of Dr. Ames' letter in the box to cause Norma some trouble, though I didn't know who had written it. I kept that will because, if it showed his feelings toward me had changed, it also went against the others.

"That night I was really at my door and did see someone come out of Father's room, only I hadn't taken those sleeping tablets, so I wasn't at all confused. It was Aunt Georgina, and she came in to talk to me. She told me she'd give me until the next day to talk. That she'd spoken to Father about seeing me come out of Austin's room that Wednesday. She wouldn't listen to my explanation but said she'd been suspicious of me for a long time.

"She was very foolish, wasn't she? I simply waited until I thought it was safe, went downstairs and got that knife from the sideboard. I spoke to her very softly, as if I were crying and very frightened. She sat up and I leaned over her. Of course it was only luck that I struck such a clean blow in the dark.

"I drew the knife out to wipe the handle, wiped my hands on the sheets, and settled her back in bed. Then I washed my hands in the bathroom. I used matches to be sure I left no traces and washed my towel and put it in the hamper. After that, all I had to do was wait and watch the rest of them acting foolishly. I was afraid to try to destroy that bottle of brandy. It was too bad that Austin had to do it.

"He knew too much about me, and I could see, now, that he had always been thinking of the money I was going to have some day. I didn't want to marry him, and I wasn't going to have him blackmailing me. I knew he would be coming up the back stairway tonight soon after we left the dining room, so I waited for him. But I was unlucky that time."

There she had stopped, signed her name, every letter of it meticulously formed, and taken out the cyanide she had carried somewhere in her clothing. Eleanor folded the paper with unsteady fingers. She said finally:

"Is this will valid? I don't want any of his money."

"It is written, dated and signed in his own handwriting," Pope said. "Of course, it will not work out as he intended, but it was a rather damning document, not only to Beatrice but to others."

Alfred Leale had left five thousand dollars each to Norma and Joseph, ten thousand to Eleanor, the same sum to Paul Taylor, his lawyer, five thousand to Theophilus Pope.

"Which is odd," Pope said. "Not that I can't and won't use it."

Rocky said: "You've earned it. I s'pose he'd have made a new one if he got married again. This was just in case."

He read on. Several hospitals were to have bequests, Dunn was to receive his ten thousand, the Spanish cook an equal amount, instead of the original sum allotted her. Leale had written:

"*I am omitting the name of Daniel Austin from this will, as he has forfeited my confidence.*" Then: "*To my daughter Beatrice, one hundred dollars. She will be further provided for by her aunt, who will understand exactly what course I would wish her to take in this matter.*" The residue of the estate was to go to Miss Georgina.

"In other words," Rocky said, "the old lady wasn't to let Beatrice starve, but that's about all.

But now I suppose the rest of them get what the old lady would have had."

"Leave it to the lawyers," Pope said. "I suppose that Leale was forcing Norma to make a decision when he said she might want to marry Ames, now. If she was never to receive more than five thousand dollars from him, she must make up her mind to marry Ames—or a richer man. Evidently he didn't care to drag the girl, Isabel's, name into this by cutting Joseph off entirely if he didn't marry her. Besides, that kind of provision is a dangerous one to put into a will."

Rocky said rather absently, "Is it?" putting his arm about Eleanor to draw her comfortably closer to him.

Presently, starting to speak to her, he saw that she was asleep. He smiled and sat watching the fire, his cheek against her hair. Some time this morning the sheriff and coroner would come panting up the white hill, and there would be a lot of talking to be done. He should stay awake and talk to Pope now, but he felt drowsy.

Pope sat watching them: the two young, slim figures, the red of Eleanor's hair against Rocky's brown cheek, with a look of nostalgia for something unknown. At last he sighed, put on his glasses, and tiptoeing quietly across the room poured the last of the coffee into his cup.

COACHWHIP PUBLICATIONS

CoachwhipBooks.com

MURDER ON
THE DAY OF
JUDGMENT

VIRGINIA RATH

COACHWHIP PUBLICATIONS
CoachwhipBooks.com

VIRGINIA RATH

FERRYMAN,
TAKE HIM ACROSS!

COACHWHIP PUBLICATIONS
CoachwhipBooks.com

VIRGINIA RATH

THE ANGER
OF THE BELLS

COACHWHIP PUBLICATIONS

CoachwhipBooks.com

VIRGINIA RATH

AN EXCELLENT
NIGHT FOR
MURDER

COACHWHIP PUBLICATIONS
CoachwhipBooks.com

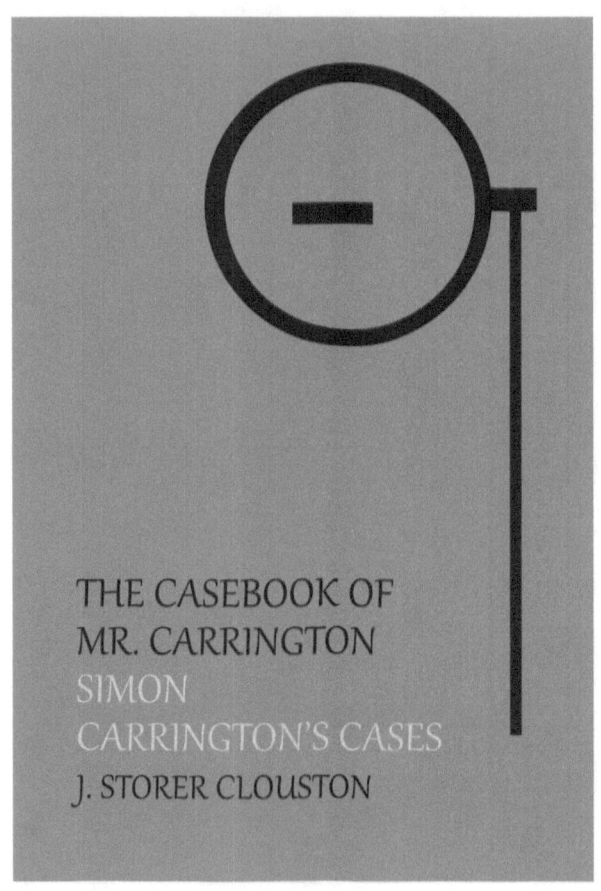

THE CASEBOOK OF
MR. CARRINGTON
SIMON
CARRINGTON'S CASES
J. STORER CLOUSTON

COACHWHIP PUBLICATIONS
CoachwhipBooks.com

3 DETECTIVES
FEMMES AUDACIEUSES
MERWIN • SOMERVILLE • FOOTNER

COACHWHIP PUBLICATIONS
CoachwhipBooks.com

DRESSED
TO KILL

Emma Lou Fetta

COACHWHIP PUBLICATIONS
CoachwhipBooks.com

ANITA BOUTELL

DEATH BRINGS
A STORKE

CRADLED
IN FEAR

www.ingramcontent.com/pod-product-compliance
Lightning Source LLC
Chambersburg PA
CBHW032232010726
47494CB00002B/462